Abigail's Exchange

KATHRYN DEN HOUTER

MISSION POINT PRESS

Readers are encouraged to go to
www.MissionPointPress.com to
contact the author or to find
information on how to buy this
book in bulk at a discounted rate.

MISSION POINT PRESS

Published by Mission Point Press
2554 Chandler Rd.
Traverse City, MI 49686
(231) 421-9513
www.MissionPointPress.com

ISBN: 978-1-943995-87-5
Library of Congress Control Number: 2018957007

Printed in the United States of America.

DEDICATION

I dedicate this book to Jim, my wonderful mate. He has been my champion during our nine years of marriage. Without him, I would still be "wandering in the desert." He willingly took on the challenge of caring for me during my widowhood, and his kindnesses and steadfastness will always have a special place in my heart.

ACKNOWLEDGEMENTS

Making this book materialize has been quite a journey. The inspiration for the book came when I read the Abigail and Nabal story with my prayer group members, Kristin, Beth, Jen, and others. Thank you for being my friends during the early days of my widowhood. It was not an easy time. I found this Old Testament story to be profoundly compelling with a perfect plot for the Women's Rights movement being waged during the late 1800s in America. It continues today.

My heartfelt gratitude goes to Jim, who with care and precision furnished the first edits of my completed book. The Window Pane Writers' Group in Vero Beach, Florida, was helpful on a weekly basis, and their encouragement and insights were treasured immensely. Tom Pine's edits were especially useful, because he took loose phrases and incomplete chapters and shaped them into a viable book. John Pahl and Doug Weaver from Mission Point Press provided incisive comments that forged new writing directions and opened up new possibilities. I always will be grateful for their efforts. It takes a village.

My phone conversations with Jenny Hope from the Woman's Exchange in Baltimore were very enlightening and spoke volumes about our shared value of helping our sisters create a better life. Also, thank you for introducing me to the book: *The Business of Charity: The Woman's Exchange Movement, 1832-1900*, by Kathleen Waters Sander. Her book clarified the context of the Exchanges. On so many levels, it is sad to see the once compassionate and effective operations of the Woman's Exchange disappear from the American philanthropic landscape. It is my hope that it will be repurposed into something even better. A special thank you to the librarians at the Enoch Pratt Free Library in Baltimore, Maryland. They diligently found information that aided my research about the Baltimore Woman's Exchange. It has been an enthralling journey.

– Kathryn Den Houter, September, 2018

CONTENTS

INTRODUCTION

From a young age, Abigail Abbott struggled to be self-sufficient in an era that was fraught with barriers. This book highlights her determination to overcome these roadblocks. Even in America today, many households are challenged by the same conflicts: How can household chores be divided fairly? How can the finances of the home be handled? What can be done about the unmanaged dark side of your spouse? Abigail and her husband Avery dealt with these same issues. For Abigail, financial equality had a special urgency, because she was the owner of a thriving business in Baltimore. Avery and Abigail established an uneasy truce as they embarked on their marital life. The real blow came when Abigail was widowed. The reader will discover what was typical during this time in history when a husband died or deserted the family.

I was reminded of the harsh treatment of widows when walking along the shores of the Ganges River in India. The guide explained the "holy" ritual of Sati, which gripped me with horror. During India's pre-colonial era, it was a common Hindu practice to place the widow beside her deceased husband on his funeral pyre so they could be cremated together. Usually, she was tied down so she couldn't escape at the last moment. Having been widowed just eight months before my trip to India, I was alarmed by this ritual. Today, the practice of Sati is outlawed, but occasionally, it is performed to exalt undying spousal devotion and everlasting love.

Abigail's Exchange depicts how widows were treated during the post-Civil War period in Baltimore, Maryland. When Avery died, Abigail had a rude awakening, but this is when her true grit came through. She overcame the obstacles and learned about a lifesaving philanthropic enterprise, the Woman's Exchange of Baltimore. Its members established enterprises that gave women a safe harbor from the vicissitudes of life.

Baltimore was a fascinating city during the 1800s. It was robust and inventive and the "first" in many things. It was just the right setting for this story. From the 1860s to the 1890s, which is the book's timeline, the firsts include but are not limited to:

> 1869 – J.S. Young Company, the first candy factory to produce licorice.
>
> 1875 – The first monument to Edgar Allan Poe.
>
> 1878 – The first animal welfare association—the American Humane Society.
>
> 1879 – The first synthetic sweetening agent, Saccharine, developed at Johns Hopkins University
>
> 1883 – The first publicly financed vocational school in the United States—the Baltimore Polytechnic Institute.
>
> 1884 – The first typesetting machine in the United States.
>
> 1885 – The first electric streetcar line.
>
> 1886 – The first free public library system (with branches)—the Enoch Pratt Free Library.

The only similarity between this story and my life's story is that both Abigail and I became widows. The circumstances that precede the loss and the outcome following this event are very different for each of us. It is my hope that my experience as a widow, though, will enrich her character and shape Abigail into a relatable young woman.

CHAPTER 1

Abbotts' Secret

❧ ❧ ❧ ❧

"*Prone?* Prone to what?" Abigail's eyes flashed with anger as she spun around on her heels and stomped out the side door, slamming it behind her. The door rattled in her wake. She didn't want an answer to her question; she just wanted to get out of there, get some fresh air. For her, fresh air was freedom.

Abigail's encounters with her mother, Martha, were never good. Today was no exception. Resentment had been building for a very long time. Being the middle child in a family of three girls, Abigail was singled out every time. It was no exaggeration, either. She wasn't about to let her mother define her or pass judgment on her. Prone? Prone? Prone to what? She wasn't prone to anything her mother might say. She'd show her what she was prone to! No matter what, she just could *not* please her mother. She had to face life by herself, trusting her own instincts.

She managed quite well sorting out her problems using her best judgment. She avoided her mother as much as she could, did well in school, and relished her father's approval. Perhaps her continual efforts to please those other than her mother created in her an eager mind and earnest demeanor. She so much wanted to succeed at life just to show her mother she could. Sewing and handcrafts were her specialty. With a lovely youthful figure and her skills as a seamstress, she always looked well turned out.

At the age of eighteen Abigail possessed unparalleled beauty. Her fair skin was offset by dark auburn hair, her chin delicately chiseled, and her face expressed a lovely symmetry. Her hazel eyes were alluring—not like those of a temptress, but of someone bright and inquisitive. Her preferred colors were autumn hues—olive, gold, brown—and a certain shade of blue. With her hair dressed neatly in a braided bun, she looked every inch a striking young woman.

"Abigail, you are prone to disobedience." Her mother's words pierced through her heart, fueling her rage. *I try so hard to be good. What have I done that makes me so disobedient? Do I have to respect and obey someone who hates me? Does my lack of love for her make me disobedient? I don't want to be like my sisters.* This explosive rage, which was focused on her mother, became irreconcilable. Beauty and accomplishments aside, this would come back to haunt her later.

Her relationship with her father was very different. They had fun together and respected each other. He owned a candy store, Abbott's Confectionary, in downtown Baltimore. They sold Whitman's chocolates in the store and a splendid array of penny candies, caramels, and newspapers for the business crowd. After school, her friends would congregate there. Abigail and her father thoroughly enjoyed this time of day, and all of her friends had a special bond with her father. They called him "Pinky" because of his short stature, baldhead, and round, pink face. He tasted his wares often, and it showed.

Pinky's store was a fun-filled place. Laughter was rampant as were squeals of delight. It was a gustatory adventure being at Abbott's Confectionary. When a new penny candy would come on the market, he would hand out free samples. The recipients talked about the flavors and aired either their endorsement or their disapproval. Abigail worked long hours at her father's store, and she loved the bustling pace and lightness of mood, which was a stark contrast to their dark family home on the outskirts of Baltimore. At the candy store, the hours went by quickly, and she dreaded the time when she had to go home.

The house was impeccable, with each table and chair accented by crocheted doilies and antimacassars. Living room chairs and sofa were a dark green, with mahogany tables standing squarely at their sides. Each table had a dainty, fluted dish filled with specialty candies from Abbott's Confectionary. Abigail's sisters, Mary and Louise, were homebodies like their mother, and they kept the house spick-and-span, with a robust practicality. They were quite a team, a team within which Abigail didn't fit.

Just before the Christmas holiday rush in 1885, her father needed to hire a new bookkeeper, a job Abigail knew she could do. She wanted to become a career woman, and this would help her toward that goal. Being with her father every day was an added plus, so she pleaded her case.

"No, Abigail. I want someone with experience," Pinky said. "You've never been a bookkeeper before. Besides, I want you to go to the Baltimore Female College to become a teacher."

"But Daddy, I can do both, I promise. Let me try it just for a month. *Please*, Daddy."

He had to laugh because she was so determined. "Okay. Okay. We'll talk about this again on the first of February to see if you can juggle everything. Don't forget January is the beginning of the fiscal year, and you'll have to do the inventory in the middle of the month for taxes. I'll pay you fifteen cents a day."

Abigail was all smiles. She immediately went into the back room to look at the ledger, her desk, and the book-keeping supplies. She wasn't interested in being a teacher but went along with his plans so as not to disappoint him. Already, she had great plans for the candy business. Understanding the importance of getting her father's stamp of approval, she was determined to proceed slowly and not make any mistakes.

Leaning back in the bookkeeper's chair, she started dreaming. She had fantasies of becoming a well-dressed career woman, both attractive and intelligent. In her dreams, her reputation as a shrewd businesswoman would be known throughout Maryland. Even men sought her advice. Realizing her thoughts were puffed-up, she conjured up more somber thoughts. *I wonder what opportunities my mother Martha had when she was my age? She doesn't think much beyond her home and garden. At least my father has given me this wonderful opportunity. What was it like for her when her mother died and her father was her only parent?*

MARTHA

સર્જ સર્જ સર્જ

"Martha! Martha!" She heard and turned around to see who was calling her name. To her surprise, it was her teacher.

"Would you clean the blackboard and erasers before you go home today?"

"Yes, ma'am," she said obediently.

The blackboard, from Medford Quarry just north of Baltimore, had just been installed, and it was quite an honor to be asked to clean it. Having a blackboard in front of the class for all to see was much more efficient for the teacher. She could write a whole day's lesson on the blackboard. Copying from the board with paper and pencil gave the students permanent copies to save, to bring home, and to study for tests. This proved to be much better than every student having to carry individual slate tablets.

After class, she went up to her teacher. "Do you want me to clean the blackboard with water?"

"No, I have a cloth in the desk drawer with two teaspoons of lemon oil in the center. That will work the best. Just put the cloth back in my desk when you're done." Martha nodded affirmatively, but her thoughts were racing. *Maybe I'm the teacher's favorite, or maybe I'm just the cleanest one in the classroom. My father always said I was the best cleaner in the whole family, and cleanliness is next to Godliness, he would say.* Humming merrily, she cleaned the blackboard with lemon oil and admired how it glistened.

Keeping the house clean, dishes washed, and beds made were Martha's mandatory jobs at home. Her father was a stoic, no-nonsense kind of person, a taskmaster who demanded that the house be ordered and spotlessly clean. Martha's mother died during one of the horrible cholera epidemics in the early 1800s, when Martha was only nine years old. There was no time for tears, for the family of five had to take on new household chores. Martha was the diligent cleaner. That was her role. If she did her job well, it would certainly please her father and secure her position in the family. She cleaned painstakingly, making sure the house was perfect—as if her very life depended on it.

After ten more years of cleaning her father's home, she was tired and looked around for something better. At nineteen, Martha, who was the baby of the family, watched her two older brothers find mates and set up their own households. She wanted this for herself, too. Penelope, her older sister, was the family cook and for all practical purposes was her mother's replacement. Penelope's relationship with her father morphed into a daughter-wife-cook role. Although it was never openly discussed, she was chosen to take care of their father until he died. Sadly resigned to this role, she became plumper and less attractive with each passing year. Martha did not want this to be her life. She dreamed of having her own husband, children, and a house of her own.

Since cleaning was so much of her identity, Martha looked for cleaning jobs when she went job hunting. Her first job was part-time, but it gave her a place to start. Her reputation as a good worker became her calling card, and she was asked to be part of the full-time staff at First

Presbyterian Church on Madison Street near their Baltimore home. The church had beautiful flying buttresses and vaulted ceilings, which gave the city of Baltimore a fine taste of Gothic architecture. For the most part, the people in the church office were kind. How she loved that place!

On one memorable Monday morning, Martha started cleaning the pews after the Sunday service. Caught up in a cleaning frenzy, she didn't notice a well-dressed man standing in the aisle by the pew she was polishing. She kept working and inadvertently bumped into him. She jostled the box that was balanced in his arms.

"Oh, excuse me, I didn't see you standing there." Her face flushed and she giggled as she reset the box so it wouldn't tip over. "What do you want? Can I help you find a person?"

"I want to talk to someone in the church office. Can you show me the way?"

"Certainly, it's in the back of the church. Go through the hallway and turn right."

His eyes twinkled as he nodded, and she watched him walk with a jaunty stride past the pews through the vestibule to the office. He was dressed for winter weather. Sporting a well-tailored gray, wool suit, with a plaid, wool scarf loosely placed around his neck, he looked quite natty. A gray, wool cabbie hat topped off his winter garb. She liked his happy-go-lucky walk . . . the lively spring in his step. *Okay, enough of that. I must get back to work.* She grabbed her rag and kept polishing. Soon, Martha was humming a Christmas tune as she worked. With a quick glance, she saw the same man standing by the pew again with the box in his hands.

"Nobody was there," he said. "I have some candy, Christmas candy. It's a gift for the children on Christmas Eve. Where should I put it?"

"I can take the box. Did your wife make them?"

"No, I'm not married. I brought them from my candy store, Abbott's Confectionary."

"Thank you. The children will enjoy it. I'll put them in the office with a note."

What a generous man. He has the spirit of the season. Generosity is so rare these days. "Merry Christmas," she said.

"Merry Christmas to you, too," he replied.

Oh, those were wonderful memories of the first time she and her husband met. Now, twenty years and three daughters later, her life was filled with disappointments and loneliness. Her thoughts turned darker as she drifted into a deeper brooding. *We've seen so much together. My two daughters, Mary and Louise, are good, obedient children. They help me clean, and there are times when we all hum together as we work. They're good workers when we garden in the summer. But Abigail, you frustrate me. You make me angry with your highfalutin' ways. You hide when it's time to clean, and you play with the dog when it's time to work in the garden. You are a disobedient child.*

PINKY

I'm a nice person. People like me and I like people. The people that work for me do what I ask, and they're all-smiles. We laugh and joke around, and the time goes quickly. Why is my home life so miserable? What have I done to deserve such torment? Enough of that, I must get back to work.

"Diane, did you order the licorice from the John Young Candy Company?" Pinky asked, refocusing his mind on his business. "I complained to John when I saw him at church last Sunday that they've got to stop sending all the licorice to New York City, because then there's none left for Baltimore."

"Oops, I forgot, Mr. Abbott," Diane said. "I'll get that order out in the mail right away. I've had many customers request licorice. Carolyn Miser said it helps with her headaches. Customers like it a lot." Diane had been with the Abbott Candy Company for over ten years. She was a loyal employee. Although the pay was a little less than average, she liked her boss and the job of selling candy. Diane liked Mr. Abbott. She never could call him Pinky the way the other girls did, because it just didn't sound right when it came out of her mouth. Even though she knew it was a term of endearment, it would get stuck in the back of her throat.

Although she never addressed him as Pinky, Diane knew that the term made sense to everyone else. He was a short, bald-headed man with a big, jolly grin. His face was pink, the top of his head was pink, and all the other skin parts that peeked out of his clothes were pink. No one knew why his skin was that color, but it was distinctive. When people asked him about his nickname, he would say, "I'd rather be pinky than stinky," with an easy chortle. Yes, he was fun to have for a boss. It was obvious he liked his job and was especially fond of the people he hired.

Diane was flummoxed by his relationship with his wife. She was such a peculiar woman. When she came into the store, it was like she was checking up on him. She would peer around the back of the counter to see if anything was dirty, or out of place, and then she would rummage around the two offices in the back. It was all very unsettling, and Pinky seemed to be on edge and defensive when she did her rounds. Perhaps he was afraid of her. Diane never knew him to be improper to her or any of the schoolgirls under his employ. It was like his wife had something on him, and that's how she kept control. She was mystified by the two of them, but there was one time when Mr. Abbott exposed a back-story to their marriage.

❧ ❧ ❧

It was the morning of a chilly, fall day. Mr. Abbott was already there when Diane opened the store. He looked uncharacteristically disheveled, as if he had been sleeping in his clothes.

"Good morning, Diane," he said, looking down at the floor. "My wife locked me out last night, and I had no other place to go except here."

When he looked up, Diane gasped, horrified. "Oh, Mr. Abbott. What happened?" On the left side of his head was a three-inch gash. It was a recent wound that needed to be cleaned and medically treated. "Let me get a fresh cloth, and I'll clean it."

"Thank you," he said dejectedly. "I just don't know why my wife gets angry so suddenly. Abigail will be stopping by soon to take me to see Dr. Kennard."

With the wound just superficially cleaned, the first customer came in the door. Diane gave a pleasant greeting as Pinky slipped through a door into the back office. Not wanting to be seen, he sat in his office away from the customers. To while away the time, he began reminiscing about some of the *good* memories he had with his wife.

The first time he met Martha, it was almost Christmas. She was lovely in her light-blue dress with a freshly starched white collar accented by beautiful lace trim. What a hard worker she was! She made the church benches vibrate with her firm polishing. Her giggle was girlish and cute, and she had intelligent, blue eyes. Oh, what a sweet smile she had. He could still see her strawberry-blonde hair glistening like spun gold. She was a real beauty!

He stopped by the church office the next day to get her name. The secretary and the minister had nothing but good things to say about Martha. Worried that maybe she wouldn't accept him, being short and bald, he hesitated to call on her. He waited until it settled down after the holidays to stop by the church to talk with her. He peeked in, and there she was, polishing the pews again just like before. It was almost comical.

"Hi, Martha. I'm Peter Abbott. I met you a few weeks ago when I brought a box of candy for the children at

Christmas time," he chuckled. "You were polishing the same pews."

"Oh, I do remember you. You wore a wool cabbie hat. Did you have a good Christmas?" she asked, hoping to continue the conversation.

"Pretty good. It was so busy at the store that I forget to slow down and enjoy the holiday. How about you?"

"It was a good Christmas, better than most," she replied with delight in her voice.

"I would like to call on you sometime. Would that be okay with you?"

"I would like that very much," she said slowly, trying to be reserved and proper.

"How about tomorrow night?" he asked. "I'll meet you at your house around six thirty. Where do you live?" There was no attempt made to make small talk; he was too nervous. He had a goal, which he achieved, and did not want to complicate it by saying something that might offend her.

"I live two blocks from here on the same side of the street," Martha said with a smile. "It's the white house with blue shutters."

"I know just where that is," he said. "My aunt lives just two doors down from that house."

"Really! Could that be my neighbor, Sally Abbott?" she asked.

"Yes," he said.

"She's my favorite neighbor," she said. "If you are as nice as she is, I'm glad I had an opportunity to meet you."

The meeting between Pinky and Martha was the beginning of something, which was both a blessing and a curse. Martha was so happy to have her own home and the chance to have children. She slavishly scrubbed, ironed, cleaned, pulled weeds, and diligently taught each of her three daughters how to cook and clean. Mary and Louise were naturals, but Abigail was so different. Even her name was offsetting. Abigail was derived from two Hebrew words—one meaning "father" and the other "happiness"—so combining them meant "my father's happiness." There was truth in that name, especially between Abigail and Pinky. Whether Martha was jealous of Abigail's relationship with her father or whether she had a disdain for her disregard of household chores, it was evident that their relationship was like oil and water. The relationship Abigail had with her father couldn't have been more opposite. They were mutually support-ive, laughed at the same jokes, and very often could read the other's mind.

Jealousy and family divisions tormented the parenting style of Pinky and Martha. This was the cursed part. It was like a dark streak of evil lurking underneath a respect-able façade, and the secret was held so tightly, it grew and festered just below the surface. It was hidden from their aunts and uncles, from their grandparents, neigh-bors, and even hidden from their own awareness most of the time. It churned in their subconscious and erupted when it could no longer be contained. They sensed that if their neighbors and relatives knew, they would be ostra-cized from the very people with whom they so wanted to belong. An uneasy peace prevailed.

࿔࿔࿔

She admitted her father to the hospital all by herself. Her two sisters and mother dismissed his injuries as minor and of no consequence.

"Are you Abigail Abbott?" Dr. Kennard asked as he approached her in the waiting room. "How did your father get those injuries?"

Abigail looked at the floor. She groped for words, but she just couldn't find them. Wringing her hands, she remained silent.

"Is there something wrong?" he asked in his quiet, deferential way.

"Yes," Abigail responded. "Daddy and my mother sometimes don't get along. She yells and screams. He doesn't want the neighbors to hear, so he tries to quiet her by holding her, but she bites and hits him. When daddy tries to get away, she'll throw things at him. She throws anything at him that is within her reach."

"How often does this happen?"

"Not often, thankfully, maybe twice a year. When it does happen, it's like an explosion, and I don't know what to do about it."

"Where is your mother, now?" the doctor asked.

"She's at home," Abigail said. "After these episodes, Mother shuts herself in their bedroom and won't come out until Daddy pleads with her to clean the house and cook for him. I'm worried about Daddy. Is he going to be okay?"

"I stitched him up and he should heal all right, but whatever hit him was pretty sharp. He will have a scar over his left eye. I need to see your mother before I'll let him go back home." Dr. Kennard shook his head as he left the room.

Why am I always stuck in the middle? she asked herself. *I seem to be the one in the middle refereeing Mommy and Daddy's fights. My sisters just look the other way and leave the house.*

Yet something told her, even then, that she would have to be the one to take care of their daddy. Being the only male in a household of four women wasn't easy for him. For sure, Mother was not an ally. She kept the house clean, and she was an adequate cook, but she always seemed cold and calculating. Sometimes Abigail wondered if she had any feelings. Daddy was so different. She felt so loved by him, and she respected him because he tried so hard to keep his wife and children happy.

As Abigail opened the door of her house, she heard her mother yelling from her bedroom. "Who is that? Is that, you, Abigail?"

"Yes, it's me, mother."

"Where's your father?" she asked, clearly annoyed by him.

"He's with Dr. Kennard at the hospital."

"What's he doing there?"

"Dr. Kennard had to stitch a deep cut above his eye. The iron you threw hit him hard. He bled a lot. I was worried about him."

"Oh," she said and fell silent. Shame washed over her since she knew she did something wrong, but she was so exasperated with the marriage. Whenever her husband tried to hold her, she felt trapped like a caged animal. She was overcome with loneliness. She was so unhappy.

"The doctor said that he needs to talk to you before he'll let daddy come home."

"What is he going to say to me?" she asked. Fear came out of her voice like a child about to be disciplined. She didn't like being exposed since she wanted the family problems to stay within the family and didn't want them shared with anybody. Even a doctor was off limits.

"I don't know, but you have to talk to him. Daddy has to go to work tomorrow."

Abigail was tired of talking through a closed door, so she knocked on the bedroom door before she opened it.

"What do you want?" Martha said. "I'm tired. I'm so tired of living like this. It's like I'm a caged animal. Nobody cares about me." She sighed and slumped in her chair, covered her eyes, and started to cry.

"Come on, Mother. You can do it. I'll walk with you to the hospital."

Her mother levered her body out of the chair and shuffled to her closet, sobbing all the way. She put on a sweater, fastened each button with a sigh, and put on walking shoes. It seemed to take forever. Abigail held the front door open for her, and the two of them headed up the street without speaking a word.

Dr. Kennard was waiting for them in his office. He heard them take a seat and opened the door to meet them. "Hello, are you Mrs. Abbott?"

"Yes, but you can call me Martha," she said timidly.

"I'd like to speak with you alone, and then I'll ask Mr. Abbott to join us."

Abigail went back to the waiting room and sat there patiently, but strained to hear what he was saying. At one point, she did hear her daddy's voice, which comforted her. She accepted that they were talking adult business, but her imaginings were on high alert. Hoping that this would put an end to the arguments, Abigail resigned herself to being seen but not heard.

After that day, life went on as usual. Daddy worked and supported the family, and her mother cleaned and cooked. Although there was no evidence of real tenderness or love between them, the arguments stopped for many months. It was a wonderful relief and stable time for the family. Abigail was the bookkeeper for Abbott's Confectionary, and she made some savvy business deals that generated unexpected prosperity. Baltimore was the first city in the United States to make licorice, so Abigail brokered a deal with the John Young Company to ship the candy to the Chicago market for a percentage of the profits.

Then one day all hell broke loose in the Abbott household. It was like a huge explosion, and the violence was worse than before. Daddy had just come home from work very tired and Mother sat sulking. He said something that upset her, and the yelling started. No forewarning, just unbridled rage. All three daughters were home to witness the brutality. This time, he didn't hold her to try to control the outbreak, but she still threw whatever was near her, always aiming for his head. It was a savage attack. Chairs, a hammer, the iron, all flew through the air. Daddy ran out the back door, his face beaten and bloodied. He needed the immediate care of a doctor. Mother, suddenly hit with pangs of conscience, ran into her bedroom and locked the door. For the first time, Mary, Louise, and Abigail worked as a team, knowing that life in the Abbott home was never going to be the same again.

They again took Daddy to see Dr. Kennard. As he was getting his wounds stitched and bandaged, the three of them talked.

"Mommy and Daddy just cannot live together anymore," Mary said. "Mommy will kill him."

The realization was shattering. They were devastated. It appeared that a very difficult decision lay ahead.

"Let's see what Dr. Kennard says before we panic," Abigail said.

Louise, the youngest, remained in shock, not saying a word. After treating Pinky's wounds, Dr. Kennard called the three of them into his office.

"Your mother and father cannot live together until your mother gets better," Dr. Kennard warned. "I recommend that she be admitted to the Government Hospital for the Insane in Washington, D.C. It's the closest Kirkbride facility and considered one of the best in the country."

❧ ❧ ❧

Gloom reigned in the Abbott household. This was the day they would take Mother to the hospital for the insane. How did it ever come to this? They saw their family as a typical one, maybe even a little better, because Daddy had a successful business. This secret about Mother was like a dark monster that lived underneath the house and came out to spook them when their guard was down. They employed every strategy to keep it in check, but finally it had reached a critical point. The misconception that they were a typical family was exposed, and they were at a crossroads. Mom needed help and would have to be separated from the family for a long while.

The skies were overcast, corresponding with the mood of the family. Pinky put Diane in charge of running the store so they all could ride the Baltimore & Potomac Railroad into Washington, D.C. Outside, it was a cold clammy drizzle, so they bundled up and carried umbrellas. Fall weather in Baltimore was sometimes like that.

Finding a place to sit on the Baltimore & Potomac train was a challenge, especially at this time of day. It was the ten o'clock train, and they had to compete for the empty seats with the commuters. Pinky and Abigail stood up while Mary, Louise, and Martha found seats where they could sit together.

Although somewhat comforted by her daughters, Martha was slumped over and seemed to be carrying the weight of the world on her shoulders. She was glum and fearful. This was the first time the whole family had taken the train out of Baltimore, and it was hard to acclimate to the jostling and rocking movements. It was very different from the horse-and-buggy rides. The screeching of the brakes as they entered Union Station was particularly startling. They stood up quickly, ready to file out at a moment's notice. Once assembled on the platform, they began searching for open air and Massachusetts Avenue. They spotted a stairway up, and they headed toward it … so good to breathe fresh air.

Streetcars were lined up on Massachusetts Avenue waiting for passengers. They chose the one heading for Anacostia Station, which was just a short walk from the hospital. The family split was always evident, even when they walked as a group. Mary and Louise flanked Martha on either side, and Pinky and Abigail walked together behind the group, bringing up the rear.

Abigail watched her mother as they ambled through the park-like area leading to the hospital. She showed no noticeable reaction, which Abigail interpreted as resignation. However, when the massive five-story structure came into view, her countenance changed and she looked visibly shaken. She had never traveled beyond Baltimore, the city where she grew up. Her simple life consisted of living at her father's home and then, once married, living with her husband in his home. Leaving her family and becoming a patient in this big building in Washington, D.C., was paralyzing for her. It was hard to imagine the amount of fear she had when she was about to separate from the only world she had ever known. Leaving her family behind was unthinkable.

As Daddy opened the large door for her, she lunged backwards cowering with fright. At that moment, two nurses came to talk to her and helped her through the door.

"Martha, we have been waiting for you," one of the nurses said. "I'm Maureen and this is Nancy. Have a seat here, and the doctor will be ready for you in a few minutes."

Fortunately, Martha listened to them.

As the nurses went back to their desks, Abigail and her sisters took their seats and waited. This place was like nothing Abigail had ever seen. There were beautiful landscape paintings on the walls. The huge, ceiling-to-floor windows emitted so much sunshine that the room virtually glowed. She didn't expect it to be like this. A prominent portrait of Thomas Kirkbride was on display above the nurses' station. Earlier, as they approached the building, she had noticed the sanctuary-like grounds and the gardens. It was lovely and tranquil.

The low tone of the doctor's voice was engaging.

"Hello, I'm Dr. Quincy," he said. His boyish smile was appealing. He shook hands first with Daddy and then Mommy. "How do you do," he said as he nodded to the three girls. "Mr. and Mrs. Abbott, good to meet you. Please come into my office."

Once again, the girls were not privy to the conversations. They had to patiently wait outside his office.

To their surprise, the nurse named Maureen approached them. She must have sensed their consternation. "Would you like a tour of the hospital?" she asked.

"Yes," Mary said without hesitation, and Abigail and Louise nodded. They very much wanted to know what their mother would be experiencing.

"This hospital opened in 1855 and was the first hospital built by the federal government. Up to that time, patients were put in prisons or poor houses, and were not treated well. Thomas Kirkbride changed all that. He was a doctor who believed in the moral treatment of patients with mental illnesses. He was convinced that providing the right environment could promote healing. He considered fresh air, sunlight, and natural surroundings essential for recovery. Our patients work in the gardens and tend to the parks on the property. They feel useful, and are active participants in their own recovery. Most of the food we eat comes from the gardens that are planted and cultivated by the patients."

"Mom likes to work and clean," Mary said. "I think this place might be good for her."

Maureen smiled and continued the tour. "Here is one of the patient rooms," she said.

It was small room but adequate, with a huge window that filled the room with shafts of light. As they continued down the hallway, they saw one of the patients in her room. She was staring out the window and completely still. *How would Mom fare in this environment?* Abigail thought. *I guess we'll just have to wait and see.*

Continuing on, their guide took them through the dining room and, once again, Abigail noticed how the sunlight filled the room. It was hard to imagine the bedlam and chaos that would soon overtake the room at dinnertime.

Their next adventure was walking the trail outside. They descended three flights of stairs and opened the door to a nature-filled sanctuary, which was surrounded by lush lawns. The grounds were meticulously groomed … so peaceful. They strolled by English flower gardens and vegetable gardens, which were filled with pumpkins and butternut squash. Fruit trees, blueberry bushes, and strawberry plants graced the property as well. The patients did the harvesting, and what they harvested was sent to the kitchen. The cooks made delicious meals from the produce of the gardens. Providing healthy nourishment for the patients was paramount to the administrators of the hospital.

"We don't have any animals yet, but there are plans to raise chickens and graze sheep. Just lately, we heard a rumor that some animals are coming in from Africa. They don't have a place to stay, because the National Zoo is still under construction, so they might stay here in the back buildings until the zoo is ready for them."

"Really," Abigail chuckled. "Mom will have something exciting to write to us about in her letters home."

As they headed back, Maureen pointed out the west wing, a treatment facility for soldiers from the Civil War, and the east wing, which was used for the treatment of the insane.

That's where Mom will be, Abigail thought. She thanked Maureen for her informative tour and then, they went back to the waiting room to find Daddy and Mommy wondering where they had been.

"We hoped we would see you before Mother went to her room," Daddy said. "We've been done for ten minutes."

"Maureen offered us a tour, and we couldn't pass it up," Mary said. "How are you doing, Mommy?"

"I've been better, but Dr. Quincy assured me that I will be happy here, and he encouraged me to give it a try." Tearfully, Mary and Louise ran to hug their mother and say their good-byes.

"Good-bye, Mom," Abigail said when her turn came, giving her a quick hug. "Be sure to write us. We'll be waiting to hear from you."

They left the room so their father and mother could have some time alone. Soon he came to join them and they walked to the streetcar together. All were solemn and quiet.

CHAPTER 2

Firsts

❧ ❧ ❧ ❧

Life had so many mysteries for Pinky, and Martha was his biggest one. Some considered marriage to be like a "box" that you share with a "box mate," an image that Pinky took to imply imprisonment, and at times for him, it was torture. Even though his marriage was filled with struggles and missed opportunities, he longed for his wife Martha. He yearned for the family times when they were all together, and the sweet sound of laughter during the holidays. Nevertheless, his work at Abbott's Confectionary pulled him back into the expected routines of Baltimore. Somehow his daily schedules kept him from going into a deep despair. His three daughters operated as an effective team, and this sustained him. Their presence in his life offered him so much comfort. Mary and Louise ran the house brilliantly, and his daughter Abigail was a fine bookkeeper, bar none.

"Daddy, I'd like to show you our profits from the Chicago licorice deal," Abigail said, handing him the ledger and pointing to the final column. Every month without exception, the John Young Candy Co. paid them ten percent of the money they received from the Chicago candy broker, Ora Snyder. Pinky smiled with approval, because those profits made the business grow beyond his own expectations and helped pay Martha's hospital bills.

"What would you say if I wrote a letter to Stephen Whitman in Philadelphia about boxing his chocolate candy for Valentine's Day?" Abigail asked. "Richard and George Cadbury are doing that in England, and it's bringing them a lot of business. The boxes of Valentine chocolates sell out every time."

"Abby, the way you think always amazes me. You are a true business woman," Pinky responded with a chuckle. "You might as well give it a try. It's a long shot, but we might be surprised."

She wrote the letter thinking that at worst they would drop the letter in a desk drawer or wastebasket but at best, they would write back. She waited for several weeks. What a great day it was when an answer came in the mail.

Dear Miss Abbott,

You and your father have been good customers; people with whom we like to do business. I have placed an order with the head of the manufacturing section of the company to create special Valentine boxes for Whitman's Chocolates, and you will be the first place of business allowed to sell them. We will mail one hundred boxes to Baltimore sometime in January 1886.

Please let us know how they sell.

Sincerely,

Stephen Whitman

One hundred boxes of Whitman Valentine Chocolates arrived in mid-January as Stephen Whitman said. A flurry of excitement filled the store when the crates were delivered. When the large shipment was opened, Abigail's jaw dropped. The boxes were heart-shaped! How did they do that? She carefully lifted the first box out of the crate and gently stroked the pretty pink velvet bow on the bright-red valentine box. Word spread around Baltimore that Abbott's Confectionary had something excitingly different for Valentine's Day. Sales were brisk for the next month, right up through the fourteenth of February.

Pinky made plans to visit Martha in the hospital on Valentine's Day. He brought one of the pretty boxes of chocolate with him for Martha. He arranged with Abigail to manage the store before he left on the train to Washington, D.C. Abigail took the job of monitoring the store on Valentine's Day seriously. She was so busy! The men of Baltimore were buying chocolates for their ladies all day long.

One such gentleman bought the last heart-shaped box of chocolates around four o'clock in the afternoon on the fourteenth of February. She would *never* forget him.

He had a thick, well-groomed, dark-brown beard and mustache, and she spotted a swath of light-brown hair under his brown felt fedora. He was so different from the captains of industry dressed in their stovepipe and derby hats. These gentlemen were all dressed up to buy the latest candy for their ladies.

The most alarming feature was the black patch over his left eye. Abigail didn't know whether to be frightened, sympathetic, or intrigued. His hands were large and masculine and his walk strong and direct. He was a no-nonsense kind of man. She showed him the Valentine box of Whitman's chocolates, and his face lit up the room. His smile was childlike, disarming, and simply irresistible. Then he gave her a curious look.

"My Sylvia will really like that. I'll take two," he said. His voice was deep and melodious.

With a voice like that, maybe he's an actor or a performer of some kind.

"I'm sorry, but there's only one left, and that's the one you're holding." she said with a pleasant smile.

"What am I supposed to get for the other one?" he said, flirting with his eyes and flashing his charming smile.

"Just maybe she'll have to wait until next year," Abigail responded in kind.

"Maybe so," he said as he took out a roll of bills.

He paid her double the cost for the chocolates. Abigail went to the till to get change, but when she looked up he was heading out the door.

"Wait, sir. I have your change." Abigail hurried to give him his money.

"Keep the change in place of the chocolates. Happy Valentine's Day."

He looked at Abigail with that engaging smile and a twinkle in his eye. He walked out the door and left her mystified.

What just happened? Is there such a thing as scary charm?

At five o'clock, Abigail closed the store and headed home for supper. She caught herself reliving the encounter with this mystery man. Sometimes she chuckled and other times she shook her head. Her sisters, Mary and Louise, prepared a great supper of chicken and dumplings. She was drawn to the tantalizing smell of the cooked chicken. Pinky arrived home from his visit with Martha just in time to join his three daughters. For dessert, they baked a large heart-shaped cookie that they split four ways. It was like they were a whole family again.

"How is Mommy?" Abigail asked.

"Your mother misses us very much. She's being cooperative but is very discouraged. Cleaning and gardening are all she does, and those are things she could do at home. She doesn't think she's getting better."

"Does she see Dr. Quincy?" Mary asked.

"Yes, once a week, but he's not telling her what to do to get better."

"Did Mommy like the box of Whitman's chocolates?" Louise asked.

"Yes, she did. It was the first time I've seen her smile in a long time," he responded, then, turning to Abigail, he asked, "How did it go at the store?"

"It was so busy! The Valentine boxes were sold out by four o'clock."

Abigail debated whether to share the experience she had with the mystery man at the dinner table. She decided to stay quiet and excused herself from the table to go to her bedroom. She shut the door, but her mind kept whirling.

Who is he? Is Sylvia his wife or his girlfriend? I was attracted to him. Why did he have a patch over his eye? Did he lose his eye in a fight? Where is he from? He wasn't like any man I've met in Baltimore. Will I see him again?

Abigail took off her dress and looked at herself in the mirror. Then, she untied her braids and let her long auburn locks fall loosely around her shoulders. She studied her hazel eyes, her oval face, her ears, her chin, her breasts, her waist, her belly, her thighs and legs. She took a long look and then sighed. *I'm okay.*

She dressed in her bedclothes and talked to the mirror. She repeated the conversation between "no-name" and her. She chuckled, smiled, and then became serious, because somehow, he tugged at her heart. *This is just such a time I need to talk to my friend Rosemary.*

Rosemary's family lived on the "other side of the tracks." Her father worked on the railroad but was injured in the railroad strike of 1877, when Rosemary was in elementary school. A member of the state militia hit him hard in the head with a billy club. He was knocked out and sustained an incapacitating head injury. He hadn't been strong enough to work since. Her mother, a seamstress, somehow kept the family going by catering to those who lived in a more prosperous part of town.

Rosemary and Abigail spent time together at the candy store after school. Some days they would fill up with candy and then explore Baltimore. One afternoon, after hearing rumors about a goat-man terrorizing teen lovers at Lover's Lane, they decided to see for themselves. They waited until early evening, and off they went to check out the veracity of the stories. Dusk descended as they approached the one-lane bridge off Acton Lane. Hiding in the underbrush, they waited for any signs of the goat-man. Hearing some rustling in the bushes, they were spooked and ran off in a panic. The next day, however, they skipped the candy store and went straight to Acton Lane to see if there was evidence of the goat-man. To their surprise, they saw cloven goat prints in the sand, which convinced them that the rumors were true.

The "Crybaby Bridge" escapade was another adventure that bonded their friendship. The rumors had it that, when nightfall came at Crybaby Bridge, a wailing sound of a baby would fill the air. When this happened, people witnessed the goat-man with a beard and horns roaming underneath the bridge. Off they went to check it out. Once again, they hid in the underbrush with the mosquitoes. They waited in the dark with their eyes and ears wide open. Suddenly, out of the dark, came a prolonged cry of grief and pain. They looked at each other and took off at a fast run and didn't stop until they were home. They didn't see evidence of the goat-man, but for sure, they heard the ghost of the baby that was thrown over the bridge into the water.

స్వేస్వేస్వే

Abigail woke up on what promised to be a particularly fine Baltimore day. She put on her everyday clothes, took a jacket along in case it turned cool, and off she went to see her friend. Rosemary partnered with her mother as a fledgling seamstress, so she was sure she would be home. Being a seamstress meant long hours by the sewing machine.

Climbing aboard the streetcar, with a plan to transfer to another one, she found her way to the other side of the tracks. All the row houses had front porches with five or six wooden steps leading up to the front door. She recalled the view from Rosemary's front window. Across the street from their house was an eight-foot-high stone fence with another five feet of wrought iron fencing on top. On the other side of the wall were the tracks. The cargo trains rattled their house with predictable accuracy every two hours. Rosemary was too embarrassed to bring classmates home, but Abigail was the exception. Their respect for each other and their adventurous spirits transcended any class differences.

Rosemary's family lived in St. Ann's parish and, as the story goes, Captain William Kennedy built the church in 1873. Having survived a brutal storm in Vera Cruz, Captain Kennedy and his crew were very grateful to be alive. This event inspired him to build a Catholic church as a token of his appreciation. This church was named after St. Ann, the patron saint of sailors.

Their street was by the train tracks and was one of the outside boundaries of St Ann's parish. Abigail walked alongside St. Ann's Church and marveled at the dark-brown brick structure so typical of Gothic revival architecture. Soon she was at her friend's house knocking briskly on the door.

Rosemary opened the door, and her mouth dropped open. "Abigail! I'm so happy to see you. What a nice surprise!" Rosemary's face beamed with joy, and while they hugged, they jumped up and down.

"Who is that, Rosemary?" Her mother queried, thinking it was a customer.

"It's Abigail Abbott." Rosemary said. "She stopped by to see me."

With that said, her mother came out of the sewing room with a big smile. She had always liked Abigail. "Hi, Abigail. My, it's so good to see you! You're as beautiful as ever, my dear."

Florence, Rosemary's mother, was her "other mother." She cared for her and encouraged her—so unlike her real mother. Abigail always appreciated her sweet warmth and the love she gave to her own daughter.

"What are you working on?" Abigail asked.

Florence brought her into her sewing room to show her the wedding gown she was making. It was gorgeous! The design was simple yet sophisticated, with material of white satin and lace, which was smooth to the touch. The bodice was feminine, a bit flirtatious with an overlay of French lace, exquisitely tailored with the neckline gracefully exposing the shoulders. Florence's skill as a seamstress was unparalleled.

"Abigail, I think you are the same size as this bride-to-be. Would you like to try it on?"

"Yes," she replied with a sheepish smile.

While Abigail took off her everyday clothes, Florence and Rosemary lifted the wedding gown off the dress form and readied it to go over her head. They smoothed out the bodice and laced her up in the back. Each gentle tug accentuated her slim waist and ample bust and, when they tied the final bow, they both commented on how nice she looked.

Abigail turned around to look at herself in the mirror and, to her surprise, she saw someone very young but strikingly elegant. *Is this kind of elegance possible for me in my lifetime? Someday, will I be a bride? I do wonder what my future holds.*

She was startled out of her daydream by a knock on the door. It was a new customer for Florence, so it was time to stop daydreaming, take the dress off, and put on her everyday clothes.

"Rosemary, is there some place where we can talk privately?" Abigail asked.

"We can't talk here, but we can go to Morency Park down the street. I'll ask Mom if I can leave for a few minutes."

Rosemary notified her mom, got her permission, and off they went to the park. Finally alone, they retold some of the funny mishaps they shared. They laughed together and sometimes at each other. Rosemary's physique was light and wiry. She moved so quickly it was like she flew from place to place. Her curly blond hair danced as she moved. Just watching her made Abigail giggle.

"You were always the teacher's pet," Rosemary teased. "They would treat you special for a box of chocolates."

"And you … if you stood on the scale in Salem, you'd be declared a witch," Abigail countered. "You're lucky you live in Baltimore one hundred years later." Their style of bantering was personal but done in a good spirit. They liked each other so much, and both knew they would be friends for life.

"I have something to ask you," Abigail finally said. "Have you ever had romantic feelings?"

Surprised by the question, Rosemary turned around and looked her straight in her eyes to see if she was serious. "Yes, I have," she said after collecting her thoughts. "Mathew, my friend from church, stops by to talk to me every couple of days. I like him. We laugh a lot about silly stuff. He's a good friend. Sometimes I feel a kind of romantic love for him. Why do you ask?"

"Something happened with a customer, and I just can't stop thinking about him."

"What's his name?" Rosemary asked.

"No name," Abigail responded.

"You don't know his *name?*" Rosemary snickered.

"Not yet. I have a hunch that I'll see him again, soon."

"What does he look like," she asked.

"Curiously, he had a black patch over his left eye," Abigail said. "If I ever see him again, that will be the first thing I'll check. That patch was a little worrisome. It made me wonder if he got into a bad fight. Otherwise, he was very handsome and quite manly. He has light-brown hair with a dark-brown beard. His manner was masculine but not gruff. I think he's probably in his middle to late twenties."

"Did you find out what he does for a living?" Rosemary queried.

"I didn't find that out. All I know is that he's very different from the other men I've met in Baltimore. He's quite unique."

"Promise me that you'll come by to see me when you meet him again. I'd like to share stories. I'll let you know if anything happens with Mathew," Rosemary said. "Well, I've enjoyed our visit, but I have to head back to help my mom."

They hugged good-bye, and Abigail went off to catch the streetcar, her heart filled with thoughts of Florence and Rosemary, her good friends. Also, the intrigue continued about the mystery man.

She spent the next two weeks going to Abbott's Confectionary to do the bookkeeping. It was her habit to read *The Baltimore Sun* every morning with her cup of coffee. On Friday, February 26, 1886, she opened up the newspaper to a front-page story that would change her life forever.

$$\approx \approx \approx$$

Abigail's disbelieving eyes were glued to the morning paper. There was a sketch of the mystery man shaking hands with one of the other landowners in the dispute. The front-page headline read:

Avery Johnson Suing the Pennsylvania Railroad

The article read: *Avery Johnson, a land speculator, is suing the Pennsylvania Railroad Corporation for a million dollars for taking federal lands that were given to them and selling the land to American settlers for steep prices. He claims they are taking the money to pay for their own personal projects. "This is the biggest land grab that has ever happened in this country," he said. "I'm claiming that the railroads are getting rich off land speculators and the common man."*

Court proceedings will start on Monday with Judge Samuel Larkins presiding.

Abigail stared at his picture in the newspaper for a long time, especially noticing how handsome he was. So, his name is Avery Johnson. That is a good to know. She saw only the right side of his face, so she didn't see the patch over his left eye. Avery wore that same fedora he had on the first time she met him. Also, she noticed he was wearing the same long stylish frock coat he wore on Valentine's Day. His beard and mustache were nicely sketched and his stance was strong and confident. He gave the landowner his full attention, and that irresistible smile jumped off the page. It looked like he was gearing up for a challenge.

Downtown Baltimore was abuzz for the next two weeks. Daily reports about the court proceedings were discussed at the store. This happened until the final verdict came down. People discussed how the railroad industry had changed their lives, which was sometimes for the good and other times, for the bad. Groups of husbands and wives came into Abbott's Confectionary to buy newspapers and candies. The women would gravitate to the candy counters, and the men would huddle together to discuss the court case. They commented on the ruthless exploitation being carried out by the railroad management. Most of them were rooting for Avery, because they wanted the railroads to be put in their place.

"I hope the judge rules in his favor. If he's a fair man, he will," one of the patrons said as he purchased a newspaper.

"Avery is on the right side," another man said.

Abigail secretly supported his position as well. Even though she was new to the field of business, she understood the importance of honesty and a level playing field. The railroad corporations flourished because they exploited settlers, speculators, and landowners. But she also knew that business enterprises had to take risks to stay ahead of the trends. Abigail found the entrepreneurs to be intimidating, making her feel uncertain about her views. At this point, she could understand both sides— the risks taken by industry and the frustration of those suffering exploitation. Her unfamiliarity with competitive industries made her too timid to stand up for her views, but she knew that the day would come when she would confidently express her opinions. In so many ways, she was handicapped by her father's attempts to protect her from the world and its harsh realities. Taking care of the financial records for Abbott's Confectionary was her sole focus, but she relished hearing the animated discussions of the businessmen sharing their political views.

Finally, the day came when the judge rendered his opinion. It was a positive verdict for the plaintiff, so it was a victory for Avery. Most of the business community was intrigued by the outcome, and the copies of *The Baltimore Sun* were flying off the shelves. The general population wanted more information. Groups of men gathered to discuss the newspaper articles; many were jubilant that Avery had won a decisive victory. The power of the railroad corporation had been successfully challenged, and, hopefully, big changes were about to happen.

Avery and a group of his comrades triumphantly walked past Abbott's Confectionary, and one of the men stepped inside to buy a paper. While the group stopped to wait for him, Avery turned toward the store and his eyes met Abigail's. She was relieved to see that the eye patch was no longer there, and his eye was intact. Locked in a stare, he burst into his wonderful smile. Abigail responded in kind and, with a twinkle in her eye, mouthed the word "*C o n g r a t u l a t i o n s*" through the windowpane. They joyfully shared that fleeting moment. It was a split second in time that caused eternal consequences. Abigail went about her business in the store, and Avery continued on to the local pub to celebrate the victory with his comrades-in-arms.

Two weeks later, when Abigail was in the back office doing books, Avery stopped by for a visit. Pinky was working the front counter.

"I'm looking for a young lady who works here. She has green eyes and a lovely smile. I believe she has red hair. Sorry, I don't know her name."

"That's got to be my daughter, Abigail," Pinky replied.

"Oh, it's your *daughter*? I didn't know she worked for her father," Avery said.

"Yes, she works for me in the store." Pinky took a little time to check him out before he spoke. "She's in the back office; I'll go get her."

Abigail heard the entire conversation and her heart started to pound. She was excited and afraid at the same time. As Pinky walked in the back office, she was poised to get up and meet Avery.

"Where did you meet him?" Pinky asked. "I think I've seen him before."

"He bought the last box of Whitman's Valentine chocolates from me on Valentine's Day. He was also in the newspaper a couple of weeks ago. His name is Avery Johnson, and he won a lawsuit against the railroad corporations. Don't worry, Daddy, I'll be okay."

She glanced at her dad for reassurance and walked out to the front counter. Her eyes met Avery's, and she smiled demurely.

"Hello, Miss Abigail," Avery said, flashing that irresistible smile. "I finally know your name. Would you like to go out to dinner with me sometime?"

"Yes," Abigail said with just a moment's hesitation.

"I'd like to take you to The Horse on Thames Street.

Edgar Allen Poe, my favorite poet, used to go there. What time are you done with work on Friday?"

"Six o'clock would be a good time," Abigail replied.

His face lit up with that boyish smile. "With your father's permission, I'll stop in and escort you there. Friday, then?"

Pinky was in the back hallway listening, so he stepped back into the front part of the store. He checked Abigail's face and from her expression it was clear that she wanted his approval. "You have my permission, sir," he said, holding out his hand for a handshake.

"Excellent. Abigail, I'll see you at six o'clock on Friday," Avery said while responding to Pinky's cordiality. He smiled, and off he went with a spring in his step.

Pinky knew that a major change was about to take place between Abigail and him. They both watched Avery leave the store. Abigail so wanted her father's blessing, but she also appreciated his deep desire to provide the best circumstances for his beloved daughter.

తతత

Every number Abigail put in the books was punctuated by thoughts of Avery and what might happen during their first time together. She was not functioning well enough to do justice to her job at Abbott's Confectionary. Her uncertainty made her edgy and overly concerned. She wanted to go home to change into fresh clothes, but there wasn't enough time, so she brought clothes to the office and planned to change just before he arrived. Her decision to wear her robin's-egg-blue dress was based on the positive comments she received from friends and family. Her deepest desire was to be ravishing for Avery, and wearing a dress that enhanced her eyes and hair color was a good start.

Six o'clock was well after the store closed; Pinky could have gone home as early as five o'clock, but he chose to stay and wait for Avery. He cleaned the counters and the shelves over and over again, and Abigail knew it was just busy work. He was as nervous as she was. *What a dear father I have! He's been both a mother and a father to me. I love him very much.*

Abigail put on her dress, then combed her hair in the small washroom at the back of the store. The tight quarters made it almost impossible to get all the tangles out of her long auburn hair. She looked in the mirror, spotted a bump of frizzy hair, and gave an exasperated cry.

Pinky came back to check on her. "Is something wrong?"

She sighed. "I just can't get my hair the way I want it."

"Abigail, you look so lovely in that dress, and your hair is just fine. A beautiful smile is the best way to hide any imperfections, and you have a splendid one," Pinky said. "I think I've talked to you before about exchanges that one has to make in life. Especially now, it is important that you hear it again. One of the hardest truths to accept is that you can't have everything. For instance, if you marry, you won't be single and free anymore. If you choose a career over marriage, having a family won't be an option. When you make a decision, you have to accept the fact that you have to give up something else. My advice to you is that you need to choose wisely, because you will always have to make an exchange."

"I will, Daddy. I will," Abigail said dismissing the gravity of his words.

"You know, usually, mothers chaperone their daughters when a young man courts them. Maybe I should go with you tonight," Pinky said.

"Daddy, I'll be fine. Don't worry about me. I'm not a little girl anymore."

"Maybe so, but you'll always be my little girl. Just remember to be careful."

"Daddy, you are the best," she said, giving him a hug.

The bell rang when Avery opened the door. No one was watching the counter, so he sauntered over to the candy case and looked at the different kinds of penny candies. His eyes and nose pulled him toward the chocolate counter where the Lancaster caramels were on display. It was a feast for his eyes ... and nose. He looked up as Pinky walked through the door.

"Good evening, Avery. How are you?" Pinky said as they shook hands.

"Good evening. By the way, what would you like me to call you?" Avery asked.

"Pinky is just fine. I'm used to it by now. Abigail reassures me that it's a term of endearment."

"How long have you been in this business?" Avery asked.

"About twenty-eight years," he responded. "I have seen so many changes, some good, some bad. How about you? How long have you been a land speculator?"

"My family has been in the land business since before the Civil War," Avery explained while offering a boyish grin. "I own land north of Baltimore in Carroll County. It's a beautiful piece of country land that is peaceful and quiet. I need that kind of place to live, because land speculating is a business that can give a fella quite a wild ride."

He turned when he noticed Abigail coming towards him. His demeanor changed. He stood tall and gave her his undivided attention. Pinky, for all practical purposes wasn't in the room. Avery and Abigail's eyes were fixed on each other.

"Good evening, Abigail," he said, flashing that smile of his. He seemed to be eclipsed by her radiance and at a loss for words. She did look beautiful that night, with her gentle smile and gorgeous eyes. A dainty lace partially hidden by her auburn hair outlined her delicate neck. Abigail's slightly chiseled chin and full lips gave testament to her loveliness. She was the very essence of youthful beauty.

Avery quickly collected himself and held out his arm. Abigail slipped hers through his and turned her head toward Pinky with a warm smile. Arm in arm, they walked down the street to have dinner at The Horse restaurant.

As Pinky watched them leave, a single tear rolled down his cheek.

The Horse was a new experience for Abigail. There was a bar in the front area and fine dining in the back. Avery had Abigail lead the way, and she did her best to navigate the crowds to get to the dining area. Everyone seemed to know Avery. He was greeted, buttonholed, and wheedled as he walked through the throngs of people. He stayed focused on following Abigail, his dinner partner. The waiter positioned the chair for Abigail, and she gracefully took her spot. Avery's movements by contrast were brusque and clumsy. He seemed to be out of his element, but once seated, he was a charming companion.

"Do you like working for your father?" Avery asked.

"My dad is a wonderful boss. Everybody likes him. He says I'm good at bookkeeping even though I taught myself. Dealing in candy is great fun," Abigail laughed. "I saw you checking out the candy counters," she chided.

"Yum!" Avery answered with gleeful smile, "Lancaster caramels are my favorite. Heavenly morsels!"

The waiter returned with the menus, and he took their drink orders. Abigail chose a Chardonnay and Avery ordered a tall glass of Guinness Extra Stout.

"Tell me about what you do," Abigail asked curiously.

"It's simple and complicated at the same time," Avery responded. "I was relieved when we won the lawsuit. The Pennsylvania Railroad had it coming for a long time. The federal land grant office and the railroads were in bed together. They left the land speculators out in the cold. My attorney said they should settle, but they wanted to go to court. They thought the judge would support them, but they were dead wrong! I think the judge picked up on the public sentiment. The long and short of what I do is I buy and sell land for the best price. My family has been in the land business for a long time. If everything works the way I want it to, I try to buy low and sell high."

"Who's Sylvia?" Abigail asked after a pregnant pause. She shyly lowered her gaze to the tabletop.

"Sylvia, the thrillvia!" he said with a snicker. "She's an old girlfriend who was two-timing me. I said good-bye to her and haven't felt better. How do you know about her?"

"When you came in the store on Valentine's Day, you mentioned buying candy for Sylvia. I wondered if you were married. I must say that I am relieved to know that you are not, and I'm especially happy to find out that she's no longer your girlfriend."

The waiter returned to take their orders. Avery ordered crab cakes and slaw and Abigail, feeling a bit adventurous, ordered scallops imported from Block Island.

"They have the best crab cakes here at this restaurant," Avery announced. "I order the same thing every time. Every day they bring in fresh catch from the Chesapeake."

"My aunt lives in Rhode Island and she claims they get good seafood from Block Island. I was surprised to see it on the menu. I thought I'd give their scallops a try."

With the drink tray in hand, the waiter carefully served Abigail the glass of Chardonnay, and he placed the Guinness Extra Stout in front of Avery. Before the waiter could set the tray down and take their orders, Avery took a big swig of beer.

"Aaah! That hits the spot," he said.

Abigail leisurely sipped her Chardonnay. When the waiter served their food, they enjoyed the aroma of freshly cooked fish. The Worcestershire sauce and the mustard and pepper smells floated through the steamy air. Abigail's scallops were covered with a delicious white sauce.

"Bon appetite," Avery said. They smiled, locked eyes, and took their first bite together.

After their sumptuous meal, they walked leisurely through the Inner Harbor of Baltimore on their way to his Concorde buggy. He took her hand and helped her into the buggy. There they were, side-by-side, looking out at the dark road, not sure what the future might bring. The buggy stopped in front of her house, and Avery walked around the carriage, gingerly taking her hand to help her down. Their eyes met.

"I had a very nice time. Thank you," Abigail said, smiling sweetly.

"Would you like to see my land sometime?"

"Yes, I would like that very much."

Uneasy and a bit clumsily, Avery extended his hand for a handshake. It seemed a bit too formal for Abigail, almost like he was finalizing a business deal. This time she was close enough to notice a red puffiness as she looked into his eyes. When the time is right, she would ask him about the patch. Even though the "good nights" were a bit unsettling, she responded with a nod and a smile.

చితిచితిచి

The next week, Avery stopped by the candy store to arrange a time when the two of them could travel to see his land in Carroll County. The trip would be about three hours; two hours by train and one hour by horse and buggy. An overnight stay would be necessary. Avery obtained permission from his parents so Abigail could spend the night with them in their guest bedroom. Next, Pinky would have to give his permission, and that was more difficult. Abigail took him into the back office.

"I have never met these Johnson people," Pinky said. "I just don't like the idea of you being by yourself with this man."

"Daddy, Avery has a good reputation, especially after he won that lawsuit. I'm nineteen now, and I have to broaden my world beyond Baltimore. I'll be okay, I promise."

"Okay, but I want you home by suppertime on Sunday. Is that understood?"

"Yes, Daddy. I'll be home by then."

Avery and Abigail agreed that noon on Saturday would be a good time to leave, since it allowed Abigail the morning to finish the books from the past week. In spite of this major change in her life, she wanted to be a good employee. To their good fortune, the cool, sunny day was perfect for traveling. They boarded the Western Maryland Railway and headed northwest to the newly built train depot in Union Bridge. Being able to see the countryside in this part of Maryland was a real treat for Abigail. Other than the commuter trains to D.C., this was a new experience for her.

Avery told her to bring some clothes for horseback riding, so she brought a carpetbag packed with her everyday clean clothes, her nightgown, and toiletries. She got the feeling that this would be a couple of rugged days. With the smokestacks blowing huge billows of gray smoke, it was quite a sight to behold. The train rattled through bucolic meadows dotted with farm animals. Other vistas offered lush, cultivated fields of hay and grains. Sitting side by side with this impressive and influential man was beyond her wildest dreams.

"I brought some Lancaster caramels for you," she said with a little bit of flirt in her eyes.

"You did? How nice of you to think of me." He took the caramel out of her gloved hand, popped it in his mouth and, with a smile, he said, "*Yummmm!*"

The two-hour train ride went by quickly with light

conversation between them. The brakes screeched to a halt, and Avery and Abigail disembarked. The Concorde buggy was waiting for them behind the station. After a one-hour buggy ride, they arrived at Avery's homestead, which was near Medford Quarry. He held claim to one hundred acres of rolling hills and mineral-rich land.

"Right now, I live in a little shack, but I have plans to build a big house with the money that I got from winning that court case," he said.

He stopped the horse and buggy in front of his little shack and then helped Abigail down. They entered the shack and, after a brief lunch, she slipped into a small, private room to change into her riding clothes while Avery saddled up the horses. He took the lead with his horse Bandit. They spent the rest of the afternoon riding the towpaths through the Bayberry bushes that were protected by a majestic canopy of stately oaks and pines. They contentedly traversed Avery's virgin land, enjoying the vast countryside.

At one point their horses whinnied, and they were off to the races. What ensued was an exhilarating ride with boundless energy and laughter. For a short while they were in sync, racing wildly through the foothills of the Maryland. Dusk settled in, and they headed back through the darkening forests. Bandit neighed an alarm, reared up, and kicked mid-air.

"Whoa! Bandit. Whoa!" Avery shouted. "Who's there? I see your shadow. Show your face!" The shadow ducked behind the trees. Avery pulled out his rifle and shot in the air. "Come out or I'll shoot to kill. You're trespassing on my land again. You got to learn to keep your filthy livestock off my property, you cur." *Pow*! *Bang*! Silence.

"I've been hit!" someone moaned. A wailing sound came from behind the trees.

"Get your stinking carcass off my property, or I'll shoot you, again!"

A frantic rustling in the trees followed a rapid scampering and heavy breathing. Avery turned to look at Abigail, but he could hardly see her through the dark. Abigail's head was down and her arms wrapped around the horse's neck, visibly shaken.

"Let's go. My parents are waiting for us. Their house is just over the hill," he said matter-of-factly.

Abigail, still shaken, was relieved. She didn't want to spend time alone with him in his shack. His rage reminded her of the violent fights that erupted between her mother and father. The situation was just too similar for her to be comfortable. His outburst was out-of-control scary. What if he turned that rage on her?

"You're awfully quiet. What's wrong?" Avery asked, sensing her consternation.

"I've never seen you so angry. It scared me."

"A man has to protect his land," he said, his tone defensive.

Abigail said nothing.

As they galloped over the hill, the newly installed electric lights illuminated the Maryland mansion. The Johnson family home was stately yet inviting.

❦ ❦ ❦

The door opened and two people were standing in the entryway waiting to greet them. Abigail's first impression of their house was that it entertained a lavish lifestyle.

The gold, brocaded drapes outlined the six-foot-high colonial windows. The red-flocked wallpaper decorated the entry, as did the oval oak frames, highlighting paintings of imposing relatives.

Most impressive by far were the recently installed electric lights. The steady glow of the chandelier radiated through the room. Abigail had never seen anything like it before, and she was determined to convince her father to install them in Abbott's Confectionary.

The short, petite woman was Avery's mother; she had a lovely smile and a curt, black bun tucked tightly on top of her head. Her smile hinted at a playful nature, which was unfortunately curtailed by those around her. Avery's father, on the other hand, was an enormous man, stern-faced, and serious to a fault. What a match! They were "the tall and short of it," as Abraham Lincoln would say.

"Mother, this is my friend Abigail. She's from Baltimore and is the bookkeeper for her father at his candy store, Abbott's Confectionary in downtown Baltimore. Abigail, this is Mallory."

"Oh, how nice. You don't often see young girls going out and working. You must be one of those modern women," she said with a muffled giggle.

Her voice was sweet and childlike. Abigail shook her hand politely and smiled.

"Where's your mother?" Mallory asked.

"My mother is being taken care of in a hospital in Washington, D.C. She's not feeling well," Abigail responded, shifting her eyes downward.

"I'm sorry to hear that," Mallory said with genuine compassion. "Your father is lucky to have you for a daughter. He must trust you very much."

"Yes, he does. I help him at the store, and my two sisters take care of the house." "How did you meet Avery?" Mallory asked.

"On Valentine's Day; he bought some chocolates from me. He said they were for Sylvia." Abigail smiled.

"Sylvia! What a puzzle she was," Mallory remarked. "She's been here to visit, and it was so hard to have a conversation with her because she couldn't sit still."

"Harrumph! I can't get a word in edgewise," Grant said in a gruff tone while extending his hand.

"Father, this is Abigail, and this is my father, Grant."

"It's nice to meet you," he said. His handshake was firm and forthright. They made eye contact and smiled. Instinctively, Abigail liked him. *I might even grow to trust the two of them, but it's hard to know if I'll see them again.*

"Avery's younger brother, Henry, is out West, seeking his fortune. He should be home for Thanksgiving. Perhaps you will meet him then," Grant declared.

"Let me show you your bedroom, and once you're settled you can come down and have a nightcap before you retire," Mallory said, motioning Abigail to follow her. Avery tagged along, carrying her carpetbag.

They climbed the expansive, winding staircase, and Mallory opened the second door at the top of the stairs. The canopy bed was covered with fresh, white linens, and lovely rosebud curtains framed the windows.

The cozy room provided the comfort Abigail needed after the harrowing evening. "Thank you. It's wonderful," Abigail said with a sigh. She was so glad to be in a safe, comfortable place; it was only her sense of propriety that compelled her to go downstairs for a nightcap. She forced herself to freshen up, and then made her appearance by descending the long, winding staircase. Mallory, with tray in hand, walked into the parlor and set the drinks on the table.

"I have found that a little bit of milk before bedtime helps you sleep, and by adding a bit of chocolate, it makes you smile while you sleep," Mallory said with a wink. Abigail took a cup off the tray and sipped it daintily. Avery and Grant chugged theirs and had a second cup. She smiled at their antics. Grant and Avery had so many similarities.

"What did you think of my land?" Avery asked.

"Like all the land in Maryland, it's beautiful," she said. "It has a lot of potential."

"What exactly do you do at the candy store?" Grant asked. "Has the store been in the family for a long time?" All the questions put Abigail on edge. She sensed that he was trying to determine the family wealth, which was something she wanted to stay private.

"I'm the bookkeeper, so I record the money made and the money owed and keep the inventory where it should be," she answered. Hoping that would be enough information, she looked at him and smiled, but he was not about to drop it.

"Was the store handed down to your father from his father?" he asked again.

"I'm not sure. I just know that my father has had the store since I was born," she said. Abigail finished her cocoa and turned to head upstairs to retire for the night. "Thank you, Mallory for the warm drink. It was soothing and delicious. Good night, Avery and Grant. See you in the morning."

Tired and ready for some time alone, she changed into

her bedclothes, settled into the comfortable bed, and quickly drifted off to sleep.

❧ ❧ ❧

Abigail woke to the noise of a work crew outside her bedroom window. She slipped out of bed, opened the curtains, and saw a cadre of lumberjacks clearing Avery's land. *He really is a man of action.* Somehow, that made her very proud of him. She changed into her traveling dress and went downstairs to find Avery.

"Good morning, Abigail. How did you sleep?" Avery asked.

"Very well, thank you," she replied with a smile. "What's happening on your property?" Abigail inquired.

"They're clearing the trees and the brush so I can build my house. I'm building a homestead, and someday I hope to have a wife and a family," he replied, looking at Abigail with a peculiar grin.

Could it be, Abigail thought, *that he's looking at me as a potential wife? Maybe I'm part of the plan,* Abigail speculated privately. *He was creating a homestead, a family residence to his specifications. Maybe this trip to Carroll County was a ruse for her to meet his parents and to see the beginnings of the house being built.* She pondered the possibilities. *Moving up in class might mean a secure financial life, and she might even be a very wealthy woman. It wasn't very romantic, although it certainly was intriguing.* But she chastised herself for thinking that way. *That's enough fantasizing. Wake up to real life, Abigail!*

She was relieved that his parents didn't try to find out

more about her mother's illness. Also, it seemed that his parents didn't condemn her working outside the home. Most of the adults in her life considered her interest in having a career to be improper. Meeting the Johnson family was something new for her, and she was determined to keep an open mind and see where it would lead. She was proud of Avery in so many ways. He won the lawsuit and had the respect of his colleagues. He was a man of action, and his family had influence.

The weeks following her visit to Carroll County, the pace of their courtship increased. They went to church together and discovered many shared values such as the importance of working hard. Most of all, they both hoped to have a family someday.

Culturally, at this time in history, there was a huge emphasis on formality in courtship. At times relationships suffered because the formalities supplanted genuine feelings. Abigail tortured herself with questions about the authenticity of their relationship. Was their relationship merely a reflection of the formalities of their time? Sometimes, their relationship seemed empty. But what often followed those thoughts was the hope that deep, loving feelings would someday materialize. Those good thoughts propelled her forward. She so wanted to share her thoughts with somebody close to her that she trusted. The two people that came to mind were her good friend, Rosemary and Rosemary's mother, Florence.

Before she could take time to visit Rosemary and Florence, Pinky wanted the end-of-the-month report for the candy store completed in a hurry. He was concerned about the recent slump in sales and wanted Abigail to help him with a plan to manage this problem with some new strategies. Little did they know that a surprise was about to come in the mail. It was a letter from Stephen Whitman in Philadelphia addressed to Pinky and Abigail.

Dear Pinky and Abigail,

I was happy to receive your letter about the heart-shaped boxes of chocolate samplers made especially for Valentine's Day. It's always good to hear about brisk sales for our new chocolate items.

I received a special request from an acquaintance. Perhaps you can help me with some ideas. Rose Elizabeth Cleveland, a personal friend of mine, wrote me and requested that I prepare some chocolates for her brother's wedding reception. It has been in the news that Frances Folsom will be marrying her brother, Grover Cleveland, in the Blue Room at the White House on June 2, 1886.

How do you think we could display the chocolates, or present favors for the wedding guests? Please let me know of your ideas as quickly as you can, because we will need ample time for preparation and delivery.

Sincerely,
Stephen Whitman

Abigail and Pinky were so proud to be recruited by Stephen Whitman. To be asked for their ideas was such an honor. The upcoming wedding was the talk of the town, and to have any kind of input or part in the festivities was a privilege. For a few days, Pinky and Abigail brainstormed ideas about chocolate candy and wedding favors.

They liked many of their ideas, but they had one that was their favorite. The idea was to create a personalized favor from the president and his new wife. The plan was that each guest would receive a miniature heart-shaped box with five different chocolates inside. On the top, the inscription would read:

Best Wishes from Mr. and Mrs. Grover Cleveland.
June 2, 1886

Abigail penned a letter to Stephen Whitman presenting the idea. It was hard to wait patiently for his reply. They hoped they would hear from him soon. Meanwhile, they prepared a new marketing strategy to help manage the downturn in sales, and Abigail organized their financial records.

CHAPTER 3

The Washington Soiree

❧ ❧ ❧ ❧

How could just three weeks feel like an eternity? Day after day, either Pinky or Abigail grabbed the mail from the mailman and hurriedly flipped through the letters. Disappointment ensued when there was nothing from Philadelphia. She went back to the books, and Pinky continued to stock shelves.

"Maybe they didn't like our idea," she remarked.

"Maybe so, but still, Mr. Whitman is the kind of person that would let us know either way," Pinky said.

The next day was a charm. "Abigail, the letter came!" Pinky yelled excitedly when looking through the mail. "You open it," he said. She took the letter in her hands, examined it carefully before she broke the seal, lifted the top flap, and read aloud.

Dear Pinky and Abigail,

Thank you for your prompt response. I shared your idea with my brother who knows the sister of the President, too, and he liked the idea. I went to Washington, D.C., to share the idea with my friend Rose Elizabeth Cleveland. She is the President's sister and is handling the wedding reception at the White House. She discussed the matter with the President, and he endorsed it.

I am happy to say that we have started to manufacture the boxes, and our in-house chocolatier is creating the smoothest chocolates with a delicious cream filling.

I will be placing the individual heart-shaped boxes in wooden crates and sending them by train to Washington, D.C. My wife is going in for surgery the day before the wedding, so I will need someone to ensure that the chocolates are in good condition and that they get from the train station to the White House. Would you and Abigail be so kind as to make sure that the candy boxes get to where they need to be on June 2nd and that they arrive in good condition? Please let me know if this is something you can do.

Sincerely,

Stephen Whitman

"That turned out to be even better than what I hoped for," Abigail said. "What an honor! Dad, you and I are a great team. Stephen Whitman seems to think so."

Pinky smiled and his face lit up. "This has been an exciting time in the candy business," he said, but then turned suddenly quiet.

"What's wrong, Daddy?" Abigail asked with concern.

"Your mother is coming home from the institution for a trial period that week. I have to stay here with her. I can't go to Washington with you." Disappointed, Pinky paused for a moment to think. "Maybe Avery can escort you."

"I'll miss you, Daddy, but that's a good idea," she responded. "I'll take the train to Carroll County and ask him."

Abigail knew that Avery was in the middle of building his house, but maybe he could break away for a few days. With this urgent request, she caught the first train heading north to Avery's land. Traveling through Maryland always inspired her. It was like a microcosm of America, with stretches of flatland, foothills, mountains, oak and pine forests, beautiful lakes, and Atlantic coastline. Who could ask for more?

The now familiar screeching of the train's brakes signaled the arrival at Union Bridge. She took a Hansom Cab to Avery's property and was amazed to see how much progress they had made with the building in just a few months. Avery worked side by side with his crew, standing on the roof trusses with a hammer in his hand. Looking out over the countryside, he spotted Abigail in the buggy.

"Hello, Abigail!" he shouted from the rooftop. "What a surprise!"

He jumped down through the rafters of the house and ran to meet her. He reached for her hand, gently lifted her to the ground, paid the driver, and motioned him back to the station. After these formalities, he took her in his arms and gave her a welcoming hug and a loving kiss. She warmly returned the kiss and nuzzled in his arms.

"What brings you here?" Avery asked.

"I have a favor to ask you," Abigail said with a kittenish smile.

"Ask away."

"Do you remember when I told you about the idea my dad and I had about favors for Grover Cleveland's wedding reception?"

"I do," Avery said with mild amusement.

"We finally received a response from Stephen Whitman in Philadelphia. He asked if Daddy and I could make sure the wooden crates filled with chocolates got to the White House at the right time and in good condition. My mother is coming home from the hospital for a visit that week, so my dad can't go. I am inviting you to escort me ... *and* the chocolate crates to the White House on that day."

"Well, there's more than one way to get to the White House," Avery said, bobbing his eyebrows. "I would be honored to escort you, my dear."

"I can't believe that it's going to happen," Abigail said. "We'll have to leave on the early morning train that Wednesday, the second of June. Would that work for you?"

"Yes, it sure will. I'm looking forward to being with you."

After having dinner together, Abigail caught the early

evening train back to Baltimore. The train ride back gave her time to sort out all the changes in her life. She felt a wave of anxiety as she worried about whether she could meet all the demands she was facing.

❧❧❧

All the fuss about going to the White House made Abigail yearn for simpler times, like the fun she had with her friend Rosemary. Their uncomplicated life had some appeal. The simple life contrasted with Abigail's hectic world of business and travel to Washington with Avery. Florence and Rosemary were hard working, down-to-earth, and fun companions. It was time to check in on them.

After finishing her records on Saturday morning, she filled a box with chocolates and took a streetcar to St. Ann's parish. Abigail knocked on Rosemary's door expectantly, but there was no answer. Mystified, she followed the path to the back of the house, and there she saw Rosemary and her mother, hanging clothes on the clothesline in the backyard. Florence spotted Abigail first and took the opportunity to play a game.

"Rosemary, close your eyes, I have a surprise for you," Florence said. "Don't peek! Can you guess who? She's funny and cute, a dreamer, and likes wild adventures. She lives on the other side of town, and she has green eyes and a lovely smile. Who do you think it is?"

"Is it Myrtle?" Rosemary joked.

"No. Here's one more hint. She's carrying a box of chocolates."

"Abigail!" Rosemary exclaimed as she quickly turned

around to hug her friend. "What a nice surprise!" She looked at her directly to fully connect with the moment. "What have you been up to?"

"You wouldn't believe what has been happening in my life," Abigail declared. "I have met the man I think I am going to marry, *and* he is escorting me to the White House on the second of June."

"Of course, he is. Tell me the one about the three bears," Rosemary scoffed. "Isn't that Grover Cleveland's wedding day? The newspapers are exploding with that news. How did all that happen?"

"Well, his name is Avery Johnson, and he has land in Carroll County, north of Baltimore. We've been courting since I've seen you last. Going to church together, having dinner at fancy restaurants, and riding on his land are just some of the things we do. I've even met his parents, who live close to where he's building his house," Abigail continued. "The White House part was truly unexpected. Daddy and I got a letter from Stephen Whitman, in Philadelphia—he's the well-known chocolatier and businessman ... you know who I'm talking about, right? He asked us to make sure his crates of chocolate get to the White House on time and in good shape for the wedding. Dad can't go because Mom will be coming home for a visit that week, so Avery is escorting me."

"That's amazing," exclaimed Rosemary.

Florence seemed dumbfounded with all the news. "How *is* your mother?" she asked gently.

"She doesn't seem to be making much progress at the hospital. She says that her life is empty without the family, so they're letting her come home for a week. It's kind of a trial to see if she feels better and if she can handle it."

"Abigail, do you need a dress for the time you're in Washington?" Florence asked. "After all, even though it's just a delivery, the ladies will dress elegantly that day."

"I have my old blue one I thought I'd wear," she responded.

"I made dresses for a wedding party last month, and they changed wedding colors, so I had to make blue dresses instead of yellow ones. They paid me for both colors but only kept the blue ones. It must be nice having a lot of money. I have a pretty yellow dress in the closet that I could alter for you."

"That would be wonderful!" Abigail exclaimed.

"Let's try it on," Florence said as she entered the sewing room.

Once again, Abigail stood in front of the mirror as she slipped the yellow dress over her head. When she looked down, she noticed lovely embroidered daisies on the bodice. The dress design was elegant and the color suited her green eyes and auburn hair. Just an enticing bit of cleavage showed, and the pastel yellow fabric draped comfortably around her arms, exposing her attractive shoulders. It needed some tucks in the waist, and the hem needed shortening, but otherwise, it was just perfect for a summer's day in Washington, D.C.

"Oh, it's a beautiful dress! I can pay you for the dress and the alterations," Abigail said.

"I've already been paid for the dress, so don't even think about it," Florence said.

"Please, let me pay for your sewing time."

"Okay, but keep me in mind for making your wedding dress," she said with a twinkle in her eye.

"I don't know when that will be," Abigail sighed.

"Everything is all so new, right now." Looking at Rosemary, she said, "Could we take a walk to the park?"

"How about it, Mom?" Rosemary inquired. "Can you spare me for a little while?"

"I'll need you in about an hour," she replied in a business-like tone.

The two chatty soul mates rushed off to share the secrets of their love lives.

"Who is this Avery Johnson?" Rosemary asked. "Is he the one that bought those chocolates from you on Valentine's Day?"

"Yes, the one and only!" Abigail remarked.

"Are you falling in love with him?" she asked

"Talk about getting right to the point!" Abigail said, chuckling. "You're the same old Rosemary. Actually, I can't stop thinking about him. He's handsome, ambitious, and respected. His mom and dad are influential and very nice."

"That's all well and good, but do you *love* him?" Rosemary insisted.

"I care deeply for him, but in all honesty, I'm a little afraid of him."

"Really? Why is that?"

"For one, I saw him shoot someone who was trespassing on his land," Abigail shared hesitantly.

"I'd be scared, too, if I saw that. Do you think he would ever hurt you?"

Abigail was silent for a long time. "No, I don't think so, but he's *very* protective of what belongs to him. Now it's your turn. Tell me about your love life with Mathew."

"There's nothing new to report. It's the same as it was before," Rosemary said. She was a little sad that she didn't have anything exciting to add about her love life. Rosemary brought up some chatty news about old friends and a teacher that they had in elementary school. The hour just seemed to fly by. "We'll talk again when you come to pick up your dress. I'll have to head back to help my mom," Rosemary said.

They gave each other a quick hug goodbye.

"Until next time, then," Abigail said. So much was left unsaid, but the dress would be done soon, so they could pick up where they left off.

❧ ❧ ❧

Abigail woke up early on the day she and Avery would be traveling to Washington. The house was quiet, so thoughts whirled inside her head spinning non-sequiturs and fantastical imaginings. What would the day bring? At the tender age of nineteen, she was thrown into the world of business and social expectations that were beyond her years. Although she enjoyed the challenge of making good business decisions, she feared making a major faux pas, either socially or financially. Abigail masked her fear well, since her countenance always seemed even and calm. Perhaps it was her symmetrical face and lovely smile that belied what was simmering underneath.

Today was one of those days that set her heart racing. The wedding was scheduled for seven o'clock in the Blue Room at the White House. The D.C. newspapers were exploding with the news, and it captured the attention of the whole nation.

"Why such a short notice of only five days before their

wedding?" women whispered to each other in hushed tones. "Maybe she's pregnant."

Abigail had just a small role to play in this wedding, but she would be at the hub of the most important news of the day, and her nerves were on high alert. She would be crossing paths with some very important people, since the train would be filled with dignitaries, notable politicians, and the press. This would be a new experience for her … both exciting and scary.

Will I be dressed appropriately? Who do I talk to, and what do I say? Will the chocolates survive this warm June day? What will I do if I find them melted? Will Avery be helpful? Such thoughts bedeviled her and gave her a stomachache.

"I better get out of bed and get the day started," Abigail said out loud as she placed her feet on the floor. "I always do better when I'm doing something active."

The beautiful yellow dress with embroidered daisies hung in her closet. She had picked it up from Florence and Rosemary the day before. It was positively lovely, even more beautiful than she remembered. She would add a light shawl and a straw hat tied with an ample yellow and white-checkered bow. She would be "as pretty as a picture." If only her insides were as pretty. Maybe a good breakfast would help calm her nerves and give her the energy she needed. She wrapped herself in a house robe and headed down the stairs.

To her amazement, Martha, her mother, was standing in the kitchen with a teacup in her hand. "Mother!" Abigail exclaimed. "So good to see you. I didn't hear you come in last night."

"Pinky took the train into D.C. after work to pick me up for this one-week home visit," Martha said. "Mary and Louise were doing the chores, so it gave us some time alone."

Abigail noticed her mother's hand shaking as she poured herself another cup of hot tea. She observed how much her mother had aged. Her hair had turned almost completely gray and her face was ashen. *Life had been hard for her.*

"How are you feeling, Mom?" Abigail asked.

"I miss my family so much. The people are very nice, and the grounds are beautiful, but I feel lonely and empty, like I have no purpose."

"How often do you see the doctor?"

"I see him once a week on Thursday, for an hour after lunch."

"What does he say?" Abigail asked

"He's very encouraging. He praises me for all the work I do around the place. I have a flower garden that I'm responsible for, and a girlfriend there helps me. We place bouquets of my homegrown flowers on the tables for dinner. I clean my room every day."

"Did he say you were ready to come home?" Abigail asked.

"He said I could give it a try. This is my first day."

"Have you heard about what I'm doing today?"

"Pinky said you were going to Washington, D.C., to make sure the chocolates are good for President Grover Cleveland's wedding. That's pretty exciting. Are you getting ready?

"Avery and I are taking the late-morning train to D.C., because the chocolates are coming in from Philadelphia on the four o'clock train. We'll be claiming the crates and inspecting them. Then, the last thing we do will be to take the crates to the White House for the reception."

"What are you wearing?" Martha asked.

"I'll run upstairs and get the dress. Close your eyes, so it's a surprise," Abigail giggled. Filled with excitement, she ran upstairs, then took the dress down the stairs to show her mother. "Keep your eyes closed, Mom. Okay, now you can open them." Abigail twirled around to reveal the dress, which she held out in front of her.

"Oh, how pretty!" Martha said with an effort to be positive. "I like that color on you. You'll be the 'belle of the ball.' I'm eager to meet Avery, too. This is a special time in your life, Abigail."

"Avery is coming in two hours, so I've got to get ready," she said as she flew up the stairs with renewed energy.

The next two hours consisted of a blur of activity from washing her face, combing her long hair, to twirling a neat bun on the back of her head. She gathered up her petticoats and was finally ready to put on her dress.

"Mom? Would you come upstairs and button me up in the back?" Abigail asked.

"I'll be right there," Martha said.

She seemed to take forever coming up the stairs, so Abigail waited patiently.

"Abigail, what a fine young lady!" she said admiringly.

Abigail hadn't heard such positive statements coming from her mother in a long time, if ever. Maybe being in the hospital is helping her. Dutifully, she fastened the buttons in the back and then sprung a surprise. She slipped her hand inside her apron pocket and slowly showed Abigail a beautiful necklace. It was a string of miniature shells with edges that were tipped with gold. It was truly an amazing piece of jewelry. She put the necklace around Abigail's graceful neck and fastened it in the back.

"Your father gave this to me before we were engaged. Wear it with pride, my dear," Martha exclaimed. "What I remember most about the gift was how your father enjoyed giving it to me. Young love is such a wonderful thing. Too bad it's so fleeting."

"Oh, Mother, thank you so much," Abigail said tenderly. They looked at each other a long time and hugged. *Maybe Mom and I can have a good relationship after all.*

A knock at the door interrupted her fantasies, and her mother went downstairs to open the front door.

"Hi, Mrs. Abbott. I'm Avery Johnson," he said as he doffed his hat.

"Come in. Come in, Mr. Johnson. It's so nice to meet you. Abigail will be ready soon. Did you have far to come or do you live in Baltimore?" she asked.

"No, I live in Carroll County about fifty miles northwest of here," he answered. "I'm building a home there on a piece of land. Most of my family lives up that way. My parents live on the land next to the building site."

The door from Abigail's upstairs bedroom opened, and they shifted their attention to her. The smile on her face spoke volumes. She was the embodiment of bright sunshine; the yellow dress and her lovely smile radiated like the freshness of springtime. Avery stood at attention and carefully took her hand when she came to the last step.

"You look lovely, Abigail," he said greeting her with his endearing smile. "We must be off to the White House, my dear." Abigail set her straw hat on her head, wrapped her shawl around her, and took her purse. Avery grabbed her carpetbag with his left hand. "It was nice meeting you, Mrs. Abbott," Avery said. They walked toward the carriage and into their own world, just the two of them. Martha no longer mattered. Off they went, riding in his horse and buggy to catch the train to Washington, D.C.

Martha found herself in a daze. *What just happened? It's like I'm reading a chapter in a romance novel when a handsome couple with a promising future goes off to discover the world together. I can't believe that my own daughter is the main character in the story and this is her plot line.*

It was so unlike her wretched life. She never experienced such love, and her life had no joy. Her relationship with Pinky was estranged and, no matter how hard she worked at it, she felt empty.

Rage came over her like a crashing wave.

കുകുകു

Abigail and Avery chatted and laughed while riding in the buggy and on the train. Anyone near them could sense their good cheer and camaraderie.

"Did you hear of the story in the Buffalo newspaper about Grover Cleveland fathering a child?" Avery chuckled. "He's a busy man."

"I read a different slant in *The Baltimore Sun*," Abigail countered. "Supposedly, he admitted it and he supported the child throughout his life. But come to find out, the mother of this child had many relationships. The scuttlebutt has it that one of her affairs was with Oscar Folsom, the late father of the bride-to-be. The article speculated that Grover took the blame, because the other men were married. Who knows, maybe it was Grover's way of being a loyal friend," Abigail said.

"Very interesting," Avery responded. "What have you heard about the bride-to-be?"

"She's a college graduate and supports women's rights. Grover was the executor of her late father's will. Supposedly, that's when he fell in love with her. Grover and Frances kept their engagement a secret until five days before the wedding. You can just imagine the gossip about that. So many tongues were wagging." Abigail said.

"Sometimes I hear people calling her 'Frank,'" Avery said.

"I've heard that too. That's just a nickname," she said. "The press jumped the gun thinking that Grover was marrying Frances's mother. The reporters were surprised the president asked Frances and not Emma, her mother, to be his bride. Frances is twenty-nine years younger than the president. It's one of those May-December romances."

As they chatted, the train chugged on, and soon the Washington skyline came into view. Crystal-clear skies heralded the promise of a beautiful spring day for the Cleveland/Folsom wedding. Washington seemed to have gained a little snap to it; like a man with a spring in his step, there was something in the air.

The train screeched to a halt at the B&P Station on Sixth and B Street.

"We're here. I wonder what the day will bring?" Avery said with measured excitement.

"I'm so glad you're with me, Avery. We've got quite an adventure ahead of us."

"The train from Philadelphia won't be in until four this afternoon, so let's check out Washington."

"That's a great idea," Abigail said enthusiastically.

⮞⮞⮞

Darkness descended into the heart and mind of Martha, and she was powerless to stop it. She was consumed by the sharp pangs of jealousy. Her bad thoughts were like gigantic waves pummeling her over and over again. She lost her grip on rational thinking. All alone in her house, envy ate at her, and evil swallowed her up.

I do everything right, I do what I'm told, but I feel empty. I only feel disdain for my husband. I hate him. Abigail has found a charming man, and she is her father's favorite. She has been such a disobedient child. How did she find love and not me? My life is over. I'm useless. I'm worthless.

Her mood shifted from depression to rage and then back to depression. And it continued ... back and forth, back and forth. Where will it be when Pinky comes home from work?

Martha ignored any gesture of love that Pinky gave her. He was not satisfied with their marriage either, but he cared about his family. He took the words "until death do us part" seriously. The loss of Martha's love made tending to his "girls" the main focus of his life. He excused his wife's behavior because she lost her mother so young and was forced to keep her family's house clean for her father, a very domineering, stoic man. Pinky was baffled by her lack of progress in the hospital. It had a good reputation and was expensive to keep her there, but they didn't seem to understand what she needed to get well. There were so many unanswered questions. He did enjoy his work, however. Abbott's Confectionary continued being prosperous thanks in part to Abigail's good business decisions.

Traffic in Baltimore was hectic and even chaotic sometimes when all the carriages headed home from work at about the same time. Pinky was right in the middle of the mass of carriages. He left work as soon as possible, knowing his wife would be all by herself in the house. This was her trial week after all, and he couldn't count on Mary and Louise to take care of her because they had housecleaning jobs and were especially busy during the spring months.

He stopped by the flower shop to buy some spring flowers for her. She liked daisies and roses. He chose some beauties. All smiles, with the bouquet in hand, he hopped up the steps excitedly and opened the door.

Horror was the only word that came to mind.

Martha was covered in blood, lying face-up on the floor. In his fright, he threw the flowers in the air and dropped to the floor to help his wife. He felt her pulse and it was strong. She was breathing but not responding. He checked for any cuts or injuries, but he couldn't find any major injuries except for contusions on her face around her right eye, and her nose was still bleeding. It must have just happened.

"Martha! What happened?" Pinky said in a panic.

"I don't remember," she responded, awakened by his touch.

Pinky peppered her with questions. "Did you slip and fall? Did someone hurt you? Were you by yourself?" He wanted some answers, but all this pressure from the questions perturbed her.

"Pinky, I already told you. I don't remember!" Martha yelled as she stood up. That's when Pinky noticed something horrible. Her blouse was open in the back exposing several long, raised, red welts that looked like wounds from a whipping. What on earth did she do? It was then that he noticed the horse whip beside her. She had flagellated herself, lacerating her back until she passed out.

"Martha, clean yourself up! We're going to see Dr. Kennard," Pinky said matter-of-factly.

Obediently, she hung her head and went to their bedroom to wash up and change clothes. Pinky readied the horses and made sure they had enough to eat and drink. Martha opened the door slowly and silently climbed into the carriage. The absence of words spoke volumes.

Dr. Kennard took one look at Martha and knew immediately what she needed. "Pinky, you need to take your wife back to the hospital," he said with urgency in his voice. "Martha is *not* doing well. You need to go tonight. Take one of your daughters for your protection and to help control Martha. She will be upset about returning to the hospital."

Pinky went home to explain the circumstance to Mary and Louise. Mary agreed to go. After they had a small supper, the three of them climbed into the carriage and headed for Washington, D.C. As the road got darker and darker, the oil carriage lanterns became dimmer and dimmer. They were not illuminating the road, but they had no choice but to press on.

෴ ෴ ෴

Abigail and Avery had made that all-important connection between their discerning eyes and the candy crates.

They conversed with the freight handler and found the two crates of one hundred heart-shaped boxes of chocolates for the Cleveland's wedding reception. Hurriedly, Abigail inspected them to make sure the candy was in good condition.

First, she noticed how exquisitely they were made. Rather than red, they had chosen a magenta box color with gold lettering—perfect for the occasion. So, off to the White House they went in a Hansom cab with the crates. Stephen Whitman had contacted Rose Elizabeth Cleveland, Grover's sister, to let her know the chocolates would be arriving between five and six o'clock. Right on time, the cab pulled onto the corner of State Place and West Executive Avenue at the appointment gate. They got clearance immediately, so they knew that Stephen had done his job. They drove up to the front door and noticed that all the windows were covered with black cloth to prevent anyone from peeking in, especially the "ghouls of the press," as Grover called them.

Rose Elizabeth opened the door immediately. "Hello. Are you Avery Johnson and Abigail Abbott?" Rose asked. She graciously reached out to shake both of their hands. Every inch of her presence announced that she was in charge.

"Yes," Avery responded. "We have the chocolates from the Whitman Company in Philadelphia. Pleased to make your acquaintance, Rose."

"Stephen told me you would be coming, but he didn't mention what a nice-looking young couple you were," she smiled. "I'll let someone from the White House staff know that the chocolates have arrived." She opened the door nearest her and motioned someone to come.

"I inspected the chocolates to make sure they were in good condition," Abigail said brightly.

At that moment, three staff members came to secure the two crates. Rose caught sight of the heart-shaped boxes and raved about the choice of color and the gold engraving. "You did a very nice job, both of you, as did my friend, Stephen Whitman. Thank you. By the way, where are you spending the night?" she asked.

"I was planning on staying with my aunt," Avery replied.

"Does she know you are coming?" Rose asked.

"Not yet," he said.

"I've secured two rooms for you at the Willard Hotel," Rose offered with a smile. "They're having an evening dance, celebrating the marriage. Then, you can take the train back to Baltimore in the morning."

"Thank you, Rose. How thoughtful," Abigail said.

By the time Avery and Abigail got in their cab, it was six-thirty, and many of the guests were arriving. Less than fifty guests were expected, and the invitees consisted mostly of the president's cabinet, their wives, and close family and friends. As the cab was exiting the White House grounds, they could hear the John Philip Sousa Marine Band tuning up. Abigail marveled at the bright and happy sound of the band. It was perfect music for a wedding celebration. Their carriage brought them through the busy, rowdy streets of Washington to the front door of the Willard Hotel, which was a signature of elegance. A porter opened the door for them and carried their luggage inside.

"Rose Elizabeth secured two rooms for us this evening," Avery told the clerk. "My name is Avery Johnson, and this is Abigail Abbott.

"Yes, I have your names right here. Rose wasn't sure you would need them, but wanted to book them for you anyway," he said. "Here are your room keys. The dance celebration will start at nine, and there is a complimentary buffet with champagne before the music begins in just a few minutes. It's not every day that there is a wedding in the White House," the gentleman said gleefully. Abigail and Avery found their rooms and were awed by the surroundings. They freshened up and met each other in the elegant hallway before proceeding to the buffet. The deafening sound of church bells greeted them. They soon discovered that Grover granted permission for all the churches to ring their bells once they had said their "I dos." What a clamorous celebration! The whole city of Washington, D.C., was commemorating the marriage of Mr. and Mrs. Grover Cleveland. Music filled the dining area. Ladies and gentlemen were lavishly and meticulously dressed. Abigail, the Cinderella of the evening, was radiant in her off-the-shoulder summer dress. Her porcelain-like skin and deep auburn hair made her the "belle of the ball." Avery glowed with pride as Abigail gracefully held his right arm. Their genuine smiles and noticeable charisma made many heads turn. They were the couple of the evening.

"My dear, may I have this dance?"

"With pleasure, sir," Abigail smiled coyly. In his arms, she had a regal feeling, since Avery seemed strong and invincible. His confidence showed as he swirled her around to the tune of the music. The waltzes suited them best. The melodies and the three-four timing fit their personal rhythm. The ebb and flow of the evening made its own kind of music, like a dream come true. The glasses clinked with champagne toasts everywhere. Laughter and joviality reigned. For Abigail and Avery, it was a truly memorable evening. At midnight, the music recessed, and they walked, arm-in-arm, back to their rooms. They stood by Abigail's door not wanting the evening to end. Avery twirled her around one last time, and they laughed. Then, the embrace followed. Her body firmly pressed against his, sparking her passion. She melded into him like metal and fire, like hand in glove. A light touch of the lips and soft whispers followed. "Abigail, I love you."

"I love you, too, Avery."

სა სა სა

Pinky pushed his team of horses at breakneck speed to get Martha back to the hospital. The intense jostling upset Martha and ignited her rage. She didn't want to go back to the hospital, but neither did she want to be at home and feel the way she did, miserable either way.

"Slow down, Pinky!" Martha yelled. "I can't see the road. It's like we're driving blind."

She was furious at him, but that didn't stop his determination to get her back to the hospital. He went faster and faster, infuriating her even more. Mary, in the back seat, was caught in the middle, not knowing what to do. Despite the intense rocking back and forth, and feeling conflicted and overwhelmed, Mary escaped by falling asleep.

Unexpectedly, Pinky spotted something in the middle of the road, but it was too late to stop. The horse's hoof got tangled and twisted in the object. It reared, and the carriage flew off the road into the ditch and crashed on its side. A brief, eerie silence was followed by a loud *whoosh*. The oil lanterns shot flames up and throughout the carriage. The wooden wheels, the carpet, the entire carriage became engulfed in flames. Pinky forced his way out of the carriage with an adrenaline rush, pulled Martha out, and then found Mary a few feet away. The horse kicked his front two legs in the air trying to untangle his hoof from the old wooden gate lying on the road. His unsuccessful attempt made him slam into the ground on his side. The horse expelled a painful bellow. Pinky knew the horse was mortally wounded. Mary was thrown from the carriage but not seriously hurt, but Pinky was so exhausted he collapsed on the ground once he knew Martha and Mary were out of harm's way

A farmer a quarter of a mile away, checking his sheep, spotted the fire on the road. He took off in a sprint with shovel in hand. Once there, he assessed the horrific scene to determine who was alive or dead. Hearing the horse moaning, the farmer took out his gun and shot him. He knew that was the only remedy.

Pinky opened his eyes, but the farmer saw severe burns over most of his body. Martha did not have a pulse. She was dead. Mary was conscious, but in shock. The farmer furiously shoveled dirt and sand onto the fire. He worked feverishly until all the flames were in a smoldering heap. Once the fire was under control, he turned his attention to the human tragedy. Mary stood up and cried as she looked at her mother and father.

"My name is Hugh. I live on that farm," he said, pointing in a southerly direction. "What's your name?"

"My name is Mary, and they are my mother and father."

"Mary, I was a medic in the Union army, so I can help your father. He has been burned badly, so we need to get him back to the house soon. Can you help me?"

"What about Mother?" Mary asked.

"Your mother is dead," Hugh said matter-of-factly.

Mary rushed to her mother, rocked her back and forth, and sobbed with deep sorrow. After kissing her, and gently placing her back on the ground, she rose, ready to help the farmer any way she could.

"I found a board in the backseat of the carriage that didn't burn. It will hold your father. We need to carry him up that long driveway to get to the house," Hugh said as he pointed to the path to his house. "Do you think you can manage that?"

"I can," Mary said with clear resolve. After placing the board next to Pinky, Hugh tucked his hands under Pinky's shoulders while cradling his head in his elbows, and Mary placed her hands under his calves. With one strong lift, they placed him on the board. Pinky emitted a mournful cry of pain. Both Hugh and Mary grabbed the ends of the board and began the long, agonizing trek to the house. They quickly and successfully navigated ruts, loose stones, and a steady incline to get to the house.

"I thought something bad happened when I saw you running toward the road with a shovel," Hugh's wife said. "I cleared off the kitchen table and covered it with a blanket, so it's ready to use."

"Annie, get Dr. Benz right away," Hugh said emphatically, and she quickly departed. She was certain it was a life-or-death matter.

Mary and Hugh lifted Pinky and placed him on the table. Hugh quietly and thoroughly examined his injuries, took some bandages and ointment out of the cupboard, and started treatment. Mary watched somberly, worried that her dad would die, too. He didn't moan or cry out, but he was immobilized, keeping his eyes shut. She sat by her father, holding his hand and speaking softly to him, occasionally brushing his forehead with her fingers, hoping and praying that he would be all right. She worked very hard to hold back sobs because of her mother. An hour might have passed, probably more, seemingly the longest hour of her life—then Annie and the doctor rushed into the room.

Dr. Benz, in fact, arrived surprisingly quickly given the distance he had to travel. Annie made sure of that. He was a slow, methodical, country doctor. He examined Mary and gave her the okay and then turned his attention to Pinky. He shook his head.

"The burns are deep, like other oil burns I've seen," the doctor said. "Hugh is doing a good job treating his wounds. All I'll be able to do is ease the pain."

He questioned Mary about where they lived and how they would get transportation back to their home. From this information, he determined that Pinky needed to see Dr. Kennard and be admitted to the hospital. Hugh offered to take them home in his carriage, which had both a front seat and a roomy backseat. Hugh and Mary had the grim task of covering Martha with a blanket and putting her in the back of the carriage. Pinky was placed lying down in the back seat, and Mary rode upfront with Hugh.

Louise was in bed when they arrived. Once apprised of the tragedy, she sobbed, heartbroken by the loss. Hugh left for home leaving behind a severely injured father and two heartsick daughters. Mary expressed gratitude for his kindness and tended to her father until Dr. Kennard arrived.

❧ ❧ ❧

Abigail and Avery caught the morning train to Baltimore. They chatted about the time they spent together and were enamored of Washington, D.C. Moonstruck by the events of the night before, they marveled at their good fortune and future prospects. All in all, it was a magical couple of days.

"The way people turned their heads when we made an entrance was incredible," Avery said, looking smug. "Rose Elizabeth even said we were a nice-looking couple."

"I can't wait to tell Mom and Dad," Abigail said eagerly. "They won't believe what happened. "

The train chugged to a stop, and they exited the train station. They hailed a cab to take Abigail home. He gently lifted her into the carriage and off they went, snuggling close, enraptured by the moment.

The cab jerked to a stop in front of Abigail's home, which signaled the end of the fairy tale. Abigail stepped down and walked toward the front door holding Avery's hand. One last hug, a quick kiss, and a wave as they parted. He was heading back to Carroll County to work on the house, and she was going back to her life at Abbott's Confectionary.

Abigail opened the front door to an empty house.

"Mom ... Dad ... Mary ... Louise? Anybody home? Abigail shouted. There was an eerie silence. Her heartbeat quickened in panic. She ran upstairs and down, looked into her parent's bedroom, and dashed into the kitchen. No one was home. On the kitchen table was a hurriedly scrawled note,

We took Dad to Baltimore City Hospital. Meet us there when you get home. Please hurry.

Mary.

She hitched the horses to the buggy and thrashed them to make haste. She couldn't get to the hospital fast enough. After a quick "hello" to the receptionist, she rushed to her father's room. Turning the corner to an open door, she found Pinky heavily bandaged and her sisters trying to comfort him. Mary and Louise ran to her, throwing their arms around her, sobbing.

"What happened?" Abigail asked with horror in her voice.

"There was a terrible accident and fire in the carriage," Mary said, choking on her words. "Mother died, I was thrown from the carriage, and Dad was severely burned trying to save her."

Abigail stood frozen with shock. Tears welled in her eyes, and her mouth fell open. After a moment, she composed herself enough to see her father.

"Daddy, this is Abigail," she said tearfully, not sure where to touch him since his face and hands were bandaged. She kissed him on his cheek. He felt it, and his eyes opened slowly but only halfway.

"Abigail," he said, his voice a husky whisper. "My dear daughter, how are you?

"I'm fine, but how are you?" she asked.

"I'm not going to survive. I'm in so much pain that

death would be a relief. When I die, Abigail, I want you to take over Abbott's Confectionary," he mumbled, mustering all his strength.

All three daughters were close to him, hanging on every word. "And Mary and Louise, my darlings, the house is yours. I know you will take good care of it," Pinky said with quiet certitude. "I love you all very much. You are wonderful daughters." He closed his eyes and breathed heavily until he was in a deep sleep.

Abigail, Mary, and Louise looked at each other, brokenhearted. Even though they understood his words and were grateful for their inheritances, they felt such despair. Their grief was incomprehensible. They decided that they would take turns watching over their father. One would be on vigil while the other two slept. The nurses gave him a shot for the pain about every six hours, but they could only give him water as needed and keep him comfortable. The tenderness and deep affection for Pinky was evident. Their love filled the room.

Mary took the first shift while Louise slept. Before napping, Abigail penned a letter to Avery, sharing all that had happened to her mother and father. The words she wrote on the page felt empty and cold, and Avery seemed so far away. When she finished, she made herself comfortable in the chair and dozed off.

"Wake up! Wake up!" Mary yelled frantically. "Daddy's breathing is changing, and I hear guttural sounds."

Mary's call of alarm startled Abigail and Louise awake. They quickly found a place close to their father. Mary said a prayer with such tender, loving care that tears rolled down their faces. The three daughters spoke in hushed tones, whispering their love to Pinky. His breathing stopped, everything was still, and they silently held hands around his bed.

❧ ❧ ❧

Finding the right caskets was no small undertaking. Burial usually occurred just a few days after death, which was the customary practice. Abigail took on the responsibility of finding two caskets for her parents, and Mary and Louise cleaned the house and made food for the funeral guests who would arrive the next day.

What a change from the jollity she experienced in Washington, D.C. It was hard to believe that all of this, from the sublime to the horrible, happened in just a few days. Her emotions went from the peak of joy to the valley of despair. It was like an emotional whiplash. Processing these disparate experiences would have to come later.

She contacted the Bagby Furniture Company about their inventory and discovered they had two beautiful, oak caskets in storage. She scheduled them for delivery to the family home that afternoon. The funeral was scheduled for the next day, but the candlelight vigil was that evening. Once the caskets arrived, Pinky was placed in a closed casket, while Martha had an open one. She didn't have a mark on her from the accident. Pinky, true to the very end, pulled his wife from the carriage first, since she was the most important person in his life.

Mary dressed Martha in her favorite black dress with a ruffled, lace collar, Louise styled her hair in a tight bun on top of her head, and Abigail adorned her with the golden shell necklace gifted to her by her mother. As was the custom, Abigail would remove it before the casket was closed. The necklace reminded her of a very special moment she had with her mother. It turned out to be the last good memory, making it more than just a necklace. It had become something sacred.

The candlelight vigil for neighbors and church members happened that evening as planned. Even Dr. Kennard stopped by to offer his condolences. Most remarked how tragic the accident was for the family. The three daughters appeared devoted to their parents. For Abigail, it was merely a façade, because she had so many conflicting feelings. It was a tragic loss, but something nagged at her saying that none of this would have happened if her mother had been a better wife. Why did she treat her husband so badly? He was so good to her. Why was she always so angry? These questions tugged at her soul. Moment by moment, she changed from feelings of deep sadness to disgust. Would this conflict ever be resolved?

The funeral occurred the next day. Avery received Abigail's letter earlier that day and dropped everything to be with her. When she saw him, her heart was ever so grateful. He became a part of the family that day. Reverend Holcombe from the First Presbyterian Church conducted the service. His church was pivotal in their lives. This was the church where Martha and Pinky met, where they were married, where they baptized their daughters, and now, it was the minister from First Presbyterian who would conduct their funerals. It was the center of their circle of life. Man's mortality and life's shortness was the theme chosen by the minister.

"Our life is over in just a blink of an eye," he emphasized. "We are made from dust, and we return to dust.

And the Lord God formed man from the dust of the ground, and breathed into his nostrils the breath of life; and man became a living soul." He read from Genesis, chapter two, verse seven.

He mentioned Martha's struggles with illness but praised her gardening skills and her three lovely daughters, the fruits of their marriage. He highlighted Pete's (Pinky's) faithfulness to his family and the joy he found in his candy business. Reverend Holcombe also shared how generous he had been to First Presbyterian Church with the contributions of candy for the children and giving ample funds to the church endowment. This generosity came as a surprise to many.

"Mr. Abbott, better known as 'Pinky,' was a good man. May he rest in peace," the minister concluded. He ended with a final prayer for the souls of Pinky and Martha and for the wellbeing of the Abbott family.

Before the burial ceremony, a light lunch was served. Mary and Louise made ham buns, golden-glow salad, and served chocolates from the candy store. Light conversations filled with memories about Martha and Pinky were shared before the procession to the cemetery.

༄ ༄ ༄

Abigail drove to Abbott's Confectionary the next morning, her thoughts deeply troubled. She desperately missed her father and felt uncertain about her inner struggle regarding the loss of her mother.

"She called me a disobedient child, but what was she?" Abigail muttered under her breath. At that moment of upset, the carriage careened off the road and almost tipped over. She managed to stop it just in time. Breathing heavily from the fright, she got out of the carriage, checked the horse, and decided at that moment not to let the tragic loss of her parents ruin her life.

Nevertheless, she envied Mary and Louise because they had each other, and their daily routines stayed much the same, while she would be running the store alone, without support. Her future looked bleak and lonely, both personally and in the business world. What a devastating loss and a hard blow it was to lose both her parents!

Despite her envy, Abigail felt responsible for her sisters because neither one made enough money to keep the house going. She would have to do that. At this time, Avery was the only bright spot in her life.

She climbed back into the carriage. After taking several long, deep breaths, and finding a firm resolve, she headed toward her future. In her thoughts, she gave her predicament another perspective. She still had a purpose and meaning for living. Thoughts of her father gave her confidence that she could continue making Abbott's Confectionary a prosperous business. She would somehow survive. With a renewed sense of purpose, she unlocked Abbott's Confectionery and placed the "Open for Business" sign in the window.

CHAPTER 4

The Proposals

∞∞∞∞

Abigail was used to negotiating her way through difficult circumstances. Agreements, contracts, invoices, and receipts were commonplace for her. Brokering and dickering were part of a typical day for her, but little did Abigail know that she would be facing three of the most difficult decisions of her life. Firmly believing that compromise was the best way to resolve conflicts, her belief system was about to be shaken.

Avery peeked in the window of the candy store with roses and a small box in his hand. His eyes scanned the store, but he couldn't find Abigail.

"Hmmm. She must be in the back office," he muttered to himself. "I'll come back later," he said as he trotted off to the bar. After a few Guinnesses, he went back to the store again, and there she was, pretty as a picture, sorting and organizing candy. He quickly opened the door and smiled. Wrapping his arms around her in a dancing position, he initiated a waltzing step with roses in hand.

"Madam, may I have this waltz?"

"My dear sir," Abigail answered with a twinkle in her eye. "I am very busy, but perhaps I can find time for just one." With that, she melted into his arms. They danced with gay abandon, twirling around the store, circling around the candy counters, laughing with hilarity. Their time together was never dull, and this was a little reminder of their Washington soiree. The waltz ended with an embrace and a lovely kiss. The bell rang, and a patron, witnessing the passion, blushed, stepped back outside, and shut the door. He peeked through the window, and Abigail and Avery quickly separated. She sheepishly opened the door.

"My apologies, sir. Can I help you?" Abigail asked.

"I just wanted to buy some candy, and I got a lot more than expected," he said, chuckling. "I'll take half a pound of Lancaster caramels."

"That's Avery's favorite candy, too" Abigail said, smiling.

Hoping to avoid another public encounter, Avery went to Abigail's office, closed the door, hid behind it, and waited for her. As she opened the door, to her surprise, the bouquet of roses popped out from behind the door. She clasped her hands over her mouth in surprise. Her eyes and smile said it all. His spontaneity always made her cheery. Taking them from his hand, she fully inhaled the rosy scent.

"*Aaaah*, they're wonderful! Thank you," she said, giving him a little smooch.

"Abigail, I have something to ask you," he said getting down on his right knee, beaming with a confident smile.

"Will you marry me?" He opened a little box with a gorgeous ring tucked inside. What followed he didn't expect. There was no "yes" or "no," only silence.

"I'm still grieving," Abigail responded sadly. "I'm not ready."

His countenance turned upside down, from confidence to disappointment.

"How long before you're ready, sweetheart?" he asked, taking her in his arms.

"I don't know. I love you, and I want to be a good wife, but I'm still so sad right now," Abigail said nervously. "I think I'll feel better by Christmas, so ask me again then."

"All right, I can wait," he said despondently. "Do you still want me to pick you up for church on Sunday?"

"Yes, I do. I enjoy spending time with you. You'll always be my first love."

"See you then," he said as he kissed her on the cheek. "Goodbye, Abigail."

Abigail was all alone with her thoughts. She had so many decisions to make, and up to this point she wasn't certain what kind of future would be best for her. Was marriage something she wanted, or did she want to be a career woman without a family? She had to know for sure before she would say, "yes." Her dad frequently discussed the exchanges that we make in our lives, reminding her often that you can't have everything. She can still hear Pinky say, "Life is about choices and the exchanges or trade-offs you make with those choices along the way." Did she want to marry Avery, or did she want to be a businesswoman? She wasn't sure at this point.

Also, she had concerns about the dowry. Would Avery insist that her inheritance be under his control and become community property? If that would happen, how would she help Mary and Louise and the upkeep of the family home? If she lived with Avery in Carroll County, would traveling back and forth be too much? If she didn't go back and forth, how would she keep the business going? Would she have to sell Abbott's Confectionary? Diane might be willing to cover her job at the store in a pinch, but the bulk of the business would be on her shoulders. Many questions, all too overwhelming! She *so* missed her daddy! He would have helped her sort through the choices.

While Abigail did the books and managed the store, she pondered her relationship with her father. She was his "little girl," and when he came home from work, he would scoop her up in his arms and give her a kiss. He gave her "monkey rides" on his back outside on the lawn. Martha would have none of *that* monkey business in the house. Most of all, he was her protector … from her mother.

He sensed she was her target. From daylight to dusk, whenever Abigail was around, Martha chastised her. Martha didn't like being challenged. She wanted complete control, and Abigail was an independent spirit who thought for herself. Pinky saw this quality as a strength and encouraged her to stay curious and to keep "why" in her vocabulary. He respected strong women who stood up for what they thought was right and just.

The most joyful times were those spent in the candy store with her friends and her dad after school. They giggled and teased each other as they tasted the new candies. Abigail's favorite as a child was the Baltimore licorice, but when she grew up it was Darby's fudge. What a wonderful discovery that fudge was; it was the kind of taste that melted in your mouth and stayed with you all day. Pinky enjoyed the sweets, too, but most of all, he appreciated the laughter and conviviality in his candy store. The joys of others seemed to radiate on his face. What a great Dad he was!

The saddest part for Abigail was her parent's marriage. Their relationship vacillated between being courteous and strained to being glumly silent and wretchedly lonely. It was especially hard for Abigail and her sisters to live comfortably in this world of estrangement. When they were in their "tight" roles, they were civil to each other. Pinky's function was to be the breadwinner, and Martha's role was to be the housekeeper. She was extremely responsible, kind of hyper-responsible. Martha was utterly convinced that she had more control over her world than she actually did. She tried hard to make sure that everything and everyone in her life was precisely ordered and predictable. Obedience was absolutely essential. Pinky tried to lighten up their home with jokes and laughter, but Martha would have none of it. For her, frivolity made her feel out of control and improper. Abigail knew something was wrong with her mother. A significant part of Martha's problem was that she tortured everyone in her family by demanding perfection and complete compliance to her rules. For the most part, they tried to conform to her wishes, but she continued to make their lives miserable. Why did she have to torture everyone else? Why was she so unhappy?

Abigail found it easier to grieve for her father because they had enjoyed life together, and the two of them created many good memories. These memories filled her thoughts. The opposite was true for her mother, since she found grieving for her almost impossible. Abigail's anger toward her mother lingered. With the baggage of those hard feelings, it was difficult to grieve her loss. She tried to bury her thoughts in the business ledgers. She didn't even want to start this difficult process. Knowing the only way to deal with those negative thoughts was to understand them, Florence, her "other mother," suggested she write a letter that she would keep secret. In that letter, she could explain *why* their relationship was so difficult. Understanding the "whys" was the first step to feeling better.

Folk wisdom suggested that she might marry a person who was similar to the parent with whom she had an unsettled relationship. Did she have unfinished issues with Martha? Was Avery like Martha? Did he lose his temper when life was out of his control? Did Martha become angry when life didn't go as planned? Of course, there were so many parallels between her mother and Avery, and thinking about those similarities frightened and overwhelmed her.

❧ ❧ ❧

Abigail busied herself by purchasing candy for the Christmas season. Ribbon candy was all the rage in England, so she ordered some. She decorated the store with red and white ribbons and placed a small Christmas tree on the counter adorned with candy canes. She added more bells to the door so it gave a cheerful Christmas tinkling sound when opened and closed. The distinctive peppermint scent floated through the store, and it seemed like all the children in Baltimore stopped by just to eye the candy. The smells and sounds announced the celebration of the season. Pinky, who loved Christmas, would have been so happy to see how she had decorated the store.

She wondered if Avery would ask to marry her again. He was not happy with her previous answer, but recently she felt more confident. Avery was more self-assured, too, since he had made some money speculating on land out West. All she could do was wait to see what would materialize during the holiday season.

This was the first Christmas without their parents, and she missed them dearly, especially her father. Abigail and her two sisters decided to display *all* the decorations and make life more festive at the Abbott household. Mary and Louise missed their mother, so as a tribute to her, they meticulously placed each ornament on the tree just like Mom would have. In spite of their grief, the Christmas decorations brought back good memories.

Abigail invited Avery over for Christmas Eve, which involved savoring Mary's baked goods and sipping mulled cider. Before they settled in for the evening, the two of them brought a large box of candy to the Presbyterian Church for the children to enjoy after the Christmas Eve program. Avery carried the heavy box, which was filled to the brim with ribbon candy, candy canes, Necco Wafers, spruce gum, licorice, Lancaster caramels, and salt-water taffy. This is one tradition that Abigail would carry on every year to honor Pinky. His generosity sparked the Christmas spirit in the church.

They returned to the house to open their Christmas gifts. Abigail bought Avery a new fedora, and he gave her a beautiful black shawl trimmed with a border of red roses. The holiday was a good one, but she received no proposal of marriage and no engagement ring. Mystified, she went back to work the day after Christmas wondering what was up. Had Avery changed his mind? The next time she saw him, she tried to read his face, but she couldn't. Maybe his game plan was to try to catch her off-guard. She had to admit that if that was his intent, it was working. Much to her chagrin, all Abigail could do was be patient and wait.

৵৵৵

It was a snowy Valentine's Day. Jack Frost stubbornly stayed through the sunny part of the day, so it was a cold one. In spite of the weather, sales were brisk. The chocolate Valentine boxes were sold out by four o'clock. As usual, there were a couple of stragglers who had to settle for chocolates in a bag. At five o'clock, Abigail closed up shop, turned to gather her things, and saw a couple of eyes peeking at her through the window. Then she saw his disarming smile and knew for sure it was Avery. She happily opened the door.

"Well, my dearest, I have a question," Avery said, looking directly into her eyes. "Will you marry me?" There was no hesitation in his voice, only confidence. Somehow, he knew that making her wait would make her more inclined to say yes. He couldn't have been more right.

"Yes!" she said. "I will!"

The ring he put on her finger was the same one but now even lovelier because she thought her heart was finally ready. Her eyes watered as she looked at his. Smitten by strong emotions, a single tear trickled down her face.

"You will always be my Valentine's Day Girl," he whispered as they embraced. "I love you, Abigail."

Their lips touched, sealing their betrothal.

చిచిచి

"Abigail, dear, the store and its income should be shared by both of us," Avery said. "I'm an old-fashioned kind of guy, and this asset is safer if I am looking out for your best interest. I don't believe women should be working outside the home. They should stay home and raise the children."

Abigail looked at him quizzically. "I'm sorry, Avery, I've got to get back to work," she said as she turned her back on him and headed to her office. "Thank heaven the laws protect me," she said in a whisper once he was out of earshot. *I can't believe Avery wanted to take Abbott's Confectionary and put it under his control and label it family assets or community property,* she said to herself in disbelief.

The thought of being disobedient haunted her, since she wanted to be a good, faithful wife, and she wanted a better marriage than her parents. But, she didn't want to give up her property rights. Women fought too hard for their financial independence, and staying current by reading *The Baltimore Sun* prevented her from being exploited. The Married Women's Property Act of 1860 was finalized after a long, hard fight, and legally, she could keep her property as if she were a single woman. By law, she could keep the *profits* from her business, and her husband could not take them away. However, she was also aware that any contracts between two people contemplating marriage would remain in full force after marriage. She knew the importance of navigating through this season of her life successfully since she wanted a good marriage. Without a doubt, these were extremely difficult choices. She scratched her head, trying to figure out how she could handle the delicate subject of her financial independence. In private moments, she yearned for her daddy to guide her.

On her ride home through the grinding Baltimore traffic, she experienced thoughts that came to her in an almost mystical way. Maybe her father actually was by her side. Clear answers came to her. It was like an epiphany. She became hopeful that she could retain the ownership of Abbott's Confectionary by dividing the profits three ways: one-third to her, one-third to her sisters, and one-third to the marital assets. The more she considered it, the more right it felt. She would maintain her financial independence, help her sisters, and be obedient to her husband.

The next part of the minefield would be the hardest, which was to convince Avery that this three-way split would be the most beneficial. Yes, getting Avery on board would be the most difficult. She rehearsed her ideas and the rationale behind them over and over again. She could almost do it in her sleep. The time finally came for her to present them to Avery.

"How's my girl?" Avery said, popping through the door. It was Friday, and they usually ended the workweek by going out for dinner.

"Pretty good, how are you?" Abigail said with a sweet smile.

"Couldn't be better," Avery said. "The outside of my

house is pretty much done, so now we'll finish the inside. It should be finished by this time next year, just in time for our wedding. I can't wait to have my sweet wife in my house," Avery said.

"I'm looking forward to that, too," she said smiling. "I've been thinking about Pinky lately. Daddy always said I made good business decisions, and he supported me because he trusted me. Because of his trust, I became financially independent. I miss him so much right now. Daddy and I talked about Maryland and how proud we were to live here because this state was one of the first to give women property rights," Abigail said pointedly. She looked up at Avery and noticed a grimace.

"What are you saying? Are you not going to obey my wishes?" Avery said, raising his voice. "I'm trustworthy, too! I have won a lawsuit, kept intruders off my land, and am building a house," he said emphatically.

"I trust you, Avery. You are hardworking and ambitious. I respect that. Do you think we can work something out that would benefit both of us?" Abigail queried.

"What are you thinking?"

"I feel responsible for my sisters, but I want to be obedient to my husband," she said. "Also, I want to be true to myself."

"So, I'm not the most important person in your life?" Avery said defensively.

Abigail fell silent for a few moments before speaking. How could she answer something like that?

"It's complicated," she said. "You *are* the center of my life, but I'm responsible for other parts of my world as well," Abigail said.

"Well, what is your proposal?" Avery retorted.

"I'm being pulled three different ways because of my husband, my sisters, and myself," she said. "Rather than being rigid and insisting on my rights under the law, I am proposing that the profits from Abbott's Confectionary be split three ways, one-third to the marital assets, one-third to my sisters, and one-third to myself," Abigail said carefully.

"I strongly disagree," Avery said loudly. "I'm going to talk with Reverend Holcombe and get some advice from him. I'm sure he agrees with me that *all* the assets should be marital ones."

"I would like to go with you," she responded.

"No, this is between men," he said as he left in a huff.

Abigail felt bewildered. She started to second-guess herself. Was she being a disobedient woman? Did Pinky give her too much independence? Was she out of line? She calmed herself by remembering why the law was put into practice. Abigail knew in her heart that she had done the very best she could, given the difficult circumstances. From her American history class in high school, she recalled how Harriet Beecher Stowe fought for the expansion of women's rights in 1869. Harriet considered the lives of women to be similar to the plight of the slave. They could not own property or make any contracts. Everything became the property of the husband, even though it might have been her fortune that she acquired through her efforts or maybe an inheritance. According to Harriet, the wife couldn't get a penny of it without the permission of her husband. Then, if the wife died, she sadly passed out of legal existence. She left no legacy for her children or other family members. It was like she was a non-person. Abigail did *not* want that for her life, since she wanted to contribute to society by doing something she enjoyed. So, her intent was to stand firm.

The next Sunday, Avery picked her up for church. Both were silent on the carriage ride to church. Neither one wanted to bring up the topic. When church was over, they shook Reverend Holcombe's hand. He pulled Avery and Abigail aside.

"Abigail, I would like both you and Avery to come to see me," he said in a whisper.

"I would like that," she said. "What time would work best for you?"

"How about next Saturday afternoon at two o'clock? Would that work for both of you?" he asked. Abigail looked at Avery, and he nodded affirmatively.

"Yes, that would work. We'll see you then," Abigail said. Avery helped her into the carriage, shaking his head in disbelief.

"Well, well. I guess I'm marrying a *modern* woman," Avery said grimly.

☙☙☙

"Come in, come in," Pastor Holcombe said with enthusiasm. "I've been waiting for you." The pastor was a short, jolly fellow, blessed with a sunny disposition, and Abigail instinctively liked him. He reminded her of Pinky. Most of all, she admired his willingness to see her and Avery together. She was hoping he was open-minded about women. From her observations, men of the cloth could be either legalistic or nonjudgmental and nothing in between. Pastor Holcombe seemed to be of a kinder ilk, more evenhanded. She especially liked his warmth.

"I'm usually up in Carroll County working on the house on Saturdays," Avery explained, "but this meeting is important for my future." Pastor Holcombe led the way to his study, and the three of them hustled through the dim corridors, the light from his study guiding them. Books and more books were piled on the shelves. Other than the sizable display of reading materials, the study was quite modest, with a large window facing the courtyard. His desk was graced with a lovely, etched, reading lamp.

"Have a seat," he said politely. "Did I hear you correctly when you said you were building a house in Carroll County?"

"Yes, I got some money from a court case I won against the railroads," Avery replied, smiling smugly. "I'm living in a shack until it's finished."

"Where are you living, Abigail?" the pastor inquired.

"I'm living with my sisters, Mary and Louise, in the family home until I get married," Abigail said. She sensed Pastor Holcombe was delicately trying to determine their assets. This motivated her to get to the point. "When Mom and Dad died, I was left with the business, Abbott's Confectionary, and my sisters were given the house. I'll get right to the point. It's important that I take care of my sisters, so I don't want my portion to be turned over as marital assets," Abigail explained.

Avery stood up suddenly and became agitated. "This makes me very angry," he said. "A married couple should trust each other enough to put all the assets under the control of the man of the house." Avery paced around the study, red-faced, spitting saliva as he shouted his opinions. "I want to have a strong union with my wife, and, if she separates me from her business world, our relationship is over. Pastor, you should know that a wife has a moral obligation to obey her husband."

Flummoxed by his exhortations, Abigail slid down in her seat, and Pastor Holcombe's countenance became stern and expressionless. When Avery's rage lessened, there was a long silence before Pastor Holcombe responded.

"Mr. Johnson, it seems to me that this matter is of major importance to you, so it's good to resolve it before you're married," he said reassuringly. "I commend both of you for seeking outside advice. The Church has had many discussions about the role of the wife to her husband, and many of them conflict. Personally, I believe what applies here are the laws of the State of Maryland. Many widows, single mothers, and their children have been left penniless and destitute following the death of a husband," he cautioned. "Women who have lost the main breadwinner of the family are at a loss, not knowing how to make a living for themselves or their children. Abigail is one of the lucky ones. She is able to manage a business. Pinky recognized her ability and gave her an opportunity." Turning his head toward Abigail, "What do you have to say about this?" he asked.

"I want to be a good wife to Avery," she said solemnly "But I feel responsible for my sisters. They have the house, but not the income needed to keep it in good repair. I have to provide for them. My dear father gave me the business, and I cherish the memories of him when I am at the store. I'm not ready to part with it. Avery *is* the center of my life, but I have other obligations that demand my attention as well."

"Let's say that a final decision has to be made, and you

disagree," Pastor Holcombe inserted. "Who would have the final say?"

"For my business, I would, but in everything else, Avery would," Abigail said without batting an eye.

"So, for matters of the household and for my business, it would be my decision?" Avery asked quizzically.

"Yes," Abigail said without wavering.

A thoughtful pause followed until the contention seemed to evaporate.

"The two of you seem to solve problems pretty well," Pastor Holcombe said. "Compromising and finding a middle ground is important for a good relationship, and the two of you are well on your way."

"What about the profits from her business? Would that become part of the marital assets?" Avery asked.

"The business is mine, but I want to be the best wife possible. My sisters need money to keep the house running, and I want some of the profits from Abbott's Confectio—"

"Wait a minute!" Avery interrupted. "Wouldn't that money be part of the marital assets? Why would you need your own money if you were married to me? I'll take care of you."

"Thank you, Avery," she said, "but, with an allotment of the funds I can reinvest back into the business and have some money for myself. This will motivate me to make more profits."

"Making money motivates *me*, too," Avery countered.

"Please listen to my plan. I don't want to be selfish or disobedient, but I would like to propose giving one-third of the business profits to my sisters, one-third to the marital assets and then, one-third of the profits for me. This seems fair to me."

Avery sat there shaking his head. He crossed and uncrossed his legs. He slumped in his chair and placed a closed fist under his chin, deep in thought.

Pastor Holcombe looked directly at Avery. "Well, what's your answer?"

"I'm thinking about my mom and dad and their relationship. My mom would be lost without my dad. She couldn't survive without him. I don't think that's the best way to go. I don't want my wife to be that helpless. I like Abigail's confidence, which she gets from being a successful business woman."

She didn't expect that answer, so she was ecstatic. She jumped up and threw her arms around Avery and gave him a kiss.

"Does that mean you'll sign the agreement?" Abigail asked excitedly.

"That would be in the affirmative," Avery responded, overwhelmed by her ebullience and her willingness to listen to his views.

"Well done, you two," Pastor Holcombe said happily. "Now, I would recommend you see an attorney to get a copy of that agreement signed. It's a good agreement. You have made a compromise!"

"Thank you, Pastor for hearing us out. We needed that," Avery responded gratefully. "I haven't talked to Abigail about this, but would you officiate at our wedding?"

"It would be an honor. Thank you for asking me," he responded graciously.

CHAPTER 5

Valentine's Day, 1888

❧❧❧❧

The choices Abigail made up to this point had been good ones, but the vicissitudes of life could change all that in a heartbeat. She counted her blessings every day. She managed a successful business, had a handsome fiancé, an imminent wedding, and an enviable future with a beautiful new home waiting for her in Carroll County. Daydreaming about her wedding day and her soon-to-be married life with Avery consumed every thought. Keeping the books and managing the income of Abbott's Confectionary paled in comparison. Her sense of duty became fervent, and somehow, she managed to keep the store running smoothly.

Avery and Abigail followed the advice of Reverend Holcombe and went to a lawyer to have the papers drawn up to secure the agreement between them. With that major difference settled, Abigail breathed easier and was inspired to plan a memorable wedding. First on the list was to choose the date. She wanted a "Thanksgiving wedding," but Avery would have none of that. Usually, the woman decides the date, but his determination was so strong.

"I met you on Valentine's Day, we were engaged on Valentine's Day, and I want to be married on that day," he said. "The fourteenth would fall on a Tuesday, and you know that old superstition: 'Marry on Monday for health, Tuesday for wealth, Wednesday, the best day of all, Thursday for crosses, Friday for losses, and Saturday for no luck at all.' Tuesday is a good day, because I want wealth," he continued.

Abigail shook her head and smiled. "Avery, Avery. You're already wealthy," she chided with a glint in her eye.

&ed;&ed;&ed;

The date was set, February 14, 1888, only six months away. Without a doubt, Avery was the decisive one in the relationship, and she would have to pick her fights and stand firm. Something in her saw this trait as strong and masculine, but it was disconcerting nevertheless. She wasn't sure how this would present itself in their future together.

With Valentine's Day as the theme, red roses would be just the right flower to choose. They would be vibrant and richly aromatic. Most of all, Abigail wanted to have the latest fashion from Paris. She worked hard for her money, and her wedding day would be her day to shine. She wanted to step out in a dress that was out of the ordinary. Her friends, Rosemary and her mother Florence, needed a visit. They would know what was in fashion for wedding dresses and would have the inside scoop on the best patterns.

It was autumn and a cool, clear-aired Baltimore day when she decided to head to St. Ann's Parish to see Florence and Rosemary. With her future wedding dress on her mind and a box of chocolates in hand, she felt like skipping. The cool air and the fall fragrances brought back memories of going to school. It was like she was a happy child again. Eagerly, she knocked on the door. Florence opened it, expecting to see someone else.

"Oh, I thought it would be Matilda's mother," she exclaimed. "What a nice surprise to see you on this Saturday. Come in, come in!"

No matter what they were busy doing, both Florence and Rosemary welcomed her with open arms. Rosemary scurried toward her out of the sewing room. She had not seen her since Abigail lost her mother and father.

"Hi, Abigail," Rosemary said. "I read about the carriage accident in *The Baltimore Sun*. What a horrible tragedy! How are you doing?"

"It has been hard not to have my parents. I've cried myself to sleep many nights. It's going to be a long time before my sisters and I accept that they're not around. I have something else that I came to talk with you about. I have some good news to share. I'm getting married on Valentine's Day next year," she said. Both Rosemary and Florence stood there with their mouths open in surprise.

"That's wonderful news!" Rosemary said. Abigail and her friend danced a brief jig together while Florence watched. She laughed at their childlike antics.

"You two are too much," Florence said. "Abigail, let me guess … you're here because you need a wedding gown."

"That's why I'm here. Would you and Rosemary be my seamstresses?"

"We would be honored, wouldn't we, Mother?" Rosemary blurted as Florence nodded in agreement.

"I want the latest Parisian fashion, a dress that is soft and flowing," Abigail said.

"I have a journal of new fashions, so let me get it," Florence said. She gestured for her to have a seat and placed the catalogue in front of her.

Peering intently at the dresses in the magazine photos, Abigail began to tear up. "I miss Mother and especially my father so much. They won't be there to see me on my wedding day."

Rosemary, sensing her deep pain, embraced her friend and let the tears flow. They held each other for a long time. "It is sad not to have your mom and dad there. I guess you have to remember all the people that will be there to celebrate with you. *I* will be there and my mom will be there. You are very important to us," Rosemary said.

Somehow, their love and friendship softened the tough blows of that terrible tragedy. Love in the midst of tears is the most we can hope for in this life. Rosemary and Florence were always supportive and kind. It was an unconditional friendship.

"You are the best!" Abigail said, trying to compose herself.

She picked up the fashion journal and searched through the pages, hoping to find just the right dress. She discovered an elegant one on the inside-back cover. It was made of organdy cloth, fresh and billowing. The skirt had gentle scallops, like soft, white petals cascading from the waist to the floor. The sleeves were full and airy with an abundance of fabric, also of organdy. The bodice was sheer with a satin lining, close-fitting at the waist. The neckline was highlighted by a wispy, delicate collar that gracefully curved around the outside of the shoulders, coming to a point at the center, showing just a bit of cleavage. It was regal and, yet, pristine.

"I want that one," she said, pointing.

"Oh my! That *is* beautiful," Florence exclaimed. "Rosemary, do you think you could sew it? I already have her measurements from the yellow dress, but I want to put you in charge of this one. After all, she is your best friend."

"I think I can do it, but I'll have to ask for help once in a while," Rosemary said.

"Go ahead and order the pattern. I know you'll do a good job. I appreciate you so much. Thank you," Abigail said.

She got up to leave and gave her two good friends a hug good-bye. "I'll stop by in a couple of weeks to see how it's coming."

❧ ❧ ❧

With that big decision behind her, Abigail was ready to expand her trousseau with linens and lace. She had heard that Mrs. Harmon Brown had opened up her house for women who wanted to sell their wares. Their handwork was so fine that they recently opened a shop on Saratoga Street. They called it The Woman's Exchange.

Abigail respected their mission. Women who were widowed or abandoned by their husbands could become financially independent by selling their handwork. The news around town was that the items were of high quality, and many goods were exquisitely crafted. To ensure a sustainable lifestyle for the consignors, the prices were moderate to high.

Because it was a respected business, it gave the women value and, most of all, dignity. For Abigail, this was paramount, because she had worked so hard to negotiate her financial independence from Avery. She knew the importance of women standing on their own two feet.

Abigail read a sign on the door, "Open, Please Come In." She entered and looked around. Amazed by the amount of handwork on the shelves, she ambled around, trying to decide what she wanted for her trousseau. The lace tablecloths were exquisite. She spotted an appealing one, pulled it off the shelf, and unfolded it to see the lace pattern. She heard a noise behind her and turned around to see a sophisticated young lady smiling at her.

"Do you like that tablecloth?" she asked.

"Yes, I do," Abigail responded.

"That item was crafted by one of the best at the Woman's Exchange. We don't use names, but her number is ninety-eight. She has other patterns. Let me show you my favorite," she said. "By the way, I'm Elizabeth Brown, Mrs. Harmon Brown's daughter."

She reached up to the top shelf and tugged at a box. She took the lid off and draped the tablecloth over the counter. What a splendid piece of handwork it was— white lace with outlines of dainty, pink roses placed in a circular pattern in the center.

"I'll buy that," Abigail said. "I've heard that you are planning to have a store on North Charles Street."

"Yes, we're purchasing the building right now, and are hoping to be all moved in by the end of next year," Elizabeth said.

"That's good," Abigail said as she nodded. She took her package, said goodbye to Elizabeth, and hustled home to show her sisters what she found at the Woman's Exchange. She ran up the steps and opened the door. She discovered Mary and Louise making supper.

"Look what I bought for my trousseau," Abigail said. She twirled the tablecloth out of the box and opened it for display.

"That is so lovely," Louise said as she reached out to feel it. "Oh! This is very fine lace."

"Will you be using Mom's hope chest to store the linens?" Mary asked.

"Yes, if it's all right with the two of you," Abigail responded.

Mary and Louise looked at each other and nodded in agreement.

"Thank you, my dear sisters. We have supported each other through thick and thin." Abigail took their hands and gently held them, so grateful to have sisters that were caring.

Over the course of the next few months, Abigail stocked her hope chest with lovely embroidered linens, quilts, crocheted pillowcases, and even baby clothes. She neatly organized them in the old oak chest and closed the lid. Her hopes and dreams for a fulfilling married life with Avery lifted her spirits and spurred her on to meet the demands of each day.

చ్రచ్రచ్ర

Abbott's Confectionary was usually busy during Christmas time, and this season was busier than most. Perhaps it was because Abigail was monitoring the store by herself, or maybe people were buying more candy out of respect for her father. The increased profits were always welcomed. The good business climate and dreams of the forthcoming wedding created lightness in her spirit, something she hadn't felt for a long time.

Saturday afternoon was her time off, and she made plans to visit Florence and Rosemary. She tucked a box of chocolates inside her satchel, and off she went to St Ann's parish. While riding the streetcar, she thought about her wedding day. Reverend Holcombe would officiate, and she was happy that he was willing to conduct the wedding ceremony in their family home. Abigail wanted to feel the presence of her mother and father at her wedding. Her memories of the dining room table being the gathering place for the whole family, the recollections of holiday fun, birthday celebrations, and of course, the fond memories of her father's playful side reinforced the idea. She wanted to feel their spirits on this special day.

Her sisters, Mary and Louise, were more than willing to clean and decorate the house. In fact, they wholeheartedly wanted to participate. There would be between fifty and sixty guests, mostly business acquaintances, and some family and friends. She invited Stephen Whitman and his wife, since they had been so kind when her mother and father died in the accident. They sent a card to all three of us, and attended the funeral. The Whitman's had become family in the larger sense.

The streetcar stopped with the sound of screeching brakes jostling her out of her contemplation. It was time for her to disembark and head to Rosemary's house.

After knocking on the door, she walked inside and saw Rosemary busily working on a dress that was draped across the dining room table.

"Oh! Hi, Abigail," Rosemary said. "You're just the person I needed to see." She seemed scattered and a bit over-whelmed, almost like she was trying to hide something.

"Is that my dress?" Abigail asked.

"Yes, it is," Rosemary answered. "Mom just scolded me for not pressing the darts before I sewed the bodice."

"Do you want me to try it on?" Abigail asked.

"Yes, if you don't mind," she said.

Abigail stepped into the bedroom, took off her street clothes, and slipped her wedding dress over her head. She looked in the mirror and was surprised about the fullness of the dress. She wanted it to be flowing and billowing, but it was fluffier than she expected. When Rosemary tied the laces in back, Abigail voiced her disappointment.

"I wanted my dress to be more formfitting," Abigail said. "Can you make some changes?"

Rosemary started crying, because she wanted Abigail to be satisfied with her work. Abigail reassured her that much of her sewing was well done, but she wanted some of the skirt fabric removed.

"I can do that right now while you're waiting, and then we can see how it fits," Rosemary said after composing herself. She turned the dress inside out and cut away a layer of fabric. "Okay, let's try it on." Abigail put the dress over her head, and after Rosemary laced her up, she turned around to look at herself in the mirror. "That looks much better! Very good. I think that solved the problem." The dress was still "floaty," but it remained elegant, which suited her tastes. There was something about organdy fabric that was fresh and virginal.

"Have you seen the pictures of the modern women in *Life* magazine?" Abigail asked.

"Yes, I have. Charles Gibson, the illustrator, proclaims them to be the 'New Women,' and I've heard other people call them the 'Gibson Girls.' They're supposed to be both feminine *and* independent. I like that independent idea, because I see so many women become dependent on a man and then become destitute at the end of their life. A lot of men can be selfish that way. So, Gibson's idea is good, because it presents us as being able to stand on our own two feet. I look at my mom. She's been able to support our home, daddy, and me through her business. She's an amazingly strong and supportive woman. The hair of these 'Gibson Girls' is so different, too. I really like the curls. I wonder how they do it?"

"I must have read the same article," Abigail said. "I think I want my hair done like that at my wedding, rather than in a tight bun."

"That would suit you," Rosemary said. "A hairstyle like that would complement your more modern wedding dress. I should have your dress done by next Saturday, so you can come back for the final fitting that afternoon."

"I'll be here," she said. Abigail took the box of chocolates out of her satchel before she said good-bye. "Make sure you share some of the candy with your mother," Abigail winked. "I'm off chocolates until after the wedding. I have to actually fit into the dress you're making, you know." Both of them chuckled. "I'll see you on Saturday."

☙ ☙ ☙

The wedding preparations went surprisingly smoothly. The invitations were mailed at the appropriate time. A simple wedding at the family home was the order of the day. Mary and Louise would oversee the caterers and help Abigail, while Henry, Avery's brother, would help the groom. At least, that was the plan. The decorations for the house, the wedding cakes, the final fitting for the bridal gown, the purchase of gloves and the little brocade slippers, had to be handled well before the event.

The flowers came the night before, gardenias for the men's boutonnieres and orange blossoms for the bride. Her sisters and Mallory, her soon-to-be mother-in-law, received a corsage of orange blossoms as well. By all appearances, it was all falling into place. However, to borrow a phrase from the old Bard, "The course of love never did run smooth." The groom and his brother Henry violated all wedding protocol by their outlandish behavior.

Henry was living it up out West and was loud and raucous, kind of a "silver spoon" roustabout, if that could be imagined. He traveled far for his brother's wedding, but he brought with him the manners of the Wild West. The night before the wedding, Avery, Henry, and five of their buddies trashed The Horse restaurant. There was a fight at the bar, and Henry was at the bottom of the pile, being slammed around by Baltimore's most unsavory characters. Henry was incensed. He pulled out his gun and fired several rounds. A bystander was hit in the shoulder, and the city police were called in to put a lid on the fracas. Still in a rage, Henry resisted arrest. They handcuffed him and threw him in jail. Avery, the big brother, had to bail his little brother out of jail.

The next day was the wedding, and it would be Abigail's first encounter with Henry, her new brother-in-law.

ॐ ॐ ॐ

It was Valentine's Day, 1888, and Abigail was up at six o'clock in the morning. It was her wedding day, and she was eagerly anticipating a joyful celebration. The house was quiet. She breathed a prayer for a blessed event, hoping everyone would enjoy the day and take home good memories.

Still in her nightgown, she tiptoed down the stairs to see the decorations. Long after she went to bed, she heard her sisters whispering and bustling about, hanging this and pulling that, and she was greeted with an extravagant surprise. It was like Christmas in February. There was a profusion of white with touches of red. The doorways were draped with evergreen garlands highlighted with red roses. The staircase looked exquisite, with white tulle and red roses winding through the balustrades. Each window was embellished with swags of white fabric, and on each sill was a bouquet of red roses with a tall white candle in the center.

The most resplendent site was the fireplace. The garlands of pine and roses were woven with white tulle and placed across the mantel and down the sides. Suspended from the ceiling was a fabricated white-feathered dove, and in its mouth was a red satin heart. This was the good luck symbol for the couple, placed just above where they would exchange vows. On the fireplace mantel, there were two beautifully framed pictures of Pinky and Martha. Abigail started crying, her tears a mixture of profound sadness and elation. She had never felt that intensity of emotion before, truly a bittersweet joy.

"Mary, Louise, wake-up!" she yelled. "Come downstairs!"

Both of them, exhausted from decorating the house in the wee hours of the morning, shuffled out of bed, rubbed their eyes, and headed downstairs.

"What's the matter?" Mary queried.

"Did we do something wrong?" Louise asked.

"No, no! It is just so perfect that I couldn't contain myself," Abigail said. "Please come down, so I can give you a hug."

She was so deeply grateful for her sister's support. All of them were left as orphans when Pinky and Martha died, but somehow, the three of them remained intact because of their loving bond. Heartfelt thankfulness rolled over them like a gigantic wave. It was the kind of wave that heals.

Once awake, the sisters scurried about the house getting everything ready for the arrival of the guests. Louise was to help Abigail with her dress, hair, and veil, while Mary readied the food in the kitchen and built the fire in the fireplace.

Abigail put on her white silk stockings, her petticoat, and then struggled to get her corset on. After all, she wanted to have that S-curve, small waist, large bust, and hips like the Gibson Girls. This corset was called the Perfect Health Corset because the front busk was removed, so the intestines weren't squished together. Louise laced the ties in the back and pulled them tight to lift her bosom and give her a tiny waist. Though not comfortable, Abigail just wanted one day where she would look like one of those women in *Life* magazine.

Louise styled Abigail's hair. Her first job was to separate the tight bun and brush her auburn locks until they shined. Then, with a magical sleight of hand, she pushed her hair up and twisted the hair into a braid at the nape of her neck. Wow! Louise had created the perfect bouffant chignon. She beamed with pride, and the hairstyle accentuated the graceful curves of Abigail's neck.

After the petticoat, corset, and hairstyling, it was time to put the gown over Abigail's newly styled hair, so Louise had to be cautious. She whisked it carefully over her sister's head and fastened the back buttons and ties.

"Thank you, Rosemary. Your sewing was masterful. It fits just right," Abigail said, speaking loud as if her dear friend Rosemary was there. Louise fetched the brocade shoes from the closet and slipped them on Abigail's feet. It reminded her of the story of Cinderella.

"Don't forget, Abigail, you need 'something old, something new, something borrowed, something blue, and a lucky sixpence in your shoe,'" Louise said as she reached in her pocket for a sixpence to put in her shoe.

"Oh! Louise, you are so funny," Abigail said as she pulled out a blue garter from her drawer. "I've already thought about that ditty. My gloves are new, and I'm borrowing your petticoat, so if you help me with Mom's golden shell necklace, which is something old, we're all set."

"Mom and dad would be so proud of you today. You are starting a new chapter for yourself and our family too," Louise said as she fastened the necklace. "I hope I'm as lucky as you are some day."

With that done, they heard the guests arriving downstairs. Mary greeted them as they entered and guided them to the chairs that were set in front of the fireplace. There were light skiffs of snow outside, so the hearth fire emitted welcoming warmth.

Bundles of gifts were delivered, and Mr. and Mrs. Whitman carried a very large box, which read "Open immediately." Mary lifted the box and took it to the kitchen to open. What a surprise! There were seventy-five bright red heart-shaped boxes filled with the finest Whitman chocolates. On the cover of the box was this inscription:

Mr. and Mrs. Avery Johnson
Betrothed
Valentine's Day, 1888

It couldn't have been more appropriate! It symbolized so much of Abigail and Avery's relationship. As Louise carefully placed each one on the credenza, the room filled with lighthearted chatter.

Avery's parents, Mallory and Grant Johnson, made quite an entrance. She wore a white fur coat and a large pink hat, festooned with an array of white plumes. Grant, quite the gentleman, helped her with her coat and hung it in the closet. She looked diminutive in the heavy folds of pink satin and white lace adorned with pearls and diamonds. This was a big day for her, to see her oldest son marry. Grant, who was tall, towered over her. They set their package on the gift table and waited to see who would come to speak to them. Soon, Mary greeted them, and they mingled and brought their cheer to the celebrating wedding guests.

The conviviality was interrupted when a loud shouting was heard at the front door. Mary hurriedly opened the door to an unwelcome argument between Avery and Henry.

"Mom and Dad always favored you," Henry shouted. "I'm tired of being the black sheep of the family!"

"I bailed you out of jail this morning. What more do you want?" Avery said. "Henry, today is my wedding day, please be civil and respectable."

Henry composed himself when he saw all the wedding guests staring at him.

"Gentlemen, come in!" Mary said as she held the door open, hoping for the best.

There was a stark contrast between the two brothers. Avery was the essence of elegance. He wore a well-tailored black suit coat with tails, white shirt, and pale-gray vest with a gold chain hanging between the watch pockets. A stiff collar stood straight, with a white bowtie around his neck. Dark-gray pinstriped, cashmere trousers reminded the guests that it was a very special day for him. He wore patent-leather button boots, pearl-colored kid gloves with black embroidery, and, of course, his black top hat.

His brother, Henry, was just the opposite of elegant. Being short of stature, his height amplified his corpulent body. People said that he got his height from his mother's side. He was a swashbuckler from the Wild West. His brown derby hat topped off a suit jacket that he couldn't button. He was just too big around. The matching pants sagged, and his boots, with spurs, were dusty from use. The white shirt, yellowed around the collar, was tight but the gold chain hanging between his watch pockets suggested a man of means. Henry was indeed a free spirit, an adventurer. He was his own kind of land speculator.

As they stepped into the warmth of the Abbott household, Henry doffed his hat and flashed an engaging smile. What he lacked in looks and character, he made up for in charm. Avery, not to be upstaged on his wedding day, took off his hat and smiled at the guests. A spontaneous round of applause erupted, and the jollity of his wedding day recommenced.

"Ladies and gentlemen, thank you for coming to my marriage to Abigail Abbott," Avery said. "People have traveled from afar to see my beautiful bride. Now, it's time to tie the wedding knot."

Mary placed a gardenia in his lapel, and Avery gave her his top hat. Reverend Holcombe and the best church musician entered the house through the back door. Officiously, they walked through the dining room to stand in front of the fireplace.

Reverend Holcombe faced the audience, the violinist positioned himself to the right of the minister, and Avery stood on his left, directly under the feathered dove with the red satin heart in its beak. The violinist played the prelude as the guests took their seats in anticipation. After a brief pause, he played a beautiful rendition of *Jesu, Joy of Man's Desiring* by J.S. Bach.

The audience turned their heads to the top of the stairs and saw the bride about to make her descent. Abigail's face was radiant, almost angelic. Avery was transfixed. Her dainty feet, clad in brocade slippers, mastered each step. Although, Pinky was not there to walk her down, she kept her focus on his picture on the mantel. Slowly and gracefully, she glided down the stairs to stand by her soon-to-be husband.

Avery gave her hand a squeeze, and she met his eyes with a smile. The fresh, clean smell of the orange blossoms gently wafted through the air. The flowers were carefully attached to her coronet, as was the silk tulle veil. In her hands she carried a bouquet of red roses with sprigs of orange blossoms. Underneath the veil and around her neck, the gold-tipped shell necklace from her mother glistened. She was resplendent with pristine beauty.

"Welcome to this blessed event, the marriage of Abigail Abbott and Avery Johnson on this Valentine's Day," Reverend Holcombe said. "Let us pray."

After the prayer, he read Proverbs Thirty-One verses ten through thirty-one from the King James Bible.

Who can find a virtuous woman? For her price is far above rubies.

The heart of her husband doth safely trust in her, so that he shall have no need of spoil (no lack of gain).

She will do him good and not evil all the days of her life.

She seeketh wool, and flax, and worketh willingly with her hands.

She is like the merchants' ships; she bringeth her food from afar.

She riseth also while it is yet night, and giveth meat to her household, and a portion to her maidens.

She considereth a field, and buyeth it; with the fruit of her hands she planteth a vineyard.

She girdeth her loins with strength, and strengtheneth her arms.

She perceiveth that her merchandise is good; her candle goeth not out by night.

She layeth her hands to the spindle, and her hands hold the distaff.

She stretcheth out her hand to the poor; yea, she reacheth forth her hands to the needy.

She is not afraid of the snow for her household: for all her household are clothed with scarlet.

She maketh herself coverings of tapestry; her clothing is silk and purple.

Her husband is known in the gates, when he sitteth among the elders of the land.

She maketh fine linen, and selleth it; and delivereth girdles unto the merchant.

Strength and honour are her clothing; and she shall rejoice in time to come.

She openeth her mouth with wisdom; and in her tongue is the law of kindness.

She looketh well to the ways of her household, and eateth not the bread of idelness.

Her children arise up, and call her blessed; her husband also, and he praiseth her.

Many daughters have done virtuously but thou excellest them all.

Favour is deceitful, and beauty is vain: but a woman that feareth the Lord, she shall be praised.

Give her of the fruits of her hands; and let her own works praise her in the gates.

Then, the vows were declared:

"I, Avery Johnson, take you, Abigail Abbott, to be my wedded wife, and I do promise and covenant, before God and these witnesses, to be your loving and faithful husband, in plenty and in want, in joy and in sorrow, in sickness and in health, as long as we both shall live."

Abigail responded in kind, adding, "I will love, cherish, and *obey*" to her vows. Then, the rings came out of Avery's pocket. They were simple gold bands inscribed with "To My Valentine with Love." They slipped them on one another's fingers, symbolizing their exchange, moving away from the life of "me" to the life of "us."

"I now pronounce you husband and wife," Pastor Holcombe said triumphantly. "You may now kiss the bride." Avery carefully lifted her veil and kissed his bride. The guests erupted in applause. They turned toward their guests, joyfully. What an unforgettable moment. "Let me introduce Mr. and Mrs. Avery Johnson," Pastor Holcombe announced. Another enthusiastic round of applause erupted.

The newly married couple bowed their heads to the audience, and the party started. Mallory and Grant were the first to congratulate them, and then Henry, Mary and Louise. A receiving line formed, and the guests shook hands and congratulated the bride, groom and their families.

They were officially married!

❧❧❧

The wedding took place at eleven o'clock, so Mary and Louise with some help from local caterers prepared a lunch for the guests. Reverend Holcombe gave the blessing and then offered a champagne toast to the new couple. Henry stepped up and raised his glass.

"I'd like to propose a toast to my big brother, Avery, and his beautiful *and* intelligent wife. You see, where I come from, the women are pretty dumb. Once, a young rancher and his wife wanted to increase their herd of cows. He takes their life savings to buy a bull. He finds someone who will sell him a bull for $49.90. He accepts the offer. He needs his wife to bring a bigger wagon, so he heads to the telegraph office only to find out that each word is ten cents. So, the farmer tells them to transmit the word 'comfortable.' The telegraph operator scratches his head and says, 'Why did you choose that word?' 'My wife reads real slow,' says the farmer, 'so she'll read: com—for—da—bull.'" The wedding guests howled with laughter.

"I, for one, am someone who likes smart women, and Avery, you did a fine job. Congratulations Avery and Abigail." Henry raised his glass and took a gulp of champagne, and the guests did the same.

The guests chatted as they found their way to the dining room for food and a piece of wedding cake. Many commented on the sumptuous array of food and the delightful red, heart-shaped boxes of chocolates.

Avery and Abigail were the first to eat lunch and have a piece of their wedding cake. They took the time to circulate among the guests, thanking them for coming.

"Nice to meet you, Henry," Abigail said as she opened her arms to hug him. "You are now my brother-in-law." They hugged.

"My brother is a very lucky man," he said, "By the way, does Louise have a fiancé?"

"You are *too* much," she responded with a chuckle. "Why don't you ask her?"

Avery and Abigail disappeared upstairs while the guests ate and conversed. In thirty minutes, they came downstairs wearing more comfortable clothes under their overcoats. The guests were ready with handfuls of rice to throw at the newlyweds.

With her bouquet in hand, Abigail and Avery dashed through the torrents of rice and slipped out the front door. A white carriage with two white horses waited for them. Before stepping into the carriage, Abigail threw her flowers into the throng of people on the steps. It was Louise who caught the bouquet. She wondered if Henry noticed.

Whether she was lucky, or not, only time would tell. Henry brought the luggage and lifted it into the carriage. As the carriage left, the rest of the rice flew through the air. Women took off their slippers and threw them toward the couple; it was said to be good luck if one of them landed in the carriage—especially if it was the left slipper.

કે કે કે

Abigail and Avery could hear the guests celebrating all the way to the end of the neighborhood street. Other than a few snow flurries, it was a mild Valentine's Day in

Baltimore, and Avery moved the carriage at quite a clip to make the Philadelphia, Wilmington & Baltimore Train to Philadelphia. From there, they would make the connection to the Philadelphia & Atlantic City Train, which would bring them to Atlantic City, New Jersey. Avery was able to keep the location of their honeymoon a secret. Only the two of them knew. They planned to spend three nights at the United States Hotel in Atlantic City. This hotel wasn't the oldest, but it was the largest. Ulysses Grant stayed there when he was president. The sheer size of it was extraordinary. It covered a complete city block and could handle over two thousand guests. Abigail was giddy with excitement. Spending time in Atlantic City was a private dream of hers, and how wonderful to be able to share it with her new husband. From some of his connections, Avery heard about a really good travel deal. The railroad offered a special package including train fare, dinner aboard, and accommodations at the United States Hotel for three nights for twelve dollars and seventy-five cents. Abigail didn't know that she married someone who was good at scouting deals. She found it to be an amusing surprise.

They didn't talk much on the train, but they sat close together and held hands. It was a reflective time for both of them. They were tired and satisfied because the day had gone well. When Abigail remembered how long the day had been, she yawned and put her head on Avery's shoulder and fell asleep. Avery's yawn was not too far behind. He closed his eyes and placed his head on top of hers. He had no idea how long he napped when a waiter accidently bumped him as he walked down the aisle.

"Sorry, sir," he said. "I need to take your orders, so I'll

be back shortly." Avery sat up straight and looked over at Abigail, who was still fast asleep.

"What would you like for dinner, madam?" the waiter asked. Groggy from her nap, Abigail rubbed her eyes and gave herself a minute to recall where she was.

"Crab cakes would be wonderful," she said.

"I'll have the same only with slaw on the side," Avery added. "By the way, this is our wedding day. Do you offer champagne for newlyweds?"

"Yes, we do. Congratulations to you, sir," he said with a smile. "I'll put the order in the kitchen." He promptly returned with two champagne glasses and a bottle of Duval-Leroy Champagne for the special occasion.

The champagne gave them a contented disposition as they pondered the events of the day. What a full one it had been! They were married in the morning, enjoyed the gusto of their wedding party at noon, and then, took the train to Philadelphia. Having made the connecting train to Atlantic City, they were on the last leg of their journey. Because this was a night train, they weren't able to see the New Jersey scenery—only an occasional black shadow rushing past the windows. They were so focused on each other and pondering the events of the vanishing day that they were oblivious to the flashing darkness whirling by them.

"Here's to my lovely bride," Avery said as he lifted his champagne glass and nodded his head. "May she always be as sweet to my heart as she is right now."

"My dear Avery," she responded, "my sweetness will depend on the freedom given to me to be myself."

"How long do you think our guests partied without us?" Avery asked clumsily, trying to change the subject.

"I would guess probably late afternoon," she said. "It was a grand celebration, and you looked so handsome, my love."

"You looked like an angel. I couldn't keep my eyes off you," he said in a hushed tone. Even though he expressed emotions awkwardly, she found them sincere. She cherished his boyish charm that was so much a part of him.

Much of the two-and-a-half-hour train ride was spent sipping champagne and smiling seductively at each other. They didn't need words to feel close, because an invisible connection like an electric current surrounded them. The unspoken shadows of their relationship were long forgotten as they enjoyed this marvelous time together.

Avery handled the details of their honeymoon like an expert. He chose the best penthouse suite for the two of them with a breathtaking view of the Atlantic Ocean. Arriving at the hotel, the bellhops greeted them and carried their luggage to the suite. They rode in a new Otis elevator. It was creaky and a bit noisy, but it was quite a ride to the top floor. Once off the elevator, they walked on plush oriental carpets to their room numbered 501 on a gold plaque. Underneath the number, it read, "The Presidential Suite." Abigail opened the door to sheer opulence. The centerpiece of the room was an intricately carved poster bed covered with a gold satin quilt. On either side of the bed were two long windows draped in red velvet. Gorgeous electric chandeliers, more oriental carpets, and fine linens outfitted the room. It was palatial bar none. Abigail placed her shawl on the bed and explored the smaller room to the right.

"Oh, Avery. Come here!" she said with surprise. What she found was a whole room dedicated to hygiene. In this smaller room was an enamel-coated bathtub prominently branded with the name John Kohler, Sheboygan, Wisconsin. The tub was encased by oak wood that was carefully engraved with grapevines and flowers. The carvings on the wood around the porcelain sink matched the bathtub. Both sink and tub had faucets, which they tried. To their surprise, when they pulled out the plugs, the water disappeared. Where did it go? The water closet was a tiny room off in the corner with a toilet that flushed when the chain was pulled. Where did that go?

"Wow! This is like the White House," Avery exclaimed. "This is even more than I expected."

It was time to get ready for their first night together. Abigail bathed first and washed away the travel grunge, loosened her hair, dabbed her body with a delicate violet perfume, then slipped into her lingerie. She demurely walked toward Avery. He softly touched her hair, caressed her face, and kissed her. He carried her to the bed, which he prepared by drawing the covers back, exposing the white satin sheets. "I'll be back soon," he said softly, walking into the washroom. He washed his body, and for this special night he rubbed the woody scent of Patchouli oil on his body. - It had a masculine scent.

She waited in anticipation, and as she did, she remembered the verses from the Song of Solomon (Chapter 2:16-17). The lover's story is as old as time.

Arise, my love, my fair one, and come away.

O my dove, that art in the clefts of the rock,

In the secret places of the steep place, let me see thy countenance,

Let me hear thy voice; for sweet is thy voice, and thy countenance is comely.

My beloved is mine, and I am his; he feedeth his flock among the lilies.

Until the day break, and the shadows flee away, turn, my beloved and be thou like a young hart upon the mountains of spices

Avery moved toward Abigail with a singular passion, wrapped his arms around her waist, and pulled her to him. His strong body was warm with ardor. Their lips touched. She abandoned her cool prudence and submitted to his will. A sudden surge of pain surfaced when his body pressed hard against hers. Her sensual self, which before was dormant, surged with his touch. Their passion sealed their fate as her virginity was exchanged for their marital union.

"You must never, never leave me, my love. You are mine forever. I need you and I love you and I will protect you always. When I want you, you must be there to love me. I love you, Abigail, my beautiful valentine," Avery whispered. "Promise me that you will never leave me? Say you are mine forever," he begged.

"I am yours, and you are mine," Abigail whispered.

And so, the journey of their married life began. The peaks and valleys of joy and disappointment, the dark shadows and bright sunlight, became all one together.

CHAPTER 6

Over the Threshold

❧❧❧❧

"What are you up to?" Abigail asked with a giggle.

Avery lifted her out of the carriage, swept her in his arms, and carried her through the front door of their new house. Abigail crossed her fingers, hoping that the ancient belief was true; that her family's demons were left on the other side of the threshold. The ancient lore declared that once inside, the evil spirits couldn't cross over into the house. Abigail knew she had many family demons, and soon found that Avery's family had some, too.

Avery took care of the horses as Abigail busied herself with the wedding gifts that Mallory and Grant brought back from the wedding. Her hope chest was carefully placed in the center of the foyer, right under their new chandelier. Grant and Mallory's house was simply a larger version of theirs, with electric lights and all. They both lived on Nicodemus Road, and were so close together that you could see the weather vane on top of their house. Fortunately, rolling hills hid the rest.

Abigail relished taking the sheets and pillowcases out of her hope chest, folding them, and placing them in the linen closets. The tablecloths and napkins were hidden away in the built-in china cabinet in the dining room. Furniture was sparse, but at least they had a bed for their master bedroom. Dressers and nightstands would have to come later. Henry was a good carpenter, so he promised to make a dresser and two small tables for their bedroom. For now, the pitcher and bowl would have to be put on the floor. She took the best sheets, blankets, and an appliquéd rose quilt out of her hope chest and made the master bed. She sighed with satisfaction, because it looked so cozy and comfortable.

Mallory shared one of her old tables and chairs with them. Abigail found them carefully placed in the kitchen by a window that revealed a beautiful vista of rolling hills, oak trees, and the shaded front lawn. She covered the wooden table with the lace tablecloth from the Woman's Exchange and sat down to write a letter to her sisters. She instinctively knew that this place where she was sitting would be her comfort spot, her "happy place." Avery's shed was just across the front lawn, so she could see him working with the horses. Soon it would be suppertime, prompting her to get the fire going and food ready.

Diane tended to Abbott's Confectionary while Abigail was away in Carroll County organizing and cleaning her house. She would do so for another week, then Abigail had to go to Baltimore to finish the books, check the inventory, and work the front counter. Feeling pulled in many different directions, she decided to ask Louise to watch the store on Fridays, so she would have a longer weekend with Avery. She was fond of her new house and planned to make it a cozy home. But, Abbott's Confectionary had a special spot in her heart, too. What an emotional "tug-of-war." She wondered if she could ever make peace with her two worlds.

In the middle of making supper, she looked out the window and saw a huge storm coming from the west. Dark clouds were rolling in fast.

"Avery. Avery. Come in! The weather is turning. It looks serious," she yelled. He came out of the shed, oblivious to the changing weather, acknowledged her comment and went back in to shut the window before he ran across the yard to the house. Gigantic raindrops came first, followed by torrents of rain flooding the yard and running down the hill.

"That came up fast," he said as water dripped off his nose, down his face. "Boy, that's a surprise. It's raining like a pissing cow." Abigail did a double take.

"What did you say? – pissing cow? I've never heard that before," Abigail said, a little amused. She grew up with sisters who were genteel and with Pinky, a candy salesman, so Avery's "man-talk" was foreign to her. Getting to know her mate and adjusting to him would take a while. Abigail had spent the good part of the day cooking dinner and was looking forward to sharing a meal with Avery, but just as they sat down, shots were heard nearby.

"What was that?" she said, startled. Looking out the window, she saw Henry wildly galloping away from Mallory and Grant's house heading toward Nicodemus Road. "Avery, you better see if your parents are okay."

"They're okay. Henry's just blowing off steam. Dad and Henry don't see eye to eye, so Henry takes out his pistol and fires shots in the air to scare him. It happens every time he stays at their house," Avery said, halfway laughing.

"Does this happen a lot?" Abigail asked, horrified by the violence. It was reminiscent of her mother's outbursts. Their family at least was trying to get help. It certainly was no laughing matter.

"Every time he's in town," he said. "That's why he's better off out West. He's been a troublemaker ever since he was a little kid. It's like he has a chip on his shoulder. It's always the same thing: Henry thinks he's the black sheep of the family, and he gets mighty angry when Dad treats him different."

"I'm going over to your mom and dad's house to make sure everything is okay," Abigail said.

"Don't worry. They're okay. Go ahead and see for yourself," Avery responded. Abigail waited until the heavy rain had dwindled to a mist before she ventured out. After carrying her empty plate to the sink, she took off her apron, and grabbed her sweater as she hustled out the front door. Mallory must have seen her coming, because before she could knock, Mallory opened the door.

"Hi, Abigail. It's good to see you. We're struggling here. Henry fired shots in the air and one of them ricocheted off of something and Grant was hit by one of the stray bullets. It grazed his right arm. It's just a surface wound, but it bled pretty badly. Thank heavens the bleeding has stopped, so he's going to be okay," Mallory said.

"What possessed him to do that?" Abigail asked.

"He's bad blood with a bad temper. Usually we don't

let him stay at the house, but he wanted to come to your wedding and didn't have a place to stay," she said.

"Was there an argument?" Abigail asked.

"My husband is so disappointed in him that when Grant just looks at him wrong, Henry explodes. So much resentment has built up over the years," she said. Abigail gave Mallory a hug and checked on Grant's wound.

"Life is hard sometimes, and I'm sorry you have to suffer," she said, her voice filled with compassion. Gently, Abigail held Grant's arm and examined the wound. "Mallory is right, it's just a surface wound and should heal well. By the way, I have one more week off before I have to go back to work, so stop over anytime," she said. As she headed back to her house, she was bewildered by the violence in the Johnson home. It gave her an uneasy feeling.

Avery didn't seem bothered by this incident, and life went on as usual. For Abigail, the two-week respite went by quickly. She wished she could stay home and decorate her house so it was comfortable for her and Avery. The thoughts of taking the train to Baltimore were unpleasant ones. What would Avery do without her? She would be staying with her sisters from Monday to Thursday and coming home for a long weekend. This was less than ideal, but she was determined to give it a try.

Filled with ambition and driven to become wealthy, Avery found plenty to do. He purchased livestock for the farm from the money he made from land sales. His dream was to graze cattle and sheep in the pastures surrounding their home. As the herd grew, he built barns for their shelter. He constructed outbuildings for his hired hands. They were employed to take care of the animals and tend the vineyards, planted for wine. Avery prospered, but he *still* was not satisfied. He was convinced that his neighbor was stealing his cattle in the night. When Abigail was not around, there was no one to keep him in check. If he heard a rustle after sunset, he grabbed his gun and stormed out of the house.

"Tomlinson, is that you?" he yelled. No answer. "Who's out there stealing my cattle?" No answer. He stalked the edge of his property for hours determined to find a prowler or a thief. Being unsuccessful, he went back home and drank himself to sleep. This happened night after night when Abigail was in Baltimore. She would come home on Friday and find whiskey bottles in the kitchen and general havoc in the house. Week after week, she would dutifully clean up his messes thinking this was her wifely duty. She tried so hard to be the loving, obedient wife, but her frustrations mounted. No matter how patient she was, his drinking and chaotic living didn't stop. It always surprised her how neat his property and buildings were outside of the house. He took pride in his barns, his land, his vineyard, and livestock. Why was he so untidy in the house? When she was gone, he didn't eat right and didn't take care of himself. He was smelly and unkempt, so Abigail decided to confront him.

"Avery, do you have a minute?" she asked.

"Not really, I have to meet Tony, my hired hand, to check out a problem in the back pasture," he responded.

"When would you have some time?" she asked patiently, waiting for his response.

"How about after lunch at one o'clock?"

"I'll have lunch ready about twelve o'clock," she said.

Off he went to meet up with Tony. Abigail had confronted him before, and it did not go well. He shouted, ranted, and didn't change much. She was not looking forward to this conversation but knew it had to happen. Cooking a delicious lunch was her top priority, since she had heard the "way to a man's heart is through his stomach." Maybe she was grasping at straws, but she wanted to have a good marriage, so she made his favorite foods, which were au gratin potatoes, chicken, and apple pie.

"What do I smell?" Avery asked as he walked into the kitchen. "Could it be your best chicken recipe and my favorite potatoes? You *are* a dear wife." He turned to kiss her on the cheek. She smiled as she took her place at the table. Abigail had butterflies in her stomach knowing that once they were done with their lovely meal, she would have to share her feelings about some difficult issues.

"I'm frustrated," Abigail said. "Both of us are working hard. You've made this place quite a moneymaker, and I am working hard at the candy store. We are a wealthy couple, but I come home on Friday to find chaos in the house with empty liquor bottles in every room. The cattle and livestock business outside the house is managed so well, but inside the house it's a disaster."

"What do you mean?" Avery asked with a sullen face. "What do you want from me? I can't do both the house and managing the property. I built this house, I've taken the responsibility for making the cattle investments work. I'm exhausted at the end of the day, and then, I make the rounds checking for trespassers every night. I stand at the end of the property behind a tree and I hear rustling. I just know there is someone out there, but they are sneaky. Every morning after counting the cattle, I breathe a sigh of relief because nothing was stolen. They know I'm out there and that's stopping them. I still hear the

141

sounds when I come back to the house, so I have a couple of drinks to get to sleep. Liquor takes the edge off."

"How can we work this out?" Abigail asked. "Reverend Holcomb said we were good problem solvers, so how do we solve this one?"

"Tony has offered to do the rounds at night. I think I'll give that a try."

"What about the mess in the house?" Abigail queried.

"I figured that you would be comin' home soon and you could do it—after all, that's women's work," he said.

"Well, I'm tired and feel overwhelmed when I come home from the candy store to find another mess I have to clean up. Before leaving on Monday, I make sure the house is clean, so I want it to be tidy when I get home on Friday. I'll do the wash, mop the floors, and dust when I get home, but I don't want to find a mess," Abigail said emphatically.

"Jeez, Abigail. I'm doin' the best I can. You don't have to be such a nag. Maybe if I can get Tony to take over the night watchman job, I can get some rest. Maybe then I can keep the house tidy."

Abigail's mother was overly concerned about cleanliness, and she didn't want to be like that. She wanted a good relationship with her husband. At the same time, she was tired of having to do everything, and she needed some cooperation. It also concerned her that Avery was drinking so much and becoming scruffy. She didn't know that about him before the marriage. He always did like his beer, but the whiskey thing was something new. After the discussion, she was hopeful that he would make some changes so they could have a better marriage. But, most of all, she wanted to be a loving, obedient wife.

With that discussion behind her, Abigail headed off to the candy store in Baltimore. Business was the slowest during the summertime, so she had some time to think things over. *Maybe Avery and I will need to have a more traditional marriage. It could be that to create a happy home, I'll have to be there all the time. What would I do with Abbott's Confectionary?* She was not one to give up easily, but realistically, living part time in Carroll County and part time in Baltimore might not work out. She would have to face that possibility. Having a career, being married, and traveling back and forth was exhausting. These thoughts overwhelmed her, so she had to refocus her efforts on her ledgers and organizing candy sales. She'll have to think about it some other time.

Wednesday morning, Abigail arrived at Abbott's Confectionary and was greeted by a courier from Western Union.

"Madam, I have an urgent telegram for you," he said.

"When did this come in?" she asked.

"Around four o'clock this morning," he replied. Abigail reached into her pocketbook and paid for the telegram, then quickly read what it said:

TERRIBLE ACCIDENT ON FARM. TONY SHOT. COME HOME SOON. AVERY.

She stuck it in her purse, opened the door, and placed the "Store temporarily closed" sign in the window. She drove home to see if Louise would watch the store while she was gone. She wasn't sure how long Avery would need her. Fortunately, Louise agreed to take over the day-to-day operations while she was away. Abigail hurried her horse and buggy to Carroll County. As she approached Nicodemus Road, she saw the county sheriff galloping toward the farm. When she got to the house, she saw Avery sobbing on the front porch with his dad beside him.

"What happened?" Abigail yelled frantically.

"Avery heard a loud sound in the middle of the night and grabbed his gun. He saw someone prowling around the cattle, so he shot the moving figure," Grant said.

"Was it Tony?" Abigail asked.

"Yes," he responded sadly.

"Is he going to be okay?" she asked.

"No, he's dead," Grant said with his eyes looking at the ground.

"Oh, no!" Abigail gasped, put her hands over her mouth, and wailed. *I don't know what has come over Avery. He just can't handle life by himself. His judgment is off.* Deeply sorry, Avery covered his face and sat in silence. Slowly, Abigail found a spot next to him and put her arms around him.

"What a tragedy. We'll help each other get through this," Abigail said as she cradled him. The sheriff and his deputy returned from the back pasture with the body on a stretcher.

"I have a dead body here, and I need some answers," the sheriff said to Avery. "Let's find a place to sit down in your house." The two of them disappeared through the front door, leaving Abigail sitting on the front porch with Grant. Not a word was spoken. The sheriff and Avery talked for a long time, and when Avery came out of the house, he looked much better.

"They're not going to press charges. He said it was a tragic accident," Avery said with relief in his voice.

Abigail spent the evening sorting out the events of the day. She knew something had to change, and she grudgingly accepted the fact that she couldn't do both, a career and being a wife. She had to decide, which made her sad on so many levels. She wanted to keep the store because it gave her daily reminders of her father, who she dearly loved. Also, giving a third of the profits to her sisters satisfied the commitment she made to them. What would they do for income if she sold the store? Abigail was mistaken about Avery. She expected better self-control and more common sense on his part. Was his behavior a temporary problem, or was this a longstanding character trait? She wasn't sure. It didn't really matter, because she saw her dreams evaporating in front of her face.

Knowing she needed a confidante to help her sort out these issues, she thought about her good friend Rosemary. She could talk to her sisters, Mary and Louise, but she wasn't sure they had enough experience to help her navigate such dark waters. Then, Reverend Holcombe came to mind. First of all, he had a warm disposition and was so understanding. Yes, she was confident that he was the right person to talk to and that he could help her. Most importantly, he reminded her of her dad, Pinky. The following week, she made a point to knock on Reverend Holcombe's study door.

"Come in," Reverend Holcombe said cheerily. "Well, hello Abigail. Come in. Come in." Abigail was pleasantly surprised that he was able to see her so soon. "How have you been doing with your new marriage *and* your new home?"

"It has been very hard," she said, bracing herself to share some bad news. "Avery killed someone accidentally. He thought his hired hand was a prowler trespassing on his land. He went out during the night when he heard a sound. He aimed and fired at a shadow in the woods. It wasn't a trespasser at all, but his hired hand, Tony. Sometimes, he's so impulsive. I don't trust his judgment."

"That *is* pretty bad. Was he like this before the two of you were married?" Reverend Holcombe asked.

"Well, not this bad, but when I made the rounds with him one night, he shot his rifle at a shadow in the woods. I thought it was just a random incident and not a pattern," she said. "It seems to me that he just can't handle life without me. There is a violent streak that runs through his family. His brother Henry accidently shot his dad when he was firing in the air." Tears welled in her eyes when she thought of Avery's dark side. "I don't trust him anymore."

"My, my. You are in a hard spot. When you're working in Baltimore at the candy store, you don't trust his good sense to stay out of trouble. You feel a strong urge to keep an eye on him at all times," he said.

"I knew you would understand. That's *exactly* my dilemma," she said. "I'm caught in the middle of two miserable decisions. I don't want to give up the store, but I am needed at home in Carroll County."

"What do you think you will do?" he asked gently.

"I think I'll have to sell the business and stay at home and be Avery's wife," she said, slowly grimacing.

"Don't forget that you have an agreement," he said. "One-third of the profits go to the marital assets, but one-third goes to your sisters and one-third to you. The store will provide you and your sisters with some valuable assets." Abigail sat back in her chair and sighed. *It is sad*

I will have to sell the business, but at least there will be a handsome profit.

"Reverend Holcombe," Abigail said. "You helped me sort out something that has been so difficult for me. Thank you so much." She stood up, smiled, and shook his hand. She felt his warmth and compassion. After all, he was her "Pinky replacement."

"Any time you need to talk to someone, I'm here for you," he said with a comforting smile.

Her life was about to make a major change, so she needed to talk to her sisters. Maybe, just maybe, Louise would like to take over the store. She needed to know for sure before she made plans to sell it. This is something they had to discuss at the supper table. Mary's cooking always made supper a special event. Tonight, it was fish—baked flounder with lemon pepper sauce. She took in the delicious smells as she opened the front door.

"I haven't told you about the struggles that Avery and I are having," Abigail said reluctantly. She dreaded exposing her misfortunes. "Avery shot and killed his hired hand in the middle of the night. He thought someone was rustling his cattle. The sheriff of Carroll County hasn't pressed charges, because he called it a tragic accident. Avery is getting more and more fearful and suspicious. He gets angry quickly, and his judgment is off."

Abigail had wrapped the problem so tight inside of her that just talking with her sisters gave her some relief. The three of them sat in silence for a long time. Having lost their appetites, they just poked at their food.

"I'm worried about you," Mary said. "Does he listen to you?"

"Yes, he does. It's when I'm not around that he drinks and doesn't sleep well."

"What are you going to do with the store?" Louise asked.

"I think I will have to sell the store," she said, looking directly at her sister. "I wanted the two of you to hear it first, because I was hoping that one of you might want the store." Mary and Louise searched their hearts for any desire to manage the store, but they both came up empty.

"I'm not motivated to run the store on a full-time basis," Louise said. "Once in a while or in a pinch, I will help out, but I don't want the huge responsibility of inventory, and the books. It's too much for me."

Mary looked glum and crestfallen, and Abigail knew without her saying anything that she didn't have the confidence to greet customers, not to mention manage the books and check on inventory. School was a huge challenge for her when she was a youngster, and their mother didn't encourage her to take risks, because Martha needed her to stay dependent on her. Mary was groomed to take care of her mother and father in their old age. Since that was no longer an option, she didn't have a purpose. Life was passing her by, and she didn't have the confidence to find a more useful life.

"Well, the first idea I have is to contact Stephen Whitman to find out what he would suggest. He has been so kind to our family," Abigail said. Her sisters knew how helpful they had been since they lost their mother and father. They both supported Abigail's idea.

"Yes, I could really use your support right now. Thank you," Abigail said. "I'm taking the train to Philadelphia to talk with him before I head back to Carroll County."

CHAPTER 7

The Sale

ৼৼৼৼ

It was an early fall day, very hot, and an uncomfortable day for travel, but so much of Abigail's life was uncomfortable. This was the only possible day to travel, since Stephen Whitman wanted to see her before he left on vacation. She caught the Philadelphia, Wilmington & Baltimore Train to Philadelphia. Opening the side window helped the outside breeze drive the heat out of her passenger car. It seemed to make it a bit more tolerable. The train had an average speed of about twenty-five miles per hour as it chugged through the countryside. It traveled through mountains and over rivers and by the meadows filled with Queen Anne's Lace and purple knapweed. Other than the trips to Washington, D.C., with her family and the trips with Avery, this was the first one by herself.

Her thoughts turned to what the future might bring,

and it seemed to her that she was the one who had to adapt to life at every turn. There wasn't much give from others around her. Furthermore, it annoyed her that the health of others and the choices *they* made determined hers. She was disgruntled with life. Although it was quite unlike Abigail, her self-pitying thoughts tormented her.

Tilting her head back on the train seat, she then closed her eyes and, with deep self-awareness, felt a comforting warmth envelop her. It was like her whole body was consumed in a state of prayer, and it was like nothing she had ever felt before … kind of otherworldly. She felt a confidence surge within her, propelling her to rise above her problems. Abigail allowed herself to turn to something eternal, something that would never change. This unexpected moment was a comforting reminder that she was in the care of the Almighty. She learned from the hardships of her mother that you can't control what happens to you, no matter how hard you try. To have a simple faith was the best way to live. Perhaps she couldn't control what happened to her, but she felt confident knowing that she was in loving hands. Although she didn't know it at that time, Abigail would refer to this epiphany on the train many times as she faced life's uncertainties.

She was eager to see Stephen Whitman again, since the last time she saw him was at her wedding. The train stopped at the new Baltimore & Ohio Station on the Chestnut Street Bridge. It was quite an architectural marvel, since it had been built on stilts. The main entrance was thirty feet above ground level, and the exterior was an unusual combination of brick, iron, and glass.

Abigail disembarked on Chestnut Street and walked toward Cherry Street to the Whitman Chocolate Factory.

As far as she knew, it was somewhere between the train station and the Delaware River. Gauging by the hustle and bustle around her, Philadelphia was a thriving city. The new chocolate factory was only a few years old, since they had to rebuild after the fire of 1880. It still had the look of a factory, but inside the four walls, there were bursts of wonderful candy smells. She walked through the door that read "Public Entrance." The penetrating aroma of sugar and warm chocolate permeated the air. This was a familiar scent to her, because it reminded her of the days when she opened the crates of chocolates with Pinky. As she veered to the right, she noticed employees working on white marble slab tables. They stirred the large vats of chocolate until the smoothness was close to perfection and then poured the melted chocolate into bite-sized molds to cool and set up.

To her left, she saw a modest one-room office filled with boxes, crates, and shelves stacked with papers. Stephen Whitman sat hunched over his desk, working on a ledger. He seemed to have aged since the last time she saw him. She knocked on the door.

"Abigail, come in!" he said cheerily. "I've been expecting you. The four o'clock train must have just arrived. How was the ride here?"

"It was hot, but the ride was without incident. I always enjoy scanning the countryside," she said.

"By the way, how does married life suit you? Are you settling in?"

"Truthfully, I'm realizing that I can't have a career and a good marriage at the same time," she blurted out. "It's been a tough decision, but I have to sell Abbott's Confectionary."

"I'm sorry to hear that. You have done a good job with the business, and I will miss you as a colleague," he said.

"Before I put the business on the market, I wanted you to have the first opportunity to buy it."

"Thank you for the opportunity, Abigail. I'll take the offer seriously. That means I need to scrutinize my books, talk with my family, and check with my attorney. Did you by chance bring the profit and loss statements?"

"Yes, I did." She opened her leather valise and pulled out several files. "Here they are. These are for the last five years, and I want you to know that the business has been steadily growing."

"Are you sure no one in your family wants to run the store?" he asked.

"My sisters are not interested, and they're the only ones I would consider," she responded. "How long before I hear from you?" She trusted Stephen, but his past letters seemed to have taken forever to get to her. She needed an answer sooner rather than later.

"I'll send you a response by the end of the month," he said. "Before you leave, let me give you a tour of my factory."

Abigail could tell he was very proud of his business. He shared the fire story with her and the nasty cleanup after the disaster. He admitted that the decision to rebuild was hard, because it set the business back several years. But, overall, the business followed the expansion and became successful. He claimed that one of his main reasons for success was his use of advertisement in the local paper. This is something that he initiated even before the Civil War. The awards for "Product Excellence" from Philadelphia and Paris were proudly displayed on the factory wall.

With a hearty handshake, they parted company. Abigail so hoped he would purchase Abbott's Confectionary and make it prosper like all of his other ventures. She left his office with a headache, which was probably exacerbated by her inner conflicts and the uncertainty of her future.

After boarding the train from Philadelphia to Baltimore, she chose to pay a higher fare to enjoy the comfort of a Pullman lounge car and hopefully ease her headache. She found a private area with a lovely velvet chair away from the traffic and train noise. The only person near her was a gentleman who sat in the overstuffed chair across from her. She surreptitiously observed him and noticed how well dressed he was. He was wearing a fine black suit with a silk vest over a clean, white, starched shirt. On his head was a slick-looking top hat, which he tipped as she sat down. A Double Albert gold pocket watch chain crossed his vest, with one end attached to a buttonhole by a T-bar. A most curious medallion-like fob studded with rubies was attached to it. Without a doubt, his appearance conveyed affluence. His face was animated, as his forehead wrinkled when he smiled and his eyes sparkled. The eyebrows were comically gargantuan. Wisps of unruly curls protruded above his eyes and infested his lavish handlebar mustache. While reading *The Baltimore Sun*, he used a monocle as a corrective lens, which suggested he was a voracious reader. Beside him, nestled in the arm of his chair, was a gold-plated cane that glistened in the late-afternoon sun.

Surprisingly, despite his commanding presence, Abigail didn't feel intimidated by him. Feeling safer after exhausting her powers of observation, she laid her hurting head on the side cushion of the velvet chair and closed her eyes. The rocking motion of the train lulled her into a restful state, half-awake, half-asleep. This seemed to ease her headache.

In slow motion, she relived the enchantment of the two days she spent with Avery in Washington, D.C. Her heartbeat quickened as she recalled the excitement of that evening at the Willard Hotel. A special euphoria enveloped them, because they were so much in love. But those merry thoughts were interrupted by the dark turn of events, and it was hard to compare her present life with the fantasy of those moments. *If I had known his dark side, would I have married Avery? Would Pinky have married Martha if he had known what would happen in their future? But, then again, who would I be? Would I even be alive?* Finally, after accepting the reality that she was not clairvoyant, she knew she had to embrace her fate. Abigail's father often reminded her that when choices are made, unknown risks are part of the deal. He insisted that our future depends on our willingness to exchange the known for the unknown. There is simply no way to pre-control the outcome. Her thoughts drifted again to her mother and father. There was so much that was concealed behind closed doors. This was true not just for her family, but for Avery's family as well. In general, the hidden identities of fellow humans often are a haunting threat, inconvenient at best and fatal at its worst. Abigail grimaced in emotional pain as she daydreamed about the cruel twist of fate that was beginning to shape her future.

"Is everything alright, Madam?" a gentle voice queried.

Suddenly awakened by his question, she opened her eyes and found herself looking directly into the gentleman's face. She blushed, not knowing what she might have done, or said, to betray her cool exterior. After a sheepish smile and a long pause, she decided to share her distress.

"I have to make a considerable adjustment in my life that I don't want to make," she responded. "I own a business in Baltimore that I will have to sell because my marriage is unstable."

Looking at her solicitously, he seemed to understand, so she continued. She had to get it off her chest, and she was pleased he was willing to listen. She would probably never see him again, so she dismissed any fears that he might gossip about her or malign her.

"My husband turned out to be much different than I thought he would be. Our married life has taken a negative turn, so I have to make some unwelcome changes."

"You seem so young to own a business. What kind of business is it?" he asked.

"It's a candy store, Abbott's Confectionary, in downtown Baltimore," Abigail said with pride. "Daddy bequeathed it to me before he died."

"From what you say, I gather your mother must have died, too," he said. "Usually the business goes to the wife to manage or sell."

"Yes, they both died in a terrible carriage accident in 1886," she said.

"I'm sorry to hear that. It's got to be hard to be on your own. I lost my wife during childbirth ten years ago, and I was left to raise my two daughters alone. It was quite a struggle at first, but now, they are the delight of my life. When I first lost my wife, I had to put my children in the care of a nanny. I'm a lawyer in a Baltimore firm, and I'm licensed as a barrister in Canada as well, so I have to travel often. I miss my wife Catharine very much."

"I'm so sorry to hear about your loss," Abigail said. "If you don't mind, would you tell me about your daughters?"

"I'd love to. Blythe is the scholar and loves to read and Samantha is the fun-loving one. She makes me laugh. I call her Sam." He chuckled. 'They are like their mother, kind in so many ways. Blythe is tall and blonde and Sam is shorter with light-brown hair. They're the light of my life, now."

Abigail smiled in spite of her sorrow. "You've had some unexpected struggles in your life, but they seem to have turned out well," Abigail said.

"I suppose they have at that. What does your husband do for a living?" he asked.

"He's a land speculator," she responded. "He won a lawsuit against the Pennsylvania Railroad a few years ago and, with that money, he built a house in Carroll County north of Baltimore."

"Is your husband Avery Johnson?" he asked.

"Yes, do you know him?" Abigail said, caught off guard.

"I do. My name is Samuel Abrams, and I was one of the lawyers for the defense. They used my services as a legal scholar," he said.

"Has the Pennsylvania Railroad made any changes in acquiring land?" Abigail asked, wondering if the lawsuit had any impact on how they do business.

"No. From my research, the Pennsylvania Railroad did nothing illegal. The jury reflected the public sentiment at the time, which was anti-railroad, but the company followed all the laws of the land, and they didn't do anything wrong. Maybe the laws should be changed, but the owners of the railroads complied with the laws that were on the books. Sometimes people resent the accumulation of wealth by large companies, but you've got to give them some credit, because they take huge risks in order to make their money."

"Avery got lots of support for his position," she said. "I was working at the store during the trial, and the businessmen would congregate and talk about the case. Most of them supported him."

"Well, the Pennsylvania Railroad was in compliance," he emphasized. "Land speculators want more of the profits without the risks, and it just doesn't work that way. They're competing amongst themselves, and it can get pretty cutthroat sometimes. I realize that land speculators' incomes are either feast or famine, so most of them are on a financial rollercoaster. It would make more sense for you to keep your business, so you could bring steady income into the home."

"It's more complicated than that," Abigail said. "When I'm not at home, my husband drinks himself to sleep. If he's scared awake by a sound, he assumes it's a thief trying to steal his livestock. He grabs his gun and heads out of the house ready to shoot anything that moves. Last month, he mistakenly shot and killed his hired hand. For me, this was a loud warning that he can't be trusted at home by himself. The only way I can see to solve this problem is to sell my business and stay home. If I had known this before we were married, I probably would have walked away, but it's too late now."

"Why don't you put him in a hospital or sanatorium? Maybe the doctors could help him," Samuel said thoughtfully. "The Government Hospital in Washington, D.C., has a good reputation and treats all kinds of conditions."

"Oh, no! I couldn't do that to my husband!" Abigail blurted out in horror.

Surprised by the fury of her response, Samuel chose not to speak. Abigail curled up in the chair, and tears started to flow. Frantically, she grabbed her purse to find a handkerchief, pulled it out, and quickly dabbed her face to dry the tears and regain composure.

"I'm sorry, sir," Abigail said softly. "This brings up a lot of emotions for me. You see, my mother and father were on their way to the very hospital you mentioned when they had that tragic accident. My mother was being treated there for her explosive anger and violence toward my father."

Seeming to understand Abigail's trauma, Samuel remained silent for a long time before he spoke again. "I'm sorry that you had to suffer such a loss," he said empathetically. "Is there anything I can do to help you? If you need someone to write a contract for you for the sale of your business, I could help you with that. Here is my business card. Just stop by my office."

"Thank you so much for listening and offering your help. You have been so kind," Abigail said with sincere gratitude. It was a surprise to her that she so freely shared her emotions.

The train began slowing as it approached its destination, and the harsh screech of the brakes signaled the end of the journey. Abigail gathered her purse, her valise, and umbrella and stood waiting for the final jerk of the train so she could disembark. Her new friend, Samuel Abrams, followed her with cane in hand. Abigail turned to look at him with a smile. She reached out to shake his hand. He responded in kind.

"Thank you for your company. I wish you all the best," he said.

They parted company for the moment, but Abigail knew she would see him again.

৵৵৵

Since she knew that her sisters would be waiting for her to have supper with them, she hustled home when she got off the train. Abigail opened the door to the delicious smells that filled every inch of their house. She tried to guess what the fare might be, maybe potatoes and ham. Mary was a good cook, and she knew Abigail loved a certain kind of food in the fall.

"What's for dinner?" Abigail asked.

"It's a new recipe. I'm trying it out on you. It's called Lancashire Hotpot. I made in with lamb, onions, and sliced potatoes."

"Oh, yum," Abigail said as she gave her sister a hug, delighted to be safely at home. Her sisters gave her comfort and a sense of normalcy; their home was a refuge from the turmoil of her personal storms.

Abigail would spend the next day checking inventory and completing the books for the month. Her efforts to organize the profit-loss statements and the day spent consulting with Stephen Whitman put her behind at the store. In order to get everything done, she would have to get there quite early in the morning. Avery had been alone for almost a week, and Abigail was anxious about what she would find when he got home to Carroll County. Sensing a foreboding, her premonitions guessed something was amiss. Her job was to set those feelings aside so she could finish her work.

Working with expedited dispatch, she finished the books and inventory in a timely fashion and caught the late afternoon train to Union Bridge Station. Her two-hour ride to Carroll County provided picturesque vistas of graceful slopes of the Maryland countryside. The autumn leaves were displaying lavish strokes of red, yellow, and burnt orange, creating a splendid contrast to the dark-green background. The shortened days and the slant of the sun reminded her of Winslow Homer's renditions of northeastern landscapes. We are a fortunate people to have such an abundance of natural blessings in this state of ours. That attitude developed within her an unshakeable strength that, no matter what happened, she could connect with nature to renew her spirits. Nature's beauty was wrapped around her like a healing shawl. Just looking out her window gave her a treasure trove of natural splendor sufficient to mend her broken heart. Having to give up her career for her marriage gave her such anguish.

The train came to a stop at Union Bridge Station, and she spotted the two horse-and-buggy cabs waiting to take the late-afternoon passengers home. She hailed one of them, climbed in, and the horse eagerly trotted toward Nicodemus Road. The early descent of the sun dimmed the landscape, and the horse and buggy created extended shadows on the road and ditches.

As they approached the front of her house, she noticed the electric chandelier illuminating the foyer. By all appearances, it was a lovely Victorian home with electric lights, which were the latest fashion trend, and Avery did a good job building their home. It was smaller than his parent's home, but just as comfortable. The driver brought her to the front door, and she reached into her pocketbook for some coins to pay him. Apprehension about what she would see when she opened the door made Abigail take a deep breath.

Other than the light in the foyer, the rest of the house was dark and apparently empty. Abigail went from room to room, turned on each lamp, and checked for Avery, who was nowhere to be found. Empty whiskey bottles were scattered from the living room to the kitchen. Aside from being a bit dusty, the house was fairly neat considering what she had found coming home from Baltimore before. Other than the mess of the six whiskey bottles, the dishes were washed and put away, the trash had been put in the burn barrel behind the house, and the beds were made. She took her lantern off the hook and walked outside to see if he was in the barn.

"Avery? Where are you?" she yelled. "This is Abigail. I'm home." She waved the lantern back and forth, and deliberately made noise while walking, to keep from alarming him in the night. Approaching the barn, she heard some rustling at the far end. She heaved the heavy doors open and spotted a light illuminating the last stall in the long hallway of stanchions. She smelled the pungent smell of straw bedding as she moved closer.

"Abigail? Is that you? I could sure use some help here," Avery said. "This heifer has been dilated for three hours, and she isn't pushing. She's plum tired out." Walking closer to him with a lantern in her hand, she noticed a sling on his arm.

"What happened to your right arm?" she asked. "Is it broken?"

"The heifer didn't know what was happening when she went into contractions, and she started to kick hard. I just so happened to be at the wrong place at the wrong time. I got in her way. She got me right in the elbow, and boy, did that hurt. The pain was so bad that I couldn't move it, so I grabbed a towel to make a sling. I might have to go to the doctor, but for now, I want to make sure the heifer and the calf survive. Abigail, would you hold the lantern up in this direction, so I can check to see if the calf is coming out right?"

It would be Abigail's first experience with birthing a calf, and the back end of a cow looked pretty disgusting. Her eyes were as big as saucers, but wanting to be helpful to her husband, she gritted her teeth and ignored any sensations of nausea that might render her useless. She took a deep breath to keep from passing out. The heifer let out a low bellowing moan when the pain was too much, followed by an angry kick. She must have felt so miserable, and that uncomfortable feeling just wasn't going away.

"Move the lantern over here," Avery ordered as he pointed in the direction of the heifer's rump. He looked inside the dilated cervix and spotted the head, "Oh, good, I see the head now." Peering closer, he noticed a hoof coming through the birth canal. "Wonderful. I think she's going to be okay," he said happily.

A forceful gush of amniotic fluid suddenly streamed out of the heifer. "I see one hoof, but where's the other one? Oh, no, it must be stuck back in the birth canal!"

Avery jumped up and lunged forward to insert his

working left hand through the cervix into the birth canal. He feverishly felt around for the other hoof. Persistently, he searched until his hand found the long, slender leg. Sure enough, it had curled backwards, stalling the birthing progress. He gently pulled the hoof forward to avert a fracture. Both hooves and the head emerged through the birth canal. It was a breathtaking moment.

"Well, we have a healthy bull calf," Avery said with pride. He was exuberant and exhausted at the same time, and completely satisfied with the success of the birth.

Abigail, still holding on tight to the handle of the lantern, was dumbfounded by the experience and realized that her life as a bookkeeper for a candy store was so limited. She was astonished by Avery's skill and persistence, and she gained a new appreciation for her husband. Her hands relaxed as she set the lantern down. The calf made her smile as he moved and breathed, still wet from the amniotic fluid. The calf's mother struggled to her feet, hobbled toward her calf, and started licking. With each lick, the calf became more animated and alert. No longer a heifer because she had given birth, the mother was now a "cow." Her next delivery would probably progress more quickly, and the birth would be easier.

Avery knew that the crisis was over and that he could finally get some sleep. The cow would discharge the placenta in a few hours, and the cow and bull calf would be fine. He would check on them in the morning. Together Abigail and Avery walked toward the house, slowly swinging their lanterns. They didn't say much, but the quiet amazement of having witnessed a miracle together strengthened the bond between them.

The sun rose in a cloudless sky the next morning. Abigail fixed breakfast while Avery went to the barn to check on the newborn calf and the other livestock. He forked the hay and hauled it to the feeding troughs, making sure they had fresh water, and then went on a scavenger hunt looking for eggs in the chicken coop. He always had trouble with the attacking rooster. It would seem like the coast was clear when, out from behind the coop, the rooster would fly down from the corner of the chicken coop, flap his wings, and peck at his legs.

"Drat, you little bugger!" Avery cursed under his breath. "The next time you do that, you're going to be food on our table the day *before* Thanksgiving. Nope, I'm not going to give you the honor of that day, you little varmint."

With the chores all done, he sauntered up to the house, enjoying the heavenly smell of bacon floating through the air. *This is the way life should be for married folk. I do the chores in the morning and my wife makes breakfast. This is a good life.*

Abigail was busy making coffee, toast, eggs, and bacon when Avery walked through the door. After washing up, he headed toward the light of the kitchen. With that irresistible smile on his face, he wrapped his arms around Abigail and gave her a big hug.

"You are my sweet valentine," he whispered.

Abigail turned around, smiled, and they embraced. For that moment, it all seemed right. Their life was the way it was supposed to be. It seemed like the bonding that marriage partners create was beginning to take shape. The friction of their marital conflict was waning and being replaced by dreams of their life together. Abigail and Avery were forging new pathways, making their closeness grow into something dependable and strong. Abigail knew in her heart that selling Abbott's Confectionary was the best path for both of them. This eased the loss she felt about selling off her inheritance. Still, she was so grateful for her father's faith in her and his hard work building the business. She also knew that every generation had to make the best decisions based on their circumstances. With a firm resolve, she eagerly anticipated Stephen Whitman's letter.

The letter arrived two weeks later, and this delay gave Avery and Abigail even more time to demonstrate their love for each other. This time together helped them settle into peaceful domestic routines. It was a period of healing unity. The letter was brief but promising, and it seemed to be a harbinger of something good in their lives.

Dear Abigail,

I have some very good news. My cousin, David Whitman, is very interested in purchasing Abbott's Confectionary. He currently is traveling in Europe and will not be returning to the United States until the middle of the month. He asked me to schedule a meeting with you at the end of the month. Would two o'clock be a good time for you? Please let me know so David can make travel plans to Baltimore.

Your Friend,

Stephen Whitman

Abigail read and reread the letter. *Is this really happening?* It seemed so unbelievable. One last time she read it, smiled, and jumped up and down, yelling, "Avery!" at the top of her lungs. This was no time for proper decorum, because this was something to celebrate.

"What's the matter? Are you hurt?" Avery shouted, fearing the worst. Running up to the house as fast as he could, he was relieved to see her in one piece and smiling.

"I got the letter from Stephen Whitman," she said. "I read the letter over and over, and I think he is serious about buying Abbott's Confectionary. What a Godsend!" she exclaimed.

Avery thought about what this sale might mean for their life. He saw it as a sign that she wanted to strengthen their marriage by staying home and supporting him. He found it reassuring that their love had grown into a more secure bond. Abigail chose to rely on faith, trusting that Stephen Whitman would be fair and make Abbott's Confectionary even more prosperous.

It was important for her to move quickly, so now was the time to contact Mr. Samuel Abrams, the lawyer she met on the train. He was such a dear man and willing to help her draft the most beneficial contract for her and the family. She found his business card and planned a trip to Baltimore. Avery drove her to Union Bridge Station to catch the ten o'clock train. Mr. Abrams office was close to the train station, so she walked the short distance and found his office, hoping to make an appointment for later in the afternoon.

Just like the affluent presence he portrayed when they first met, his office had the same feeling of wealth. The rich orange-rust tones of the oriental carpets and the carved mahogany wooden settee with matching chairs were richly trimmed with crewelwork on velvet. Abigail's favorite autumn colors—shades of green, muted reds and golds—were displayed tastefully and elegantly in his waiting room. His secretary said nothing but was attentive when Abigail spoke.

"I would like to see Mr. Abrams," Abigail said. "Later today, if possible."

She waited for a very long time for an answer from Lydia, his secretary.

"Mr. Abrams is in court until two o'clock today," she said with an irritating whine. "It's now about half past one, so he should be here soon. If you want to wait for him, have a seat."

Abigail was perplexed by her apparent rudeness but quietly turned around and found a place to sit down. Two hours later, Abigail's patience was rewarded when Samuel Abrams barreled into his office. Seemingly preoccupied, he mumbled something to Lydia and opened the big wooden door to his private office. Lydia followed him.

"Mrs. Johnson has been here for two hours," she said. "She would like to speak with you."

"Oh, I didn't see her," he said. "Send her in."

Abigail stood and entered his office. She noted the myriad of books on the shelves and the flurry of papers on his desk. He recognized her immediately and seemed pleasantly surprised to see her.

"Good afternoon, Mrs. Johnson," he said cordially.

"Hello, Mr. Abrams," Abigail said. "Thank you for seeing me. I have some good news. David Whitman, Stephen Whitman's cousin, is interested in buying Abbott's Confectionary. I remembered what you said on the train. Are you still willing to help me with the purchase agreement and the contract?"

"I would be happy to be your legal representative," he

responded. "First, we need to schedule a time when all of us can meet. Is there a time that works best for you?"

"Any time at the end of the month," Abigail said. "Do you have some time to talk about the purchase agreement? I need some help deciding on the price and how to split the profits."

"Lydia," he called to his outer office. "Before you go home, please come in here and schedule a time for Abigail and me to meet with the Whitman gentlemen."

Lydia approached his desk carrying a ledger and abruptly opened the appointment calendar to an empty page.

"There is an opening on the twenty-eighth of this month at two o'clock," she said. Sam looked at Abigail, and she nodded in agreement. Lydia wrote in the book and stomped out of the room, giving Abigail a strange look as she shut the door behind her.

"You'll have to excuse Lydia. She's very protective of me, especially when it comes to other women," he said. Abigail gave him a smile, understanding his predicament.

"What about the purchase price for the business?" she asked. "Do you have any idea of what would be a good price?"

Sam jotted something down on a paper and handed it to her. She perused the instructions and put them in her purse.

"A good price is whatever you can get, but you have to build a case for it," he said. "What I wrote will help you with that. Perhaps we can schedule you at one o'clock on the twenty-eighth, so we can go over the contract before they arrive. I'll be mailing you something soon, so please fill it out and get it back to me as soon as you can. Also, I'll have Lydia contact Stephen Whitman in Philadelphia."

"Thank you very much for all of your help," Abigail said.

"Glad to see you again," Mr. Abrams said. "I'll be getting in touch with you about the paperwork."

They shook hands, and the firmness of it made her feel confident that she had placed her trust in the right man.

By the time the business was done with Samuel Abrams, it was too late to catch the train to Union Bridge, so she resigned herself to spending an overnight with her sisters. She would miss Avery, but her sisters needed a visit, too.

෴෴෴

When Abigail opened the front door, she found Mary crying. "What's wrong?" she asked as she approached her sister.

"Oh, Abigail, I didn't want you to catch me crying," she said, dabbing at her tears with a hanky.

"What's wrong?" Abigail asked again.

"Louise met someone when she worked at the candy store, and she hasn't been home to have supper with me this whole week. I'm just feeling sorry for myself." She slumped in her chair, shrugged her shoulders, and blew her nose.

Abigail chuckled as she bent down to kiss her sister's forehead. "Mary, you are such a worrier. You remind me of Mom. Louise meeting someone might not be *all* bad. If he's a nice young man, it could be a good thing for her. Have you met him?"

"No, and I don't *want* to meet him," Mary pouted. "I'm afraid Louise will get married just like you, and I'll be in this house all by myself."

"My dear sister, it's like you have a raincloud hanging over the life that you haven't lived yet. You're worrying about something that probably won't happen," Abigail said, trying to reason with her. "You can't see into your future. It could be something wonderful. You don't know."

"Maybe you're right," Mary said. "I made some supper. Have you eaten yet?"

"No, and I'm starving," Abigail answered. "Mary, I want you to know that I love you and we will stick together through thick and thin."

Mary smiled back at her and then busied herself with finishing the cooking of the beef stew. The rolls that were baking in the Dutch oven smelled so delicious. Hungry and tantalized by the smells, Abigail set the table and waited for Mary to bring the food for them to share. Louise didn't come home until after Mary and Abigail finished eating. Louise said her hellos and then ran upstairs and shut her bedroom door. Mary and Louise were puzzled by her behavior, so Abigail went upstairs and knocked on her door.

"What do you want?" Louise asked.

"Want to know if you're okay."

"Come in, if you dare."

"What's the matter?" Abigail said as she opened the door.

"Nothing."

"Something is wrong. Let me help you," Abigail pleaded.

Louise sat at the edge of her bed, tears streaming down her face. Abigail reached in her pocket to find a hanky and gave it to her. Abigail wrapped her arms around her sister to remind her she wasn't alone and that she was deeply loved.

"I met someone in the store about a month ago who I

really liked," Louise said between sobs. "We've gone out for dinner a few times, and he took me for walks in the park after work. Today... he told me he was married." The sobs swelled, and Abigail held her tighter.

"I'm sorry you have to deal with that. Some men are not good that way. I know you'll find just the right person for you when the time is right," Abigail said, trying to comfort her. "Did you have supper?"

"No."

"I'll bet Mary would make a plate of warm food for you," Abigail said. "Let's go downstairs." Holding hands, the two of them went downstairs, and Mary greeted Louise with a warm hug. The three of them were a healing unit that hopefully would last a lifetime.

The next morning, after Louise had a good night's sleep, she rode with Abigail to the candy store. She planned to work the counter while Abigail caught up with the books and checked the inventory. The busy season was just around the corner, and more preparation was always necessary. Abigail discussed the sale of the store with Louise, and she was pleasantly surprised by the possibility. She didn't relish going to work every day, but she knew she would do what was necessary. Louise expressed worry about getting enough income for their lifestyle. After all, their house was older, and keeping it in good repair took time *and* money.

"How are Mary and I going to keep the house running without the income from the store?" she asked.

"When I sell the store, I will give you and Mary one third of the profits, and if you invest it, and bring in money from your housecleaning jobs, the two of you should be fine," Abigail said as they arrived at the store.

Louise placed the "Open" sign in the window, and Abigail rushed around getting her books and inventory in order. Being in a hurry to catch the train, she quickly made the necessary additions to the books and reviewed the inventory accounts. Pleased with the work Louise had done last month, she decided they had enough inventory until after the sale. Abigail thanked Louise for her good efforts and said goodbye as she headed to the station to catch the ten o'clock train to Union Bridge.

What would she find when she got home? This trip to Baltimore made her really miss Avery. The train ride from the city to the country had taken its toll, and she was quite ready to stay home to do some cooking, sewing, and other domestic chores. As she was leaving the station, she noticed that one of the passenger cars was filled with dignitaries. As they disembarked, a row of Clarence carriages was waiting for them to take them somewhere. She spotted a ticket master standing by the door of the station.

"Who are these men, and where are they going?" she asked him.

"They're from the Baltimore & Ohio Railroad, and they're heading to Medford Quarry," he responded.

"That's where I live. I wonder what's going on?" Abigail muttered under her breath.

CHAPTER 8

The Blast

❧ ❧ ❧ ❧

"Driver, hurry please," Abigail called to the driver of the Hansom cab. "Stay behind those carriages ahead of us. I'm curious about where they're going and what they're doing."

She craned her neck around the backend of the horse to keep the entourage in view. The carriages pulled over and parked at the intersection of Nicodemus Road and Medford Road, just across from her house. She had the cab driver stop next to the last carriage. As she was about to ask questions, she saw Avery charge out of the house with a shotgun.

"What the hell is going on here?" he shouted. "Take your gussied-up ways and your dandy clothes back to where they came from."

The officials huddled together to formulate a plan and chose a spokesperson to confront Avery. "We're from the

Pennsylvania Railroad, and we're here at the invitation of the owner of Medford Quarry," the spokesman said.

Avery raised his gun and shot in the air. "I don't care who you're a guest of. This is my land, and I want you out of here!" Avery shouted, fire in his eyes.

At that moment, Mr. Tate, the owner of the mine, trotted up to the intersection. "What's going on here? Are you from the Pennsylvania Railroad?" he asked the dignitaries.

"Yes, we are," they responded.

The owner waved his hand, motioning them to follow him into the quarry. The officials quickly climbed into their carriages and followed Mr. Tate into the mining operation, disappearing from Avery's watchful eyes.

"Hi, Avery," Abigail yelled as she had the driver head toward him on Nicodemus Road. "What's going on?" She braced herself for some catastrophic news.

"I don't know," he said. "I smell a rat. I'm heading over to Westminster to talk to somebody from the county. Want to come?"

"Sure, let me pay and dismiss the driver. I'll put my satchel away and clean up while you get the horses ready," she said. Abigail was eager to see if Avery had kept the house up while she was gone. She walked in the front door and the house looked clean with only a couple of whisky bottles on the kitchen table. Pleasantly surprised, she considered it noticeable progress. Greatly relieved, after freshening up, Abigail met up with Avery and gave him a warm kiss. "I missed you," she said lovingly.

"Let's find out what's going on," Avery said as he gave his hand to help lift her into the carriage.

Off they went to talk with the county officials. Hank Withers, the county administrator, wasn't in his office, so they talked to his associate, Dan Metter, who had no information about the Pennsylvania Railroad officials visiting Medford Quarry.

"Nothing has been reported to us, but I suggest you talk with Peter Tate, the owner of the mine, and find out from him what's going on," Dan said.

Avery shrugged his shoulders in frustration. "Do you know where he lives?" he asked. "I want to talk to him."

"Yes, he lives just a couple of blocks from my house on Oak Street," Dan Said. "I think 213 is the house number."

Hopefully, Peter Tate was still at the mine because Abigail sensed a confrontation coming between Avery and Peter. She did her best to stay calm and unflappable so as not to inflame the situation. Because his anger was like a brush fire, easily ignited, she stayed cautiously vigilant. Without a doubt, he was fiercely protective of his property, and it was important to her not to incite his anger.

The two of them drove to 213 Oak Street in Westminster, which was the county seat of Carroll County. They passed lovely homes with well-manicured lawns and mature shade trees, finally arriving at Peter Tate's house. Abigail insisted that she accompany Avery as he went to knock on the door of his home. A young woman opened the door.

"Is Mr. Tate here?" Avery asked.

"No, he's out at the mine."

"Are you his wife?" he asked. She nodded and warily watched the couple in front of her. "Maybe you could tell me what's going on down by the mine," he said.

"All I know is that Pennsylvania Railroad is negotiating with Pete about sharing the cost of the railroad spur they plan to build by his mine."

"Have they already decided to build a railroad there?" Avery angrily leaned toward her. Abigail grabbed at him to hold him back and struggled to get him in the carriage. He was fit to be tied.

"Those sneaky, money-grubbing tyrants! They're going to ruin my life. I'll have to take those lyin' scoundrels back to court. They think they can run roughshod over me. All I want is to live my life in peace out in the country," Avery shouted.

Abigail took the reins and drove them back to their house with a furious Avery beside her. She could feel his anger quake through the footrests on the buckboard. Once in the house, he snatched his whisky out of the cupboard and started drinking. Abigail felt helpless as she witnessed an upsurge in his ranting.

"My land will be worthless with the spur running right beside it," he bemoaned. "Those railroad engineers always start with a spur, and then the bastards continue to build through the countryside. My cattle won't be able to graze there, and the quarry will send huge loads of rocks and slate and carry many loads to Baltimore. This will happen often every day. My peaceful life in the country will be over."

In a quandary about what to do, Abigail prepared a hot meal for both of them, but she ended up eating all by herself while Avery drank his supper. With every swallow, he worked himself into a fury the likes of which she had never seen. She soon lost her appetite and left the kitchen. She remembered the angry fits of her mother and how she would hurl objects at Pinky to injure him and inflict pain. Avery was different; he was not violent toward her but was merciless to those who threatened his property and livelihood. He was driven to kill out of revenge, and he was impulsive and ruthless. Abigail realized she was in over her head.

In a drunken stupor, Avery grabbed his shotgun out of his shed and headed toward Medford Quarry. Being liquored-up, the alcohol played havoc with his judgment. All he could see was *red*. Impulse-driven without the ability to process the consequences, he was determined to confront Peter Tate. Abigail spotted him out of the corner of her eye. Frantic, she ran after him as he bolted over toward the ledge of the quarry.

"Avery! Avery!" she shouted. "Stop! We'll find a better way. Stop!"

Running with all her might, she managed to grab onto his shirt to hold him back, but his shirt tore. He shoved her back and kept going. Abigail clasped her hands over her face and wailed in horror. Pressing on toward the precipice, he stopped momentarily to see the Clarence Carriages exit the quarry with Peter Tate leading the caravan. He shot several rounds in the air and then at the carriages. The group was too far away for him to aim accurately. It was highly unlikely that he would inflict injury with his shotgun, but the horses spooked and took off in a mad frenzy. Avery heard the thunder of hooves and saw them disappear into a cloud of dust onto Nicodemus Road.

Defeated, Avery went home. He met Abigail on the way, and they walked silently together toward the house.

"Let's talk in the living room," she said.

Avery's shoulders were hunched over and his deflated spirit made him look ten years older. Fortunately, his rage subsided.

"We have to find a better way," Abigail said. "Firing your shotgun isn't helping. So far, nobody has been injured that we know of, but you've killed a man thinking he was stealing your livestock. If you would shoot someone, you would end up in jail. I don't want that for you or for us."

"I just don't know how to stop these people from the railroad," he said. "They're not listening to me. Maybe I'll contact the lawyer that helped me win the case against the railroad in 1886. I'll have to track him down, because he moved to a new office in Westminster. Maybe using a lawyer is the only way to stop the bastards."

"Avery, I want your guns off our property," she demanded, looking him straight in the eyes.

He was dead silent as he returned her gaze. Taking his guns was like taking his manhood away. How could he protect himself? His job was to keep the family safe. Their land was part of the family belongings, as was Abigail. It was unthinkable that he wouldn't have access to firearms. He didn't know how to respond.

Abigail's mind was spinning rapidly, trying to find a solution and a way out of this mess. "Maybe we could have your parents lock up your guns at their house and keep the key for safety," she said. "After all, they're just over the knoll in the front yard. If you needed a gun, they could get it out of the gun case for you."

He sat there motionless for a long time, shook his head, but seemed to warm up to the idea. "That's a lot better than selling them or throwing them away. One of the guns was a gift from my grandpa, and it's important to me to keep it in the family. He was a nice old man. Do you want me to talk to my folks?"

"I'd like to go with you," she said.

There was an unexpected knock on the front door. Abigail jumped up and opened it to find a mailman delivering a registered letter. She signed the receipt, gave it to the mailman. He gave her the letter and she noticed the return address read: *Samuel Abrams, Esq.*

"The papers for the sale of the confectionary came from my attorney. I need to fill them out and send them back before the meeting with David Whitman. But, let's go to your mom and dad's house first and take care of the guns. Then, I can complete the paperwork when we get back."

Abigail was relieved that Avery was willing to consider her suggestion. They were acting like a team again, and this made her more optimistic about their relationship. Mallory and Grant, Avery's parents, liked to keep to themselves. They were always polite to her, but she didn't feel comfortable talking to them about Avery's dark side. They really didn't even want to know about it. That part of him was perplexing to Abigail, and she had to figure out much of it all by herself. No support from his parents made it a lonely marriage for her.

With a quick hello from Grant and an invitation for tea from Mallory, Avery and Abigail found a comfortable seat in their opulent living room. A little bit of chitchat about the weather and, then, Avery broke the news.

"Mom, Dad, Abigail wants to get rid of the guns in our house," he said.

"Why would you ever do that?" Grant asked. "Isn't that shotgun a gift from Pa? I don't think that's a good idea. A man has got to defend his property."

"Ever since I shot Tony accidently, she gets jumpy when I bring them out," he said. "Maybe you could lock them up in the case downstairs, and I can get the guns if I need 'em. I already have a bone to pick with the railroad about a spur they're putting in near my land. It may be best this way."

"What do you think, Ma?" Grant asked.

"It's alright with me if Abigail feels safer."

"I get so tired of the railroad and how they grab land, it just gets my ire up," Avery said. "I'm going to talk with my attorney to see if anything can be done to stop them. It's going to affect my grazing cattle and change our peaceful country life. It shouldn't bother you as much, but it's going to abut my property line. I'll see and hear it every single day. It's a damn shame!"

"Progress doesn't happen without some inconvenient change," Abigail added. "It's too bad when we have to be in the middle of the inconvenience. We'll see what Avery's lawyer has to say."

"He's a smart man. He sure helped me in eighty-six," Avery said. "Thanks for the tea, Ma, and I appreciate you doing us a favor. It's always good when the little woman feels safe."

Avery and Abigail walked side-by-side back to their home. Abigail turned her attention to completing the papers from Sam Abrams, and Avery went about doing his late-afternoon chores. He always enjoyed checking on the new calf he named Spot. He also enjoyed gathering fresh eggs from the chicken coop. In a way, it was a relief not to have the guns around the house, because it forced him to think about other ways to protect his property.

The next morning, it was chilly and rainy, but that didn't deter him from going to Westminster to talk with Mark Simon, his attorney. Having finished all her paperwork, Abigail rode along to mail the documents to her attorney. As they trotted past the entrance to Medford Quarry, they saw several stacks of lumber and numerous steel sections of train track being stockpiled. They surmised that it was there to begin construction very soon.

"They're further along than I thought," Avery fumed. "Those varmints are going to try to sneak around the wishes of their neighbors."

"You'll have to find out from your attorney what your rights are first," she said.

Sensing his anger about to erupt, she made every effort to stay calm, which wasn't easy, considering the enormous fear inside of her. The steady rhythm of the horses' trotting was comforting and, at times, lulled her into a false sense of security. What would their future hold? This unknowable outcome was both a blessing and a curse. When hope was present, she could take it one day at a time and feel a blissful calm, ignorant of future problems. The curse, however, was not being aware enough to prepare for stopping a tragedy. What will it be … domestic tranquility or a gruesome nightmare? Abigail didn't know. She charged ahead to meet those unknown challenges whichever way they went, but she continued to be consumed by doubt.

The first stop was at his attorney's old office to see if there were directions to the new office. There was a new address posted on the door, and it was only a couple of blocks north. Avery and Abigail walked there together to make an appointment. The office was a step down from his previous one, and he didn't have a secretary. Avery knocked on the inside door, and Mark Simon opened it up.

"Hi, Avery," he said turning to Abigail. "Who do I have the pleasure of meeting?"

"This is my wife, Abigail," Avery responded. Mark and Abigail shook hands and both nodded a greeting. "I have another concern about the Pennsylvania Railroad and wanted to set up a time to talk with you."

"I'm scheduled to be in court after lunch," Mark said. "If this matter will take less than an hour, we can confer right now."

"That should be enough time," Avery said.

Simon invited them into his office and offered them a seat. A quick glance around his office indicated that he had run into some bad luck. It was sparse and run down. Avery got right to the point.

"The Pennsylvania Railroad is planning to build a spur for Medford Quarry right next to my land. They're driving me crazy. I want to know the rights I have as a landowner."

"Are the tracks on your land?"

"No," Avery said. "What bothers me is the noise that the trains will bring, and also, that's where my cattle graze. Right now, the quarry ledge is a natural boundary for them. They know enough not to go over the rock ledge. But, if they put a railroad through there, who knows what would happen to that ledge, and there's nothing that will protect my cattle. Can you imagine how difficult it would be to put a quarter mile of fence into that quarry rock? If I can't build the fence, I might have to put cattle guards all along there. That's a lot of time and expense."

"Well, I'm sorry, but the railroads have all the rights here. They call it 'railroad clearance of right of way.' The law protects the railroad business. In this case, it's the quarry and the railroads. The railroad doesn't build a fence to protect its tracks, because it's up to the landowners to protect their own property and cattle. There have been lots of cattle killed by the trains, but the landowners lose in court every single time."

Chagrinned, Avery just shook his head and was confused about what to do next.

➮➮➮

Avery paced the floor, anxiously waiting for Abigail to leave for Baltimore to close the sale of Abbott's Confectionary. While doing the farm chores, his mind conjured up ways to get even. He just could not stop thinking about it. His anger would surge, and then a plan for his revenge would materialize. His first idea was to steal dynamite from the storage shed near the quarry rock. Every once in a while, they would blast the quarry walls to free the stones for crushing. If he did it at just the right time, which would be in the early morning hours, no one would ever know. However, he knew there was just a small window of opportunity. He would have to discharge his plan while Abigail was conducting the sale of Abbott's Confectionary in Baltimore. He realized the timing of that plan would be too risky. His next plan seemed more plausible. He would talk to his farmer friend at the Grange in Westminster on Saturday to see if he had dynamite for blowing up stumps. This was a ruse to cover up his real plan of dynamiting the building supplies being stockpiled for the construction of the spur.

Pennsylvania Railroad wasn't listening to him, so this was the only way he could see to solve the problem that the railroad and Peter Tate, owner of Medford Quarry, created.

He'd have to wait for Abigail to be away before he could execute the scheme, and it seemed like she was taking forever to leave. She was busily packing her clothes and other items for a weeklong stay at her sisters' home while she transferred the business to David Whitman. The clicking sounds of Abigail's heels on the floor upstairs unnerved him. Impatiently, Avery charged up the stairs and offered to help Abigail carry her bags to the carriage.

"If I didn't know better, it seems like you want me out of the house," Abigail chuckled as she hastened her packing. As soon as she finished, Avery grabbed the satchel and the suitcase and carried them outside. Abigail put on her shawl, found her purse, and headed down the stairs through the open front door. He lifted her up into the carriage, and off they went to Union Bridge Station.

"Are you going to be okay while I'm gone?" Abigail asked. She was genuinely worried about him because of all the stress he was under from the planned spur construction at Medford Quarry. "If you need me to come home, send a telegram to Samuel Abrams office, and he'll make sure I get it."

"I should be okay," he said. "I've got chores to do, and I want to finish the re-roofing project on the shed before winter, so I'll be busy."

The rest of the ride passed in silence. Avery was thinking about the spur and Abigail was thinking about selling the store. He gave her a peck on the cheek and dismounted from the carriage. After lugging the suitcase and satchel to her side of the carriage, he offered his hand to lift her down. She bought her ticket while he heaved the luggage onto the train. With a final wave goodbye, the train rattled down the track, dwarfing Avery in the distance.

Hopping up into his carriage, Avery slapped the reigns and sped away, excited about launching his plan to impede and, hopefully, destroy the building of the track. He put his switch to the old mare and clicked his tongue to keep the momentum going. Off they went, homeward bound. He slowed down as they passed the quarry just long enough to visually mark the spot where he would implement the plan.

The stockpile grew to fill almost half of the quarry before the workers clocked out on Friday. This infuriated Avery. Instead of curtailing their efforts, they were accelerating their plans. *What I want doesn't matter. I'm just the little guy, and they don't care about me. I'll show them. I'll disrupt their work, and thwart their plans. The delays will hinder the progress and make them frustrated so they'll give-up. Nobody is going to ride roughshod over me!*

He rode right past his house and headed straight to the Grange office to see his friend Hubert Anderson. "Hey, Hubert," Avery said. "I've got some stumps on my land that need to be blown up. I need some dynamite."

"Well, I have some sticks for small blasts," Hubert said. "How many do you need?"

"I've got some pretty big oak trees that I had to cut down," Avery said. "It takes quite a bit of power to uproot those giants."

"You'll probably need four sticks for each stump, so eight in all," Hubert said. "All you need is a match. They'll work real good."

"I'll buy eight," Avery said as he pulled the money out of his pocket. "Thanks, Hubert."

So, motivated to take on those "damn bloodsuckers," Avery spent countless hours inside his little shed on Saturday meticulously planning his attack. Sunday was the day he chose, because no one was working in the quarry. He didn't want any collateral damage. He didn't have a quarrel with the workers of the mine who were just trying to make a living for their families. Instead, this was a dispute between the railroad and him. He took the time to draw the quarry to scale, adding the stockpiles of construction materials into the design. He worked feverishly all day in his shed. The placement of the dynamite had to be perfect. He wanted the maximum amount of damage with the least amount of personal risk.

He figured he would put four sticks about a third of the way into the stockpiles and the other four by the shed located at the base of the stockpiles. The dynamite in the shed would probably ignite, and a fire would burn it down along with the building materials. Planning the blasts was tricky, because he would need to detonate two blasts in rapid succession. He wanted to get out of there as fast as he could without getting caught. It all had to be done under the cover of darkness, so he wouldn't arouse suspicion. Even though he was familiar with the terrain, laying the cord and planting the dynamite would be tricky.

Four o'clock in the morning seemed like the best time. He would make it look like spontaneous combustion because when the dynamite sweats nitroglycerin, it explodes. That would be the last act, because he needed to be in his house robe and looking like he just woke up from the loud blast when his neighbors congregated to the spot.

Avery organized his supplies, checked and rechecked to make sure he had everything he needed. Most importantly, he removed any information that might be on the sticks of dynamite. Tracking down the manufacturer of the dynamite got other railroad strikers in trouble. He wanted to make sure that didn't happen to him, so he went over and over his plans again to make sure he hadn't forgotten anything. The arms on the clock moved slowly as his heartbeat quickened in anticipation of his ultimate revenge. Just thinking about how he was marginalized and victimized made his blood boil. He had more than enough indignation and outrage to fuel his villainy.

In the deep dark of night, he headed out with several bags of paraphernalia. Stealthily, he walked across the pastures through groups of cows and sheep until he came to the edge of the quarry. Finding the lowest ledge, he jumped to the base of the mining operation and walked to the pile of construction materials, placing the four sticks of dynamite under the sections of tracks. He laid the fuse all the way to the far end of the quarry. The other four sticks he shoved under the storage shed and, further down, placed the fuse parallel to the other one. When he took the matches out of his pocket, he noticed that his hand trembled from either fear or excitement. He wasn't sure which, perhaps both. He lit the first fuse, transfixed by the hissing flame as it traveled toward the blasting cap. He stood there in a trance, and then burst into a run to hightail it to safety

The blast was ear splitting, and the blistering heat at his back told him he hadn't used enough fuse. The blast almost caught up with him. Metal pieces of the track flew like projectiles through the air, and some rained down on him. The acrid smell of smoke permeated the quarry, and the intense blaze that followed the blast was a dusty, angry, red-orange billowing burst of gases.

Eyes wide open and wild, Avery ran-lunged around the eruption to ignite the second fuse that went under the shed. He lit it and then barreled back to the house and locked the door behind him. The distance deadened the sound of that blast, but there were several eruptions in rapid succession, and the multiple explosions lit up the inside of his house.

Avery got rid of as much of the evidence as he could, scrubbed his body to remove the pungent smell of the dynamite residue, put on his house robe, and waited.

CHAPTER 9

Ravaged

❧ ❧ ❧ ❧

The sky shifted from dark to light at the dawn of a new day. Deafening sounds of the two dynamite blasts woke the neighbors on and around Nicodemus Road. They gathered together to make sense of the sounds and acrid smells. Some neighbors, in various stages of undress moved quickly and urgently, while others moved slowly and cautiously. Many wore a jacket over their nightgowns, others were shirtless under their coats, yet others already doing morning chores were in full dress.

The groups gravitated toward the quarry, which seemed to them where the sound originated. Avery joined them at the tail end of the group, hoping not to be noticed. He wore his house robe and slippers to give the appearance of being awakened suddenly, and was convincingly acting the part of a concerned neighbor.

When the people looked over the quarry ledge, they

were aghast. Billowing smoke and churning gases filled the floor of the mine. Everything was charred and blown to smithereens. Avery clasped his hands over his mouth as he peered over the edge, feigning astonishment.

"The mine is ravaged," a neighbor said. "Who would have done this … and why?"

It was obvious from the destruction that it was intentional. All the equipment, the building supplies, the storage shed, and the mine trolleys were destroyed. There was nothing left of the track building materials deposited by the Pennsylvania Railroad. It was completely ruined, as was any hope of bringing greater prosperity to Medford Quarry. The remnants were nothing but worthless pieces of twisted metal.

"Someone's got to get Peter Tate and the sheriff," a man shouted while getting on his horse. "I'll go and chase them down. We've got to find whoever did this and get some justice for the workers and their boss."

Avery slunk away, heading back to his house. He scanned the people to see if he could find his mother and father, but they weren't there. His worry started to torture him, and his thoughts were spinning around inside his head, almost making him dizzy. *Will the sheriff track me down? Will I be sent to prison? Oh, no. What have I done?* His thoughts kept niggling at him and making him crazy. His fear turned into a mountain of anxiety, which mushroomed into paranoia. Did paranoid thoughts create paranoid actions, or was it the other way around? Like the chicken and the egg, which came first? Either way, one's paranoid thoughts or actions can be calamitous when they mushroom out of control and create a "perfect storm."

Once inside his house, Avery desperately looked for whiskey to calm his nerves. His body felt clammy with sweat, his extremities ice cold, his face flushed and his breaths, short and quick. *Where's the Wild Turkey?* He desperately looked in the cupboard and spotted a half-filled bottle. He grabbed it, guzzled it down, and decided it was not enough, so with a sense of urgency, he went to town to stock up. Quickly, he hitched his horse, climbed into the buggy, and went off to get his favorite tonic, Wild Turkey … *nothing like bourbon from Kentucky.*

The four miles into Westminster seemed to take forever. Then he witnessed the posse assembling in front of the courthouse by the sheriff's office. The whole town was abuzz, trying to find the culprit. He was alarmed by the snippets of conversation he overheard, worried it would all impact his future.

"It must have been someone who hated either the railroad or Peter Tate, because the explosion set them back many years. Peter Tate's livelihood is in shambles. He's going to have to start over from the ground up … someone has to pay for the crime and needs to be put behind bars for a long time. We don't want this to happen again," the Marylanders of Westminster County shouted.

Hearing the admonishment from the townsfolk worried Avery. He scratched his head trying to recall what his brother had written in the letter he received from him last month. Avery was able to remember the important parts of the letter since he knew it was relevant to what he was facing right now. He would purchase the whiskey and head back home to reread it.

He recalled what his brother said in his letter about how some some local citizens and farmers joined in the fight against the railroad because of the Chicago, Burlington and Quincy's usurpation of local villages and farmlands. Officials from the CB&Q railroad hired Pinkerton detectives to investigate, which proved to be a slow process, because all they had to go on was small fragments of paper wrapped around the dynamite. The investigation broke loose when they found the trademark of the dynamite manufacturer on one of the fragments. The trademark was the giveaway, and from there, they tracked down the men who purchased the dynamite.

Avery read and reread the letter from his brother Henry. He knew for certain that he had carefully removed any trademark or any other identifying information from the outside covering of the dynamite. He even removed the manufactured date, so he was confident that they wouldn't be able to trace the dynamite. Avery kept his fingers crossed that they wouldn't call in the Pinkertons. They had a reputation for being pretty clever and thorough in their search to find evidence.

He picked up the local paper to see if there was any information about the quarry. It was devoid of news about the mine, since it had just happened, but as he rode by the *American Sentinel* office, he noticed the reporters being dispatched to the quarry. Two reporters hitched up their horses and headed in the direction of Nicodemus Road. Avery's heart beat faster and faster, prompting him to quicken his horse's gallop to the liquor store. The next issue of the press would be sent out on Wednesday, so surely, they would have it covered by that time. *Why am I so worried about what the newsmen would write?* He pushed on to the liquor store, which was the real reason he came to town. Knowing that the liquor would alleviate his anxiety, he bought and paid for two crates of *Wild Turkey* and made haste back to his house.

He parked his buggy by the shed, took care of his horse, and carried his stash into the house. Once inside, he locked the door and closed the curtains. With each drape pulled, the house became darker and darker. It became eerie and tomb-like. After grabbing the bottle of *Wild Turkey* and plopping into the overstuffed living room chair, he started to drink … *heavily* throughout the day. In a stupor, he heard a knock at the door. Not wanting to answer it, he sat quietly and motionless for a very long time, but the irksome knock persisted. Pulling himself out of the chair, he managed to tidy up a bit. Shoving the whiskey in the closet and biting into a clove of garlic, he curled his fingers and raked them through his hair. When he opened the door, he found his parents standing in front of him.

"Are you okay? It looks like you just woke up," they remarked. "Did you hear the explosion early this morning? We didn't see you with the rest of the neighbors, so we came to check on you."

"Yeah. I heard it," Avery said. "What a racket. Woke me up, so I went to check it out. What a big mess. I don't think they'll be building a spur at Medford Quarry any time soon."

"I wonder who did it? Do you think it might be an unhappy employee?" Grant asked.

"Maybe so," Avery responded, looking at his mother, who said nothing. "Could I fix you some tea?" he said, trying to get past an awkward pause.

"Thank you for offering, Avery, but we have to head to Baltimore in a couple of hours," Mallory said. "I have to do some packing. When is Abigail coming home?"

"She's planning on coming home at the end of the week after the sale of the store is done," Avery said.

"Take care of yourself, dear," Mallory said as they left. She was eager to get home to get ready for their trip.

"I will, Mom," Avery said.

Not long after the two of them left, there was another knock on the door. Avery answered it without hesitation, thinking his parents had forgotten to tell him something. To his surprise and irritation, he found two men and the county sheriff standing in his doorway.

"Mr. Johnson, I have some questions to ask you," the sheriff said while standing outside. "Do you know who set off the blast?" There was a pause before the sheriff said, "Peter Tate thought you might have something to do with it."

"Oh, he did, did he?" Avery retorted. "Well, I don't know what he's talking about. Why does he think it's me? There are a lot of people that are not happy with the railroad."

"He said you stopped by his house looking for him," the sheriff said. "He wasn't there, so you talked to his wife. She said you left angry."

"Just because I left angry doesn't mean that I would dynamite his mine," Avery responded.

"So, you're saying you didn't have anything to do with it?" the sheriff queried. "Is that correct?"

"Yes, that is what I'm saying," Avery said.

"I won't take you into custody right now, but don't leave town," the sheriff responded. "I have more questions, and I'll need to talk to you again."

Avery shut the door on the sheriff and his small posse. He was glad to be done with them. Even though the liquor calmed him, his anxieties were bubbling up and messing with his mind.

Without Avery's knowledge, just a little way down the road, trouble was brewing at the mine. The mine workers were angry and fiercely hostile toward the person who destroyed their livelihood. The destruction of the mine not only affected them but their families too. How were they supposed to feed their kids? Finding employment especially during the winter months was nearly impossible. They also, liked and respected their boss, Peter Tate. He had worked hard to make the mine safe for them and a profitable company for everyone. The mine crews met together, looking through the rubble, trying to make sense of it all. Despondency turned into a deep resentment. Where did the culprit get the illegal dynamite? They were determined to find out.

 ‍
rₒ rₒ rₒ

The day had come when Abigail would lay all her fortunes on the table. The inheritance from her family and her pride and joy, Abbott's Confectionary, was changing hands. She would have to turn over all her interests in the business to David Whitman. It was her resolve to have a peaceful domestic life with Avery, enjoying the Maryland countryside. Selling the store in Baltimore would be the first step toward her new life. Per the instructions of the letter from the attorney, Samuel Abrams, Abigail got to his office early to finalize the details of the sale. Lydia, his secretary, gave a greeting and asked her to have a seat in the waiting room.

"Hello Abigail," Sam said as he opened the door to his office. "Welcome. Come in." Abigail followed him into the office. "Have a seat. I've drafted a contract for the sale that I think you will be happy with. All I have to do is write in the figures. One-third of the monies from the sale will go into a bank account for your sisters, one-third will be put into a checking account held jointly by you and Avery, and the last third will be for you. We have to decide on the asking price. Do you have any idea of what price you'd like to ask for the business?"

"In all honesty, I'm not sure. I'm relying on you to give me advice about that," Abigail said.

"What were your gross earnings last year?"

"We earned $3,220," Abigail said, nervously rummaging through her papers.

"Okay, now, how about your Seller's Discretionary Earnings? That number will give the buyer a realistic prediction of return on his investment," he asked.

"The business operations were $1,150," she answered. "My SDE was $2,070, but my business has grown in the last two years, and Abbott's Confectionary has a good reputation. That reputation should count for something."

"Certainly. That's called goodwill and is very important for the purchaser to know that they're buying a respected business," Sam said. "I checked on the value of the property, and a store in downtown Baltimore is valued at $5,200. So, if he offered you $10,000 for the purchase price, store and business combined, it would be a good deal for both you and the purchasing party. What do you think about that sum?"

"That sounds good to me," Abigail replied with a smile.

"If it sounds alright to you, I'm first going to ask for $12,000 to get the negotiations started. I fully expect that he will make a counter offer. If he does, it will be best if we stay firm at $10,000, with the buyer paying the closing costs," he said.

"Well, that seems like a good plan. That sounds like a lot of money to me. Actually, that is the most money I've ever made," she said.

"How's Avery?" he asked, changing the subject.

"He's pretty upset that the Pennsylvania Railroad is planning to build a spur at Medford Quarry. This is the mining operation that is adjacent to our land. What he finds most upsetting is that Peter Tate, the owner of the mine, and the railroad company never asked for our input. Seems like our quiet country life will never be the same. The livestock will be endangered, because the train runs right along our property line where our cattle graze. Our horses will be imperiled as well. They startle every time they hear a train whistle blow. He has talked to his lawyer, and there isn't much he can do because the local government favors the business interests of the quarry, which is a hefty part of their tax base."

"Do you worry that he would grab his gun and get even?" Sam asked.

"He'd have to clear it with his parents first, since he locked up his guns in the basement gun case in their house. The best thing about that is that they have the key," Abigail responded.

"Mr. Abrams, David Whitman is here," Lydia announced through a crack in his office door. "Would you like me to send him into your office?"

"Yes, please send him in," Sam said while glancing at Abigail to see if she was ready to make the final sale. Selling her business was a huge step for her. She nodded just as David Whitman entered.

David Whitman was a tall, slender man with peculiar mannerisms, a bit dandyish in appearance. From his dress, Abigail could tell that he had a good sense of detail. He wore a vested suit with formal coattails and a stiffly starched white shirt with a high collar and an ascot tie to match his paisley vest. His high-pitched giggle accentuated his unusual style.

"David, I'd like you to meet Abigail Johnson, the current owner of Abbott's Confectionary," Abrams said with stiff formality.

Abigail offered her hand for a handshake and he gently lifted it to his lips to give her a gentlemanly kiss on the back of her hand. "Delighted to make your acquaintance. I've heard nothing but complimentary words about you from my cousin, Stephen," he said with a burst of nervous giggling.

"Good to meet you as well," Abigail responded.

"Well, let's get down to the business at hand," Mr. Abrams said. "As you know, Abigail and her father have built Abbott's Confectionary into the thriving business it is today. The store has a stellar reputation in Baltimore because the business has grown substantially over the last few years. I'm sure your cousin Stephen has given you the records for you to review."

"Yes, he has," David said. "And, he will be investing his own money into the business. The majority of the financial support will be coming from him."

"We're asking $12,000 for the business and the building," Sam said as he handed him the list of business assets. There was a pause in the conversation, giving David a little time to digest the opening price. "I'll give you a moment to review the business assets. Just let me know when you're ready to inspect the breakdown of the $12,000 asking price."

David carefully analyzed the list of assets and then nodded to indicate he was ready to examine the breakdown for the asking price. He looked at the document, and then, quite sheepishly, pulled out a small sheet of paper from his pocket.

"I brought this note from Cousin Stephen. He has put a cap on how much he is willing to spend on the business," David said as he nervously cleared his throat. "It's indicated here that the top dollar he is willing to spend is $10,500. I'm sorry, but that's all he is willing to invest. He also says in the note that the seller needs to split the closing costs with him. I'm sorry, but that's the best I can do." A long pause followed.

"Let me confer with my client," Sam said as he motioned Abigail to step out of his office. "Well, Abigail, what do you think?" he asked as he shut his office door.

"I didn't know that Stephen was investing his own money," she said. "He's a capable businessman, and he'll do what he needs to make the business successful. I'll accept the offer."

"Are you sure?" Sam asked.

"Yes. It's a good offer, and Stephen is a good businessman," Abigail said.

Abigail and Sam reentered the office. "My client is willing to sell Abbott's Confectionary to you for $10,500 and is willing to equally split the closing costs with you," Sam Abrams announced.

Sam brought the papers to Lydia to make the final changes and to add a phrase about the arrangement for the closing costs. Lydia plucked away on her typewriter as Abigail and David chatted.

"Do you plan to keep the name, Abbott's Confectionary?" Abigail asked.

"Most definitely," David said. "Patrons associate the name Abbott's Confectionary with quality candies."

Abigail's smile beamed with satisfaction. Her daddy would be so proud. Sam placed the documents to be signed on the table and passed them to both parties along with a bejeweled fountain pen. Once the signatures were secured, David happily reached out to shake Abigail's hand, and she responded in kind.

"I'll have the funds transferred to your bank in Carroll County," David said. "It has been good doing business with you."

"I'll meet you at the store tomorrow morning about nine o'clock to show you a few business tricks and explain how I do inventory," she said.

"I would appreciate that very much. Thank you." He tipped his hat as he left the office.

"Thank you, Sam," Abigail said.

Before she left the office, Lydia gave her a telegram dropped off by Western Union. The messenger came while she and David Whitman were finalizing the sale. She quickly opened it, and read it under her breath. *What happened?* After rereading it, she sat down, trying to comprehend what was written.

**SHERIFF THREATENED TO TAKE ME INTO CUSTODY
THINKS I HAD SOMETHING TO DO WITH BLAST AT
MEDFORD QUARRY   COME HOME SOON   AVERY**

Her hands shook uncontrollably. She felt ill. She knew
he was fully capable of dynamiting the mine and destroying someone's livelihood. Any trust she had in her husband had dissolved. With an overwhelming sense of
dread, she instinctively knew her life had taken an unwelcome turn. Her face turned ghastly white, and her body
searched for a chair to sit down to regain her composure.
Sensing something was very wrong, Lydia fetched Mr.
Abrams from his office.

"What's the matter, Abigail?" he said with urgency.
"Are you feeling okay?"

"I'm not sure how to deal with this," Abigail said, bewildered. "The county sheriff suspects Avery of dynamiting
the Medford Quarry. When I'm away from our house, I
leave fearing the worst. I don't know what will happen.
When he finds his holdings imperiled, he gets violent. It's
hard to admit it, but he very well could have done this
dastardly deed."

"I'll talk with my friend Bill Garrett; he's one of the
local bosses with the railroad and oversees that region.
His office is just up the street. How much time do you
have before you have to take the train to Union Bridge?"

"I can take the early evening train, so I have about three
hours," Abigail answered.

"I'll head to his office right now," Abrams said. "Lydia,
please look after Mrs. Johnson while I'm gone."

Abigail's head was spinning as Mr. Abrams shut the
door behind him. The hours crept by slowly as Lydia gave
her water and made sure she was comfortable. Finally,

two large, imposing men barged into the office, Samuel Abrams and Bill Garrett. They were on an urgent mission.

"Abigail, I want you to meet Bill Garrett. He represents the railroad and would be able to answer any questions you might have."

"Pleased to meet you, sir," she said. "I do have questions about the incident at the mine. Was anyone hurt? Were there any damages?"

"Fortunately, no one was injured or killed in the explosion, since it was dynamited early Monday morning when no one was at the worksite," Bill Garrett responded. "But all the trolleys, the storage shed, and the building supplies were destroyed along with the income for Mr. Tate and nineteen mine workers. This morning, we hired Pinkerton to investigate. Once they discover where the dynamite was purchased, they'll be able to track down the suspect."

"Could I ask you a personal question?" Abigail asked.

"Certainly."

"If you were me, what would you do?"

"That's a tough question, but if the mine workers find out who's the culprit, they're going to get mean," Bill said. "They're a rough bunch. I guess I would get home as soon as I could and assess the situation. He *is* your husband, so I would listen to what he has to say and protect him the best way you can."

After a long, still pause, Abigail responded. "That makes sense."

She gathered up her things and summoned some courage to face whatever came at her. Ever so grateful for their concern and helpfulness, she smiled, shook hands with them, and departed for the train. While on the train, she fell into a deep despair. It was all so ironic. She was convinced that she needed to sell Abbott's Confectionary to save her marriage, but maybe Avery was so firmly set on self-destruction that there was no saving the marriage.

Maybe he didn't do it. After all, he willingly locked up his firearms in his parents' gun case. Deep down, she knew he was capable of doing something that horrible, because he had a dark place inside of him that was uncontrollable. She couldn't control it, either. It was a scary, untouchable place. *I do know he has an endearing side. I know he can love deeply. Even though I feel lost and alone, my vows are strong, and I will be his wife forever.*

Her emotions were a jumbled mess, and her thoughts became stuck and unstuck, racing endlessly. She just had to stop them. After taking a deep breath, she   slowly exhaled all her tension as the train entered the Union Bridge Station.

She hailed a cab and headed home to Nicodemus Road. The quick clopping of the horse's hooves brightened her spirits some, but she plunged deep into thoughts of what might happen when she saw her husband. It wasn't long before she came across a large group forming, a congregation of mine workers and neighbors mingling together, creating a cacophony of loud noises. Animated gestures and caterwauling over the din of a crowd filled the air. *What's happening? Who should I talk to? I need to find someone who knows something.*

"Driver, please stop! I want to talk to the person who's cutting across the road," Abigail declared. "Mister, mister, what's going on?" she yelled, hoping to get information.

"The sheriff has been questioning Avery Johnson. He's

the main suspect," the onlooker said. "They hired the Pinkertons this morning to start an investigation."

"Who told you so?" Abigail asked emphatically.

"The sheriff and his posse have talked to Peter Tate, the owner of the mine, and the information has spread like wildfire. Whoever did this is a son of a bitch, pardon me, ma'am, and he's going to get his comeuppance. They will be assembling a group of men tomorrow morning over by the hill. Peter Tate is joining the group, and someone said Bill Garrett, the railroad man, is taking the train to Union Bridge from Baltimore."

In a panic, Abigail motioned the driver to press on. She wanted to check on Avery and unload her baggage. As she rushed into the house, she found Avery passed out on the living room floor with an empty bottle of Wild Turkey by his side. She grabbed the bottle and threw it in the garbage. The rest of the evening, she did the chores that Avery didn't do. She wanted to make sure all the animals were fed and watered. Once the routine chores were done, she went back to thinking about her predicament. *Oh, Avery. What do I do with you? You've made such a mess of your life and mine. It is so hard to be a devoted wife to you. I certainly don't want our neighbors to see you this way. You'll be labeled the town drunk. I guess I'll have to find the strength to deal with this by myself.* Abigail reluctantly resigned herself to attending the gathering at the quarry the next morning. First, she needed to unpack her belongings, tidy up the house, and try to get some sleep.

A fitful night's sleep was followed by a golden-hued morning. Avery was still sleeping off his drunken stupor. The Wild Turkey had done its job. Doing the morning chores was not a choice but a necessity for her. It was important to Abigail that the animals were okay. She cleaned up, got dressed, and walked over to the rally at Medford Quarry. With renewed resolve, she faced the anger of the crowds and began looking for Peter Tate and Bill Garrett. *Maybe they'll listen to me, but where are they?* She waited patiently until she saw Bill Garrett's carriage pass by. She waved frantically, hoping he would see her, and, thankfully, he did see her. The carriage stopped, and he stepped out away from the crowds to talk with Abigail. His presence exuded an air of authority.

"Abigail, I heard the news," he said. "Have you talked to Avery? I fear the worst. This group could become a lynch mob if I'm unable to stop the momentum. Where is your husband?"

"Mr. Garrett, I'm ashamed to say it, but my husband is out of commission and in no condition to meet anyone."

"Here comes Peter Tate," Bill Garrett said. "I need to talk to him alone. Wait here until I'm done. I think we can work something out." She waited patiently as Peter and Bill talked privately on the other side of the carriage, hidden from the crowd. Just a few minutes seemed like an eternity. Abigail felt the chaotic energy of the men behind her. She turned around to find all eyes on her. They were anticipating some words of assurance from either Bill Garrett or Peter Tate. When the two of them appeared, the crowd became excited. Bill Garrett sought out Abigail, and Peter Tate approached the crowd hoping to quell their anger.

"I got more details from Peter," Bill Garrett said. "He has been talking to the Pinkertons. Day and night for two days, they've been investigating the sabotaging of the mine. Avery purchased the dynamite used in the explosion for stump removal the day before the blast. He bought the explosives from Hubert Anderson at the Grange office. The paper covering on the dynamite that Hubert sold to Avery was purple, and that's what the Pinkertons found at the base of the mine. All evidence points to Avery as the guilty party."

"Oh, no!" Abigail groaned. "I was afraid of that."

"Peter said that the men are angry, mostly because the nineteen mine workers are out of a job," Bill Garrett continued. "They lost their livelihood and their families will suffer. Many of them live paycheck to paycheck. I want to talk to you about a possible restitution to avoid a lynch mob. That should give us some time so at least Avery will be able to get a proper trial."

"Mr. Garrett, I understand the anger and frustration that the mine workers have. The source of their income is gone. Now would be the time to talk with Peter Tate to find out what would make sense. Would you take over talking to the crowd so I can ask him some questions? Maybe we can work something out."

"All right. I'll send him your way," Bill said as he hustled up the hill. He pulled Peter aside to relay the message, and Bill took on the task of addressing the mob. Peter walked toward Abigail.

"Hello, Mr. Tate," Abigail said deferentially. "I have some questions for you, and I'm hoping that we could work something out so my husband will be safe until his trial. How much do your mine workers make per day?"

"Well, it's a forty-eight-hour work week, and on average they make four dollars a day," he responded.

"How long before you can get the quarry back up and running?" Abigail asked.

Tate shook his head, scratched his chin, and thought for a while. "That's hard to say. Winter is just around the corner, so it makes it a little harder, but I think we should have it up and running by early spring next year."

Abigail started figuring the costs. *If I could pay each worker for lost wages until the mine was up and running again, that should help both Avery and the mine workers. I have seven thousand dollars from the sale. There are nineteen mine workers, so that would be seven thousand six hundred dollars. I have one thousand two hundred dollars of savings in the bank. If I added six hundred dollars from my own savings, I could offer each mineworker one hundred days of pay.*

Even though Abigail had very good mental math skills, it was apparent she skipped a step. There was no thought of getting Avery's approval. After all, Avery was in a drunken stupor and not fit to make any decision. Right or wrong, he was left out of the equation. Without his input, she made her proposal, and about half of the money was part of their joint assets.

"I will pay each of your men four dollars a day for one hundred work days," Abigail offered. "With that money, they can feed their families through the winter. Your workers would be okay until the quarry is back in business in the spring, Mr. Tate. I'm sorry, but restitution for *you* will have to come after the trial."

"Your offer is very generous," Peter Tate said. "That should silence their protests and make them less angry. I'll announce the offer." He summoned his courage and faced the angry mob. "Mrs. Johnson has made you a very generous offer," he shouted.

"She's the wife of Avery Johnson and probably in cahoots with that lowlife!" someone yelled.

"What about our families?" another complained. "I've got mouths to feed. They deserve something!"

"Gentlemen, hear me out," Peter Tate exclaimed. He struggled to pitch his voice above the noisy belligerence of the crowd. "She is willing to pay you four dollars a day for one hundred work days. By that time, the mine should be back in business."

The crowd fell silent. Whispers of disbelief traveled through the crowd. All eyes were on Peter Tate and Abigail, who stood next to him. "Are you willing to accept this offer?"

The loudest protester stepped forward, acknowledging Abigail by taking his hat off and placing it on his heart. "My men and I appreciate your kindness, ma'am. Thank you for your generosity," he said.

Another man standing behind him shouted, "When will we get our money?"

Peter Tate took Abigail aside and quickly conferred with her before he made an announcement. "I'll have a clerk at the north entrance of the quarry tomorrow at ten o'clock in the morning. He will have the money ready and waiting for you."

"Yay!" the men shouted, throwing their hats into the air. The atmosphere changed magically from voices of rage to exuberance. The crowd disbanded with a renewed sense of hope.

Peter Tate and Bill Garrett shook Abigail's hand and nodded in approval. They were pleased to have averted a possible disaster. She felt a deep relief, too, but the most dreaded part was still ahead of her. She had to explain what she did to Avery. Abigail headed home to get the money ready for Peter Tate and to see how her husband was doing. *What will I find when I arrive? Will he be sober or in a stupor?* She had to face the problem head-on, because the next step was to hire a competent defense attorney. The head prosecutor in Carroll County was known to be sharp and ruthless. Avery needed good representation.

"Hi, Avery," she said when she saw him in the living room. "How are you?"

There was no answer, and when she got closer to him, what she saw was frightful. He sat, propped up in the chair, and didn't move. His skin was cold and clammy and his breathing was quick and shallow. He reeked of alcohol; the overpowering smell came out of every pore. She checked his pulse, finding it weak and slow. Her first impulse was to get a doctor, but instead she ran over to his parents' house to get help.

"Mallory! Grant! I need help!" Abigail shouted as she banged on their door.

"What's wrong?" Mallory asked. "Has something happened?"

"Yes, Avery's not doing well. Someone should get the doctor."

"I'll get Grant, and we'll come over right away," Mallory said.

"Good. I'll head back to check on him."

When Abigail arrived, Avery was up and walking around like nothing happened. "Are you feeling better?" she asked.

"I just had a little too much to drink," he said. "That's all. I'm fine, now."

Mallory and Grant also checked in on their son, who was a bit disheveled but responding normally.

"Are you okay, Avery?" Mallory asked.

"I'm just fine. Why is everybody so concerned?"

"Abigail, did you hear the ruckus over by the quarry about an hour ago?" Grant asked. "It sounded like a pretty angry group of people."

Not sure how much she should divulge, Abigail shared only essential information. "A lynch mob was forming against the culprit who destroyed the mine with a dynamite blast on Sunday," she explained.

"Do they know who did it?" Mallory asked.

"They found out that the dynamite was purchased at the Grange Office for stump removal," Abigail said. "Hubert Anderson gave Pinkerton the name and the color of the paper covering the dynamite. That person is now the main suspect." She knew if she gave out any more information without Avery's consent, she would be in big trouble, so she sealed her lips.

Avery waved goodbye to his parents as they headed over the hill to their house. He shut the door firmly, pivoted around, and gave Abigail a piercing look. Her insides turned to jelly and, shivering from the fear of his rage, she braced herself for his rant, hunkering down for the expected onslaught of verbal attacks. She reckoned she would be in the hot seat for a long time.

"Who told you about Hubert Anderson and the Grange?" Avery shouted.

"Bill Garrett."

"Who in the *hell* is Bill Garrett?"

"He's the manager of the railroad in this area."

"You'd listen to someone from the railroad before your *husband?*" Avery shouted, incensed by her lack of loyalty.

Avery came at her with both barrels. He had never hit

her before, but she knew he was fully capable of hurting her without any remorse. To his way of thinking, she was a disobedient wife. Abigail remained silent, knowing this was not the time to tell him the rest of the story.

Avery interpreted her silence as submission, so he backed away and poured himself another drink. Her deepest desire as his wife was to hear the truth from his lips so, despite her better judgment, she pushed him to explain.

"Avery, did you do it?" Abigail asked, holding her breath.

"Did I do *what*?" he uttered through his clenched teeth.

"Did you blow up Medford Quarry?"

She could see Avery was ready to explode. His face contorted in pain, his eyes bulged and oscillated while he paced back and forth, shaking his head.

"I only did it to keep the railroad from running over us and destroying our home in the country. Hubert Anderson had to spill the beans and make a mess of everything. I was sure they couldn't trace the dynamite, because there weren't any labels telling where I got it. I'm wondering how Pinkerton knew that it was from the Grange?"

"The Pinkertons found the paper that encased the dynamite. It was exactly the same type that was used by the Grange," Abigail said. "How do you plan to get us out of this mess?" Abigail asked disdainfully, gaining confidence from his confession.

Avery poured another glass of *Wild Turkey*. He guzzled it down and flopped onto an overstuffed living room chair. She could see he wanted to go to sleep in the worst way to forget any of it ever happened, but she knew they needed to find a solution to this problem. He knew he had to as well.

"I guess I need to get myself a good attorney," he said after a long, pregnant pause.

"There's something you need to know," Abigail said haltingly. "When I returned from Baltimore, a raging band of protesters assembled by the Medford Quarry. The sheriff told Peter Tate that you were the main suspect. That information traveled to the protestors. Once the men heard this information, they were ready to take the law into their own hands and were ready to hang you."

"Why didn't you tell me?"

"You were passed out when I got home," Abigail said. "I had to face the angry mob by myself. I couldn't count on you."

Avery filled his glass again, but this time he just sipped it, listening to every word she spoke.

"Peter Tate and Bill Garrett tried to quiet the crowds," Abigail continued. "But, they were out of control. Their biggest complaint was the loss of jobs for the mine workers. That's what stuck in their craw. Bill Garrett said if I could offer them some kind of restitution for their loss of wages, it might settle them down. Then, at least you could get a fair trial."

"Restitution? What did he mean by that?"

"Well, I started figuring. I had made seven thousand from the sale of the store. Thirty-five hundred was for me and the rest was for our marital assets. Peter Tate said the mine workers made four dollars a day, and he thought the mine would be up and running in the spring. That would be one hundred days through the winter, so it would cost about seventy-six hundred to get them off our backs. I had the monies from the sale and six hundred from my savings account. Once I realized I had enough, I promised them the money."

Avery stood up, started pacing the floor, and glared at her, livid with anger. "You took *our* money and gave it away without asking me? You stupid, stupid woman! What were you thinking? I've seen lynch mobs before, and they chicken out when push comes to shove. You gave away the farm! Now, I will never get a fair trial, because making restitution is an admission of guilt. Hiring an attorney would be a waste of time."

Avery foamed at the mouth like a rabid dog. He grabbed her by the shoulders and shook her hard. "You are the *dumbest* woman I've ever known!" he screamed, spitting the words right in her face. Abigail went limp, crying hysterically. "We have no future. It is over for us," he said as he pushed her against the wall, grabbed a bottle of *Wild Turkey*, and walked out the front door, slamming it behind him.

My offer was to keep that angry mob at bay, but instead of appreciation, Avery scorned me. Could it be that we both were wrong? Weary from the events of the day, she felt exhaustion coming over her. Sleep was what she needed more than anything. She didn't want to see Avery that evening, knowing he would be drunk and belligerent. She tiptoed to her bedroom, locking the door behind her. Sorting all this out would have to wait until morning.

It was morning when an unusually loud whinny from their horse, Gunther, awakened her out of intermittent sleep. Now, fully awake, she dressed and headed downstairs, expecting to find Avery asleep on the sofa, but he was not in his usual spot after a night of heavy drinking. She became concerned.

"Avery? Avery!" Abigail called as she walked through the house. He was nowhere to be found, so she went outside to look for him. "Avery, where are you?"

There was no answer. She walked over the hill to his parents' house to see if he was there. As she passed by the back of the shed, she saw him sitting motionless with his back to the wall with a bottle of Wild Turkey in his hand. She rushed toward him, noticing his pale skin and that he was not breathing. She laid her hand on his neck to check for a pulse, and there was none. Her eyes widened in horror. Avery Johnson, her husband, had come to a bitter end.

❧ ❧ ❧

She sat on the grass next to him, devastated and sobbing. Her heart ached. She reached for his hand and held it in hers.

"I'm so sorry, Avery, and I so regret last night," she said mournfully. "What I did, I did because I wanted to take care of you … and keep you safe. If I disappointed you, I'm sorry."

Her despondency weighed her down, and she stayed stuck to the ground for a very long time. Finally, with every bit of her strength, she pulled herself up to tend to more perfunctory matters. She was uncertain of her obligation to Avery and his parents. She gently took the bottle out of his hand and set it in the shed before she left to tell his parents. Her feet felt like concrete as she climbed over the hill to their house. Forlorn and worried, she knocked on the door.

"Who is it?" Mallory shouted.

"It's Abigail."

"Come on in," she said, holding the door for her. "What brings you here?"

"I have some very sad news," Abigail said with tightness in her throat. "Avery died last night."

"*What*? What did you say?"

"Avery is dead."

"What happened?" Mallory asked, stunned.

"I'm not sure why he died," Abigail said. "Avery got so angry that he was out of control."

"Where is his body?" Mallory said, beginning to tear up.

"I found him sitting up behind his shed. That's where he is right now."

"Grant is at the neighbors right now. I'll go and get him. Please stay here while I run over."

"Okay, I will," Abigail said.

Mallory rushed out the door, and she found a place to sit in the foyer. Her emotions were so muddled and complicated and her mind raced with the whirlwind of those wretched events. *Why was Avery so angry? Couldn't he see that I was just trying to be helpful? Most of all, I think he was mad at himself. He had hopelessly backed himself into a corner with no way out. He must have felt trapped.*

"What happened?" Grant said as he flung open the door. "Mallory said that Avery died last night. Is that true?"

"Yes," Abigail said gravely, her head bowed.

"He was my oldest and favorite son," Grant said, sitting down hard on a bench. He brought his hands to his face and began to sob. Mallory, crying herself, sat beside her husband, put her arms around him, and wept with him for a long time. In her silence, Abigail grieved, too.

Grant, being a man of action and recovering somewhat, tried to formulate a plan in spite of his tears and agony.

"Mallory and I will take care of his body and request an autopsy, but let's make plans for the funeral together. We'll buy a coffin, send the invitations, and get the carriages. Mallory will give you some black crepe to cover the clock and drape your house. Abigail, please find suitable clothes for his burial."

"Okay, I'll do that. Would you like me to contact our minister?"

"No, we want *our* minister for his funeral," Mallory said.

ৡৡৡ

Abigail busied herself with stopping the clock at the approximate time of Avery's death and covered it with black crepe. According to convention, the clock was to be frozen in time until after his burial. She drew the curtains, closed the shutters, draped the fireplace, and twisted crepe through the chandelier. Even though Abigail wasn't necessarily superstitious, she decided to blanket the mirror with black cloth in deference to the belief that the spirit of the deceased would be forever trapped in the reflection of the glass. She didn't want Avery to be trapped but wanted him to be swiftly received into the Kingdom of Heaven. Two wreaths draped with black crepe on the front doors was the last act that indicated the house was officially in mourning.

Browsing through Avery's closet, looking for his brown frock coat, she felt the ache of broken dreams and empty promises. She remembered his engaging smile and how handsome he looked in that very coat and his brown fedora. The black patch over his left eye the day she first met him added to the mystery. Fortunately, it was only a remedy for an eye infection, as she found out later. She recalled his ambitions of being a wealthy landowner with a family living in the beautiful Maryland countryside. Then, her mind traveled to a very dark place, where she remembered his obsession with intruders and his paranoid thoughts about people trying to steal from him. The more anxious his mind became, the more he needed to drink. He created a trap for himself in so many ways.

"Oh, Avery, I am so sorry that it came to this," Abigail said as she carefully laid his favorite tie on top of the folded clothes. The last item she needed to find was his wedding ring, which he seldom wore. He claimed he didn't want to scratch or nick it when doing chores. She rummaged through his drawers looking for a jewelry box and found a tin box way, far back in his bottom drawer, a long, rectangular cigar box filled with official looking papers. She reviewed them one by one. There was a contract between Avery and his parents, a promissory note from his brother Henry, invoices for building supplies, and bank statements, but she couldn't find a will. Often, people have their attorney file a copy, so she wasn't concerned. Abigail decided to meet with her attorney, and after that visit, she would go to Westminster to talk with his attorney. Before she put the box in the drawer, she retrieved the ring she found with the papers.

The next day, six men brought Avery's closed coffin into the parlor. It was an impressive one with elaborate woodcarvings and gilded edges, which bespoke a high class. She slowly opened the coffin and touched his face, feeling the coldness and absoluteness of death. She bent over and kissed him.

"Goodbye, Avery. There was so much promise for our future together. It was cut short so fast. I'll always love you. You were my first love." Tears welled up in her eyes, she gently closed the coffin, and the deep pain of grief filled her heart.

Mallory and Grant busily prepared for the funeral. They personally delivered the handwritten invitations to their neighbors, the wealthy and ruling class of Carroll County. The black band around the handwritten card was wide and broad, expressing the depth of their loss. Abigail was motivated to sew her own black dress of expensive Parramatta silk, hoping to rise to the occasion. On the day of the funeral and every public appearance for two years and a day, she would wear all black during her "deep mourning" period. Her bonnet, her gloves, her dress and long veil would all be black.

During her "second mourning," which lasted six to nine months, she would be able to exchange the black collar and cuffs for white ones, a shorter black veil, and add a touch of white lace to decorate her dress. "Half-mourning," or the last six months, she could make subtle changes in her dress. Lavender silk, lace, colorful bonnets, more jewelry, and bolder print dresses were acceptable. Abigail thought the social mores seemed too rigid, but she chose to go along to get along, since Grant and Mallory were influential people. Being a respected daughter-in-law was more important that her individual wishes.

The funeral was held in the house Avery built. The viewing and the service went smoothly, and there was no talk about the destruction of the mine. The invitees were too polite for that. Behind their backs, however, the community spread lots of nasty scuttlebutt about Avery and his role in the explosion.

Henry, Avery's brother, came to the funeral, and he was the coordinator who organized the procession to the cemetery and the catered meal after the burial. It gave Abigail the freedom to focus on her role as the grieving widow. The hearse, embellished with black ostrich plumes on the front sides and bedecked by two brass lanterns, carried the casket and was pulled by two black stallions. The hearse had quite a presence. Each guest was provided with a carriage for his or her use, and Henry drove the carriage carrying Abigail, Mallory, and Grant.

The cemetery was a small, well-kept place near the family's church. The tombstone was exquisitely designed, with a broken column representing a life taken too soon. Avery was at peace; no more fits of rage, no more fear of thieves, no more self-torture. And Abigail was left with sorting out her emotions and memories.

こうこうこう

With all the rituals and social expectations behind her, Abigail was eager to make changes in her life. She needed to take a trip to Baltimore to visit her sisters and to meet with her attorney, Samuel Abrams. She brought the tin cigar box with all the papers, so he could help her sort out Avery's estate. She also planned to speak with Avery's attorney about his will.

Having set quite an agenda, she boarded the train at Union Bridge and headed into the city. Of course, she wore all black to verify her widowhood, but she refused to be a helpless victim. Her father encouraged her independent thinking and instilled within her an ever-present courage. Those strengths were still there and ready to be tested. What would her future hold?

Walking into Sam Abram's office brought back memories of the sale of Abbott's Confectionary. This would be another milestone he would have to help her navigate.

"Hello, Abigail," Lydia said in a pleasant voice. "Are you here to see Sam?"

"Yes, I was hoping I would find him here this morning."

"He should be coming in soon. He usually arrives between ten and eleven a.m. Have a seat."

Abigail found a comfortable place, and just as she was settling in, Sam came through the door.

"Hello, Abigail," he said softly. "It's always good to see you, but I wish it were under different circumstances. Please accept my sincerest condolences on the death of your husband. Come on in."

"How did you know about Avery's death?" she asked.

"I heard about it from Bill Garrett. How are you doing?" he asked.

"I'm holding up, but just a bit uncertain about my future," Abigail replied, taking a seat in his office. "I brought a box that I found in one of Avery's dresser drawers, and I wanted you to help me figure out his estate. I have no idea what he left."

Abigail handed him the box, and he carefully read each document. She watched him sort them into two piles.

"Well, I don't think he wrote a will, but to be certain, you might want to check with his attorney. Some of the papers have important content and some of them don't.

He pointed to the two piles he made. "These four documents are about his estate, and these are not," he said. "One of these documents is signed by Avery and his parents and states that, upon Avery's death, the land and house and the livestock will be turned over to his parents, since they own the land where the house was built. This other document is a promissory note from his brother, Henry, stating that he borrowed twelve thousand dollars from Avery last year for land speculation in Wyoming and that he promised to pay the loan back when he sells the land. Bank statements from this last year state that he has one hundred seventeen dollars in the bank. That money will be yours. The last document states that all the items in the house belong to you, but you do *not* get the contents of the barn or the shed.

"I'm leaving this marriage almost empty-handed," Abigail lamented. "The money I made from the sale of Abbott's Confectionary I used as restitution for the mine workers' loss of wages. The land and the house belong to his parents, and any money from the marital assets except for part of the money he loaned to Henry. I'm going to have to start over."

"I'm afraid so," Sam said. "Be sure to check with Avery's attorney. It's very possible that his attorney has filed his will."

"I will. Thank you for your help."

Abigail checked with Avery's attorney after she returned to Carroll County only to have him confirm what Sam told her. There was no will.

CHAPTER 10

The Exchange

❧ ❧ ❧ ❧

"Many who dance in jewels one year are shivering in the garrets the next. It was but a week ago that a respectable woman, reduced from competence to poverty by sudden calamity, traversed the streets of our city for two or three days in search of some employment by which she could earn bread for herself and her children." ~ Horace Greeley: *New York Tribune,* October 14, 1845

It was well known in the late 1800s that a wealthy, secure woman was but one man away from being penniless. Economic equality did not exist. It was a myth. Status and financial success, except for rare circumstances, was dependent on the male gender.

Abigail fell victim to this horrendous inequity. All the plans for her life backfired, and she was mired in the awful reality of financial ruin. Her sisters Mary and Louise were her only support, and they were just as surprised as she was that life dealt her such a cruel blow. They had deeply admired her because in their view she had it all—a husband who came from a respectable family, a new house in Carroll County, and a large sum of money from the sale of Abbott's Confectionary. But suddenly, everything turned on its head.

Soon after Avery's death, Abigail discovered he had left a huge financial mess in his wake. He sent most of their marital assets to his hapless brother Henry, who was indiscriminately buying land hoping to hit the "big time." All his investments came up short, and his financial dreams, as well as Avery's, collapsed. She also discovered that Avery built their house on property that was owned by his parents. Before they were married, a secret contract was signed between Avery and his parents stating that, if anything happened to him, his parents would get their land back and the house. Abigail was left out in the cold.

An evil wind encircled her like a shroud, choking out any life in her. Just thinking took effort. Where would she go from here? Her future looked bleak, and any hope-filled dreams were far away and obscured. At least she was certain that she could live with her sisters. It gave her great comfort knowing that she had shelter and a place where she could get warm food.

Incredibly, her fortune had changed so abruptly it left her breathless. Just a month previously, she secured money for Mary and Louise and herself from the sale of the family store. This money was to pay for expenses of the home they inherited from their parents, but now the tables were turned, and her sisters were *her* providers.

So many times in her young life she had turned to her good friend Rosemary and her mother Florence. A visit to her friend felt so right to her, so maybe they could advise her about what she could do. After sleeping on her idea, she woke with a clear resolve to visit her friends. Donning her widow's weeds, black bonnet and coat, she was off to confront the cold, frosty air. The trolley stop was a brisk walk from Rosemary and Florence's house.

Arriving in St. Ann's parish, she heard the train rumbling on the tracks close to where they lived. Unfortunately, they had to endure the brunt of the railroad noise as the train sped through the east side of Baltimore. Today was no exception. She quickened her pace as she got closer to their house. She smiled when she spotted it, climbed the stairs, and knocked on the door.

"Hi, Abigail," Rosemary said as she opened the door just a sliver. "Mom and I have been talking about you. We heard upsetting news about your husband, and we're trying to put the pieces together. Come in." The door opened wide, and Abigail and Rosemary hugged as they usually did, a warm, happy place for both of them.

"What did you hear?" Abigail asked.

"We heard he died suddenly of unknown causes," Florence said as she came out of her sewing room.

"Yes, he did. It's hard to say it, but I'm a *widow.*"

"We also heard he was the suspect in the explosion at the Medford Quarry. Is that true?"

"I'm afraid it's all true," she said.

"Oh, Abigail. I'm so sorry you've gone through such a hard time," Florence said as she drew her into the comfort of her arms. "You have had so much happen in your young life."

Abigail sighed, "It's so good to see both of you. One good thing is that I will be closer to you, because I'm moving back to Baltimore to live with Mary and Louise."

"You're not going to stay in Carroll County in your new house?" Rosemary asked.

"The house and land don't belong to me, they belong to Avery's parents. I'm out on my own. I'm not sure what's next."

"Did his parents buy the house from you?" Florence queried.

"No, Avery signed it over to his parents before we were married. He built the house on their land."

"Did that catch you by surprise?"

"Yes, it did. I'm all on my own now." There was a sorrow-filled pause.

"I have something that will make you smile," Rosemary said, trying to lighten the mood. "I bought some candy from Abbott's Confectionary, which you know has changed hands. I have some pralines in the kitchen."

"Pralines? I've never heard of them," Abigail said.

Rosemary left to get the candy. "Help yourself," she said, offering her some. The smell of the brown sugar and butter was delicious. They were creamy morsels, a bit larger than bite-sized, and filled with pecans. "According to David Whitman, this new candy is coming up from Louisiana, and the recipe calls for real cream. I think Pinky would have loved them."

"They are delicious, both sweet and salty," Abigail exclaimed. "Nice buttery flavor… melts in your mouth. Yes, I'm sure Daddy would have sold them in the store. How is the store doing?"

"Very well," Rosemary said, "but I miss those times

when we went there after school. Those were the good old days."

"Me, too. That was so much fun being with you and our other friends."

"So, what's next in your life?" Florence asked.

"I don't know," Abigail said with a sweet smile. "That's why I came to see you. I thought you and Rosemary would have some good ideas. After all, that's what friends are for, right?"

"I have something I'd like to show you," Florence said as she retrieved an item from her sewing room. "This is wedding lace that I had repaired at the Woman's Exchange in downtown Baltimore. They have excellent craftsmen there. Surprisingly, they are able to make a living wage with their handwork. Women meet together to learn from each other. Their needlework, crocheting, smocking, knitting, and lacemaking are the best that I've ever seen. I can picture you making beautiful *dentelle aux fuseaux* for the wealthy ladies of Baltimore. You have fine hands for such delicate designs."

"I appreciate your confidence in me, but do they have teachers that can train me? I've never done it before, so I'll be starting from the bottom."

"I would think so, but I don't know for sure. I have seen the ladies meet in groups and share ideas. You'll have to check that out for yourself," Florence said. "I know that you have the ability and most of the basic skills. I think you ought to give it a try."

ಇಳ ಇಳ ಇಳ

Wearing her best black dress and bonnet, Abigail took the streetcar to the corner of North Charles and Pleasant Streets. The Woman's Exchange was a bustling place. It was ten o'clock in the morning, and the cooks were already making food for the lunch crowd. Having read the menu in the glass case near the front door, she drooled over the entrees of a variety of soups served with warm bread and butter. Other offerings were soft-shelled crabs, sock-eyed salmon with cucumber slices, kidney-giblet stew, a chicken salad plate with deviled eggs, and the famous Baltimore crab cakes.

Also, the desserts sounded particularly delectable. Included on the list was a French dessert called "floating island," butterscotch and lemon tarts, *and* Charlotte Russe. She raised her head from the menu because her nose was lured by the onion-peppery smells of the oyster stew and clam chowder cooking in the cast iron pots. They were open for lunch until three o'clock in the afternoon. As she peeked through the window, she spotted an older, official-looking lady with pen and paper in hand. She opened the door.

"Hello, my name is Abigail," she said.

"Nice to meet you, I'm Mrs. Harmon Brown. Are you here to purchase something from the Woman's Exchange?"

"No, I am thinking about participating with your group. I am here to find out more about your organization. Before I was married, I purchased a tablecloth and linens for my trousseau. Now, I'm looking for a way to support myself, and I'm hoping that the Woman's Exchange can help me."

"I see you're wearing widow's weeds. Have you been a widowed long?"

"A little more than a month. A friend of mine suggested that I check out the Woman's Exchange for selling handwork and heirlooms. How long have you been in operation?"

"We've been doing this work for about nine years now, and our Tearoom is getting more business than we can handle, so we need help there. We have quite an array of handwork and crafts for sale as well. What kind of handwork do you do?"

"I have sewing skills, but my friend thought I would be best suited learning how to make lace," Abigail said.

"There's a big demand for lace, so if you do quality work, you should be able to make a good living. There is someone who works in the mornings upstairs who makes exquisite bobbin lace. If you're interested, plan on coming here about nine o'clock tomorrow and you can meet her. Her name is Julia Scott."

"I'll be there at nine o'clock," Abigail said as she reached out to shake her hand. "Thank you, Mrs. Brown.

Abigail had endured so much over the last two months. She had one heartache after another, and this was the first time she had a little glimmer of hope. She noticed a lightness in her step that she hadn't felt for a very long time. On one level, she was pleased that David Whitman was doing well with his candy store, but on another level, she hoped maybe he would want her to take it back. Her common sense told her that she needed to leave that behind her and find another path.

The mission of the Woman's Exchange was to help women who were impoverished by life's circumstances, and that was *her* life in a nutshell. Being able to live with her sisters was creating a safe harbor for her as she moved forward. Life was hard, but at least she had a place she could call home, and now, maybe, she had found a place where she could make a living.

Nine o'clock the following morning came quickly. Her happy steps were matched only by her eagerness to meet Julia Scott and to find out more about the Woman's Exchange. As she walked in, she spotted Julia sitting in the corner, soaking up the sun's rays and concentrating on her lace-making. Her hands moved quickly as she picked up and moved the bobbins to form the lace pattern. Even Abigail's movement toward her did not disrupt her focus. The rapid movement of bobbins and pins looked like she was playing a minuet on the piano. Abigail sat down to watch the symphony of gestures. She was an older woman whose hands were bent with arthritis; nevertheless, those fingers moved with the suppleness of youth.

"Hello, are you a lace-maker?" Julia asked as her fingers stopped and her eyes met Abigail's.

"No, but I want to be. I'm hoping you could get me started. Mrs. Harmon Brown told me you would be here."

"Would you like me to give you a lesson?"

Abigail nodded. Julia dug into her bag of supplies and pulled out a hard, round, covered pillow and a box of pins, some embroidery floss, and a couple dozen bobbins. She threaded the bobbins and hung them on the pins.

"I'll have you start with a bookmark. Here, you take over."

Feeling like she had ten thumbs, Abigail picked up the bobbins and waited for her instruction.

"Now, cross the threads with the bobbins, and then place the pins in the marked pattern and cross the threads again. Repeat this over and over again until you see a pattern emerge." Abigail did just as Julia said and was excited to see the design appear.

"Well, you seem to be picking it up quickly. With some practice, you'll do well. You seem to be a natural," Julia said enthusiastically. "I'm usually here three days a week, Monday, Wednesday and Friday," she added. "You can join me anytime."

"I'll see you on Friday, then. Maybe at that time, you can let me know where to get the supplies."

Abigail left, knowing this was something she could learn. The prospect of being able to make a living by lace-making intrigued her. It would give her some dignity. Women working in a factory were treated like chattel, and she did not want to suffer that humiliation. After all, she was used to being her own boss. She wanted nothing less for herself.

"Abigail, I have something to ask you," Mrs. Brown said as she was about to leave. "We need some help in the Tearoom tomorrow. Would you be willing to come in from noon to three?"

After a considerable pause, she replied. "I think I could. What do you want me to do?"

"I would like you to wait on tables. Have you ever done that before?"

"No, I've never been a waitress, but I owned a candy store, and I know how to serve customers."

"You owned a candy store ... in Baltimore?" she asked.

"Yes, Abbott's Confectionary."

"I bought candy there for the holidays for years. Someone

in that store really knows how to decorate for Christmas. My husband bought a heart-shaped box filled with chocolates for me on Valentine's Day. My, my, isn't it a small world." She shook Abigail's hand with even greater respect.

"I'll see you tomorrow at noon," Abigail promised.

❦ ❦ ❦

Abigail was reminded of the story of the Phoenix, which she learned in high school while studying Greek Mythology. After the bird died, it was reborn and it rose from the ashes to fly off into its own renewal. Abigail felt like that, too. The horror of the last few months was like the death of her spirit, but she felt a yearning, a desire to create a new life within her that would be even more radiant.

Today she would be a waitress and get a better understanding of the Woman's Exchange. Three other women and Abigail met in the kitchen. Their job was to take the orders and bring the food to the tables. Easy enough. Abigail watched the ones with more experience, namely Jane and Susan. They put on aprons, slipped a small tablet and pencil inside the pocket, and filled the water pitchers. Before the guests arrived, they covered each table with a crisp, white, linen tablecloth, graced the table with fresh flowers and carefully positioned each place setting. Even though their menu was limited, they were painstakingly elegant in the presentation.

She knew she would have to muddle through her first day, so she sharpened her skills of observation to learn the tricks of the trade. The customers entered the Woman's Exchange to a room filled with displays of new lace handwork, needlework, crafts, and heirlooms for sale. In the next room was the dining area crowded with impressive ladies from Baltimore and beyond. The laughter and lively conversations were contagious, and the kitchen was abuzz with food preparations.

"Good afternoon, ladies. Would you prefer clam chowder or oyster stew?" Abigail asked.

"We're from New York, and we've heard that your clam chowder rivals ours. We'd like to give it a try," the lady with the plumed hat said. Abigail called in her orders, waited for the high sign, grabbed a serving tray with the soups, breads, and beverages, and navigated through the crowd to her table. Abigail felt the pressure to perform, and wanted to impress Mrs. Harmon Brown. The huge psychological blows she experienced over the past year resulted in unearthing deep insecurities. Nevertheless, she pushed herself to perform, but still, there was something in her that yearned for the private office she had as a bookkeeper.

She felt intimidated by the patrons at the Tearoom … maybe it was their elegant deportment. Their feathered hats, furs and gloves denoted status and wealth. Even their overpowering perfume bothered her. Abigail was nervous, which was manifested by her shaking hands and awkward fingers. As she set the hot soup on the plates, the lady with an ostrich plumed hat made a quick turn with her head and the feather knocked the bowl out of Abigail's hand. Steaming chunks of hot soup decimated the feather and dripped down the side of the woman's dress.

"My heavens! You clumsy girl! Oh no! My hat has been ruined," she moaned. Standing up abruptly, she knocked the chair over, the sound reverberated through the dining room. Abigail blushed. The lady took the hat off her head and looked at it.

"Well, my plume looks pretty sick, but at least *I* didn't get burned," she said. Abigail grabbed a napkin and gingerly picked off the chunks of soup, wiped her dress and feather, making it as clean as she could.

"I'm sorry, madam," Abigail said sheepishly.

"Oh, don't worry, child. It seems that Baltimore's chowder has it all over ours," she quipped. This made the ladies laugh. Even Abigail chuckled as she went back to the kitchen to get another bowl of soup.

At 3:30 in the afternoon, when the serving time was over, Mrs. Harmon Brown called a meeting. She talked briefly about when they would get their pay and then questioned them as a group. "How many of you would like to be a waitress tomorrow?" All the other women nodded their heads, but Abigail was silent. "I'll see you then," she said to the others. When they left, she gave Abigail a nod suggesting that she come closer.

"Was it a tough day for you?" Mrs. Brown asked softly.

"Yes, I was nervous around the customers."

"Well, maybe you would prefer working for the catering service we started. We make food for the fishermen going out in the morning and for boaters who give holiday excursions for their patrons. That means you would have to arrive at six o'clock in the morning. Would you be interested?"

"Yes, I would like that. I've always enjoyed preparing food."

"I won't be in that early, but Mildred will be here fixing the picnic baskets with you."

❧❧❧

The next day, Valentine's Day, would have been the first anniversary of her marriage to Avery. She woke up in the dark, recalling the calamitous experiences of her past year. What a tragic outcome for an event that had so much promise.

Living with her sisters was quiet and predictable, just what she needed now. Life seemed more manageable in her solitude. She did her weeping in private and noticed that the episodes of intense sadness seemed to get farther and farther apart. She would be able to earn a living through the Woman's Exchange by selling her lace, needlework, and food preparation. By bringing home some money, she could contribute to the expenses of the house. Today, she was up early, harnessing the horse for the buggy ride to the Woman's Exchange. Soon dawn appeared and touched the sky with pink roses. It was a beautiful morning in spite of her personal mourning.

When she got there, she found the Woman's Exchange still locked. Nobody was there. Where was Mildred?

"Are you Abigail?" someone said as they walked briskly toward the building. Abigail turned around to see a little old lady.

"Yes, I am. Are you Mildred?"

"Yes. Well, let's get the job done."

Abigail smiled. She might be older, but she was feisty. Mildred opened the kitchen door, picked up a sheet of paper, and read the order sheet out loud.

"We've got five picnic baskets to make this morning. We'll do the orders for the fisherman first, since they stop by about seven o'clock to pick them up. Put three jars of clam chowder wrapped in warm towels in the baskets along with a heated stone, sardines and crackers, banana bread, and cooked vegetables. You get the jars of soup and the sardines, and I'll get the rest."

Abigail bustled around the kitchen, getting the fire going in the wood stove to heat the soup. After pouring the warm soup in the jars, she covered them with warm towels and placed them in the baskets. That certainly would taste good after fishing the Chesapeake. She wrapped the smoked sardines and crackers in waxed paper, and Mildred handed her the bread and the jar of steamed vegetables. She placed the hot stone inside each basket, along with some napkins.

"Please put these three baskets out on the front porch with the cash bag, and they'll pick them up," Mildred said. "Abigail, you have made my job so much easier. Thank you. When you come back after the delivery, we'll start on the two baskets for the boaters."

"One of the fishermen was waiting for his basket, and he paid me directly. The other two baskets are still there," Abigail said as she returned.

"Good. Just set the money on the table. The picnic baskets for the boaters are fancier. Sometimes they even bring along wine for their adventure. We'll make deviled eggs, liver pâté sandwiches with relish, and of course, macaroons and petit fours. The desserts have already been made, so you make the sandwiches, and I'll do the deviled eggs. Then, those baskets will be done."

It took Mildred and Abigail a little over an hour to make the picnic baskets.

"Would you be able to come tomorrow?" Mildred asked. "We have eight baskets to get ready tomorrow."

"I'll be here at six o'clock," Abigail replied.

❧❧❧

Once again, the day started early, but she enjoyed sharing the kitchen with Mildred, who was a hard worker. The two of them were early risers, and they knew how to tackle a kitchen. Day-by-day, Abigail gained a greater appreciation of the Woman's Exchange.

"A mix-up happened yesterday," Mildred chuckled. "One of the boaters picked up the basket of sardines instead of the petit fours and macaroons. The lady in the boat took exception and dumped the sardines overboard, but the fisherman that took their basket was more than pleased. They took a liking to the macaroons and pâté sandwiches. Ha-ha! All in a day's work! By the way, Mrs. Harmon Brown said she needs you in the lunchroom tomorrow. I'll miss you."

"I'll miss you, too," Abigail responded. "It has been fun waking up in the morning with you."

❧❧❧

Perhaps it was the esprit de corps of the Woman's Exchange or maybe the hubbub in the kitchen that helped her keep her grieving at bay, but whatever it was, Abigail looked forward to the days when her name was on the lunchroom schedule. Even though she was wearing all black in contrast to the others with their crisp, white blouses, she felt like she belonged to this group.

Eight ambitious women "aproned-up" and worked together: two on set-ups, two on soups, two on bread, and two on desserts. Each woman could have done her job while sleeping. That was true for Abigail, because her job was making the clam chowder. She spent the morning chopping onions, carrots, potatoes, and celery, and once the chopping was done, she made the soup base with thick cream, butter, and flour. It took lots of stirring and an abundance of patience.

"Hey Abigail! Hand me the chopping block," Esther commanded. "Looks like you're done with it." Esther was an impossible punster, a bit mischievous, but the two of them liked each other. They had an unwritten bond.

"You got it, friend," Abigail said without hesitation. "Trying something new with the oyster stew?"

"Yeah. I'm adding fresh garlic and celery today. We'll see if the guys like it. Did you hear about the Italian chef that died?"

"No," Abigail said.

"He pasta away," Esther said, laughing at her own joke.

Abigail knew she had been outwitted, so she retaliated in kind. "What did the French chef give his wife for Valentine's Day?" she asked.

"I don't know," Esther said, playing along.

"A hug and a quiche! Have you heard about the sauna that serves food?

"Nope," Esther said.

"Their specialty is steamed mussels." They both laughed at that one.

"You're getting pretty good at this," Esther said.

"I got them from the *Ladies Home Journal.*"

Finally, the noisy lunch crowd arrived as the kitchen crew made their final touches on the fixings. Some of the waitresses went upstairs to take the orders from the ladies in the Tearoom, and the other ones went to the basement to a counter-style restaurant called The Down Under Club, for men only.

Ever since the Exchange moved into the new headquarters on the corner of North Charles and Pleasant Streets, they had expanded their lunchroom options. Upstairs, they had the elegant Tearoom with white linen tablecloths for the ladies. It became a place for non-Baltimoreans from Western Maryland, Washington, and the Eastern shore to meet, have lunch, and go shopping. Some deposited their luggage and bags at the Woman's Exchange and then reclaimed them before leaving on the train. It had a reputation for being a safe meeting place for travelers.

The men became envious of the good food that was served exclusively to women, so they cajoled them into making lunch for them in the basement. This was a boon for the Woman's Exchange and, in the year 1888, the profits made from the lunchrooms surpassed the money made from the handworks.

The Woman's Exchange movement was proliferating along the eastern seaboard and throughout the Midwest. The success was unanimous. The spirit of philanthropy was alive and well, creating a wellspring of opportunities for women in need. This phenomenon was frequently highlighted in newspaper articles. One such article was published in *The Richmond Exchange.* The local Exchange boasted that nationwide over one million dollars had gone into the consignors' hands in the past twelve months. The change in attitude about "women's work" was translated into prosperity for these women, all of whom were destitute at one time or another. The Woman's Exchange was hailed as giving women the magic to turn tears into smiles and stones into bread.

෫෫෫

The catering service suited Abigail, since she enjoyed working with Mildred, but Mrs. Harmon Brown had other plans for her.

"I need someone in the consignment shop next week," Mrs. Brown said. "I'll be there but will need help because the Abell estate is being settled, and they've donated heirlooms to the consignment shop."

"I don't know anyone by the name of Abell," Abigail said naively.

"Arunah Shepherson Abell owned *The Baltimore Sun*," she replied. "He died last year, and they're tying up the loose ends of his estate."

"What kind of heirlooms did he donate?"

"We'll see. I'm not sure, but a wagon full of them is coming on Monday. Can I count on you to be there at eight o'clock in the morning?"

"I'll be there," Abigail stated energetically.

So far, her experiences with the Woman's Exchange had been lace-making, waitressing, cooking, catering and, now, it had come full circle with her once more minding the store. Rubbing shoulders with Baltimore's elite was an unexpected advantage of being a part of the organization.

Early the next morning, with no one around, she rode up the cobblestoned streets to the Woman's Exchange. It was like she discovered this place all over again. She looked at the grand old building, standing four stories tall, built around 1815. It featured a Gregorian architectural design with reddish brown brick and black shutters in contrast to the white trim. The curved archway above the door created a graceful entrance. Creaking sounds from the doorjamb reminded Abigail that the upper stories were boarding rooms, and the sounds and smells were from hard use. The steps and floors were white marble tiles bespeaking an earlier elegance. Inside the consignment shop, the high ceilings were sheathed in pressed tin, while wood wainscoting covered the lower part of the walls. Ambitious crews of women were good stewards of the building, because they made sure it was cleaned and painted when necessary. The salesroom of the consignment shop was lovely and clean. Finding this place on North Charles Street would sustain its mission for the women of Baltimore.

"Well, hello Abigail," Mrs. Harmon Brown said warmly. "You're right on time."

"I'm looking forward to learning about this part of the Woman's Exchange," Abigail responded.

A creaking of wooden wagon wheels alerted them that the items had arrived. Mrs. Brown ran outside to direct the cargo to the side of the building, and Abigail followed her. The wagon was filled to the brim with boxes and containers of unknown items.

"This might be like going on a treasure hunt," Abigail said smiling.

One by one, they began carrying the boxes to the basement for sorting. Mrs. Brown and Abigail did most of the lugging, but Neil, the coachman, helped with the heavier ones. The smells from the boxes hinted at their previous location. The telltale musty smell of a basement was on some of the items, and others had absorbed hay and straw smells. The most pungent was the moldy smells from boxes with water stains. This started Abigail on a sneezing fit. She fished in her pocket to find a hanky. Then, she started her quest by finding the biggest box on the top section of the stack. She rocked it back and forth enough to destabilize it until it came down toward her and her body braced it against a fall.

"Oh, my! What is this?" she exclaimed as she opened up the box. "This must have been cages for something—something with feathers. There are dried bird droppings stuck to fuzzy remnants on the bottom."

Mrs. Brown looked her way and laughed uproariously. "Mr. Abell was quite the character," Mrs. Brown said. "He was known for getting the news out fast, so he used everything, including carrier pigeons. He also used trains, ships, and pony express. Nothing was off limits. My husband told me he even created new routes with the *New Orleans Daily Picayune* to get the most current information on the Mexican-American War. In fact, he heard about the U. S. victory at Veracruz before the White House did. I wonder what else we'll find in these boxes."

The next box Abigail opened was much smaller and smelled almost sweet. Inside Abigail found two baptismal dresses, one made with white silk and adorned with petite red rosebuds and another made from unbleached linen embroidered with a green leaf pattern. Underneath the dresses were two sets of darling crocheted booties.

"I wonder if the family made a mistake donating these?" Abigail asked.

"I don't think so," Mrs. Brown said. "They have culled through most of these heirlooms already. Abigail, please grab the ledger and write down what you think would be a fair selling price. We allow some dickering, but the price has to be reasonable. We'll fill in the amount paid, and that's how we check on profits over the years and the amount of inventory we had over the past year."

She came over to watch as Abigail began her list. "You've got a nice hand. I can easily read your figures, so I'm hoping you can be the bookkeeper for this project. You might need to go before the Board of Directors to inform them of this shipment."

Abigail didn't object and, deep down, she was pleased that Mrs. Brown trusted her.

"We'll work for another hour, and then we'll call it a day."

Abigail opened a colorful hatbox next and found a treasure chest of splendid jewels. Cameos, heart-shaped lockets and fresh water pearls, which were keepsakes that at one time adorned the necks of lovely ladies. The most intriguing among them were the delicately carved intaglios of Roman gods, goddesses, and nymphs.

Her nose was drawn to the penetrating smell of eucalyptus. To her surprise, at the bottom of the hatbox, there was a rather large box made of eucalyptus wood. Inside there was a set of scrimshawed tusks with vignettes of an African safari and seafaring scrimshaw with delicate scrollwork on whalebone. It was evident that Mr. and Mrs. Abell traveled the world to have acquired such an array of jewels and relics. The cost of these artifacts would be anybody's guess, but Abigail did her best to determine a fair price.

"Well, let's stop for today," Mrs. Brown said. "Can I plan on you for tomorrow?"

"I don't have anything planned, so I'll be here."

Abigail gathered her belongings and left for the day. It was a bit of a walk to her horse and buggy, and the sky was an inky black, conjuring up a storm. Her footsteps quickened, and she hoped to get home before the rain came, but as her pace accelerated, she heard footsteps coming up behind her. She turned around to see who it was.

"Abigail," a familiar voice shouted. "I have to ask you something." By this time, she was close enough for Abigail to recognize her. It was Florence.

"Hi, Florence. Is everything okay?"

"Yes," she said, catching her breath. "How is everything at the Woman's Exchange?"

"It's going very well. Thank you so much for the suggestion. What can I do for you?"

"I need someone to make lace for a wedding so I thought of you. It's a gold lace made from pure gold, so I need someone who knows what they're doing. I thought of you. Do you have time to spare?"

"I'll make time for you, because you've helped me so much. How much do you need?"

"I need twelve feet."

"Twelve feet? That's a lot," Abigail remarked. "When do you need it?"

"I need it by the end of the month."

"That's possible. What's the pattern of the lace?"

"I have a sample in my purse, but I would like you to come over and see the dress before you start."

"How about right now? I'm eager to see this dress. It must be magnificent."

"Yes, I'm using spun gold."

Florence and Abigail hurried to the carriage to beat the storm, but it was not to be. As they climbed into the buggy, torrents of rain slammed against it, and thunder rumbled. The hood of the carriage was extended, but it failed to protect them from the slanting downpour. By the time they arrived at their destination, they were drenched from head to foot. Rosemary started to put her arms around Abigail to greet her but pulled back because she was dripping wet. Rosemary helped her remove her cape, skirt, and shoes. She placed them carefully by the fireplace to dry. The smell of wood smoke from the fireplace was warm and cozy.

"Would you like some tea to warm up?" Rosemary asked. Abigail was happy to see her friend again, relieved that their friendship was something constant in the midst of all her changes.

"Sometimes you know me better than I do myself. You're right; I could use some hot tea right now."

Rosemary went into the kitchen to get the tea going, and she had some crumpets in the cupboard as well. Tea and crumpets on this cold, rainy day sounded good to her. Florence and Abigail relaxed in their petticoats, warming by the fire. "Rosemary, what have you been doing?" Abigail asked, curious about her relationship with Mathew.

"Not a whole lot," Rosemary said. "Thanks to Mom, my sewing business is doing well. The two of us have built a good reputation. Well-known Baltimore families choose us when they need elegant dresses for special occasions. You'd think it would be scary working with them, but most of the time they are very nice people. The dress with the gold lace is for one of the Bryce girls. She's getting married in June."

"How is it going with Mathew?" she asked. "Anything new?"

"Not a thing. We see each other once a week or so. We go to sporting events around the city, mostly baseball games."

They chitchatted a bit more about their lives and also about the Woman's Exchange. It was a wonderful treat for Abigail to relax by the fire with her friends. It would take a little while for her skirt and shoes to get dry.

"Florence? Whose buggy is that outside?" a gruff male voice shouted as he stomped up the back stairs.

Florence rose to greet her husband. Abigail was caught off guard. After all, it had been quite a while since a man had seen her in her petticoat. Was it Don?

"Abigail is here checking out the lacework I need her to do," Florence said.

"My, my! What do we have here?" Don said, looking at Florence and Abigail.

"You never know what we do when you're gone," Florence said, laughing.

"Maybe you shouldn't stay away so long!" Rosemary teased. All was said in jest, because she knew her dad was in Pennsylvania helping his parents with early spring planting. He was always helping somebody.

"We got caught in the rainstorm and got drenched," Florence explained. "Our skirts are drying by the fire."

"Abigail, it's so good to see you. I haven't seen you in a 'coon's age.'" Abigail was primed to shake his hand when he swirled her around and up into his arms and gave her a big bear hug.

Don always had a special spot in her heart, even when she was a youngster. Rosemary's daddy was her second daddy when she was in elementary school with Rosemary. Don was a victim of the railroad strike of 1877. President Hayes dispatched soldiers to reopen the Baltimore & Ohio Railroad. One of the soldiers split his skull with the butt of his rifle, and he suffered a severe head injury from that blow.

Abigail remembered so vividly the horror of that strike, which was known as "The Great Upheaval." Over one hundred railroad workers were killed, and nothing was gained. At a tender age, her sense of fairness had been violated. The wages of those hardworking men were reduced for the third time. The angry railroad workers rioted to defend their dignity and secure their livelihood.

Don was never the same after the injury. He lost the vision in his right eye, and that side of his face was paralyzed. The left side of his body was severely weakened as well. His facial disfigurements gave him a demonic appearance, but even though he lost so much during that nightmarish time, his heart was golden. He protected and loved his wife and daughter with everything he had. No longer able to work, he helped his parents and anyone who needed a hand. In so many ways, Abigail was his other daughter.

"My wife keeps me informed. Much has happened in your life!" Don said. "Are you doing okay?"

"Yes, I'm doing fine, thanks to your wife. She's the one who suggested that I get involved with the Woman's Exchange," Abigail responded.

"I hate to interrupt, but I have to show Abigail this dress before she leaves," Florence said. Abigail followed her into her sewing room, and she immediately noticed the dress on the mannequin. It was a stunning creation, simple and elegant. Sheer cream-colored fabric lined with satin was complemented by a V-neckline and snug bodice. A slightly asymmetrical seam running down the front of the gown offset the V-neckline. It had a uniquely modern look.

"It's beautiful!" Abigail exclaimed. "Where are you putting the lace?"

"The spun gold lace will follow the V-neckline and the seam line down the front, and then around the bottom of the dress," Florence explained.

"Will twelve feet be enough?" she asked.

"Yes, I measured it twice," Florence said as she handed the gold thread to her. "I got a shipment of gold thread from New York City yesterday. It's expensive, and I don't want any waste, so I ordered less than what we need. When you know exactly how much you'll need to finish, let me know and I'll order some more."

"I'll let you know. My friend Julia Scott will be at the Exchange tomorrow, and I'll see if she can help me with the project."

"Let me check to see if your skirt is dry," Florence said as she walked to the fireplace. "Yes, it sure is, dry *and* warm. A hot fire is the fastest way to dry clothes." They slipped their skirts over their petticoats and were greeted by a little snicker from Don and Rosemary.

All dressed and dry, Abigail approached Rosemary and Don. "Goodbye, Rosemary, see you soon," she said with a hug. "Don, it's been good to see you again. Take care of yourself and my good friends, okay?"

"I'll take care of them, don't you worry," Don said with a smile. "You take care of yourself, too. Hopefully, I'll see you soon."

A warm hug followed. Abigail stepped outside their

home, relieved to find that the storm had cleared, which made her ride home much easier.

❧❧❧

Most of the work was completed for the Abell estate. The boxes were emptied, and her exhaustive lists of items and estimated prices were compiled. Abigail was careful to be as accurate in her descriptions and pricing of the items as possible. She wasn't sure what else needed to be done.

"Good morning, Mrs. Brown," Abigail said cheerfully. "What would you like me to do this morning?"

"Well, we have to clean the items to get them ready for consignment. Once we've decided which ones to sell, we'll put a price on them and take them upstairs to the shop."

Most of the articles cleaned up nicely with a damp rag, but the ones with mold spots needed special bleach added to the water. It was interesting to see how Mrs. Brown made the choice of which ones to sell and which ones to store. Since both Christmas and Valentine's Day were past, those were stored, but spring and summer items were at a premium, so they were set aside to go upstairs. Pricing the articles was the next step. Abigail handed Mrs. Brown her estimated pricing sheet. She put on her spectacles and scrutinized the list.

"Very well done, Abigail," Mrs. Brown said. "We are in need of a new treasurer, since our current one is resigning at the annual meeting. Would you be interested in taking on that role?"

Abigail was stunned by the offer. Mrs. Harmon Brown had the reputation of being a no-nonsense Quaker woman with high standards. *I'm surprised that she thinks that I could do the job. I don't know if I can manage the task—it seems much more complicated than Abbott's Confectionary.*

"I don't know what to say," Abigail answered. "Thank you for your confidence in me, but let me think about it, and I'll let you know tomorrow."

"That would be fine," Mrs. Brown said. "Let's get these cleaned-up objects upstairs in the consignment shop, and then we'll be done for the day."

Having been released for the day, Abigail found a copy of the bylaws for the Woman's Exchange. In the document, she found a job description for the treasurer. It read:

"The Treasurer shall collect, receive, and have charge of all the funds, and make disbursements of the same, subject to the approval of the Finance Committee. The Treasurer shall keep an accurate account of all moneys received and expended, shall present to the Board a monthly report showing the condition of the finances, and shall also make an annual report to the Board."

Abigail had to do some clear thinking and make an honest self-assessment. Would she be up to doing the task? Mrs. Harmon Brown's endorsement gave her confidence, but was that enough? She remembered all the years of being a bookkeeper at Abbott's Confectionary and recalled how successful the business was.

She decided at that moment she would say "yes" and work diligently to do right by the Woman's Exchange. This was a wonderful opportunity.

CHAPTER 11

Bill Garrett

❧❧❧❧

Abigail went to the annual meeting and found a seat in the back row. When the elections resumed, Mrs. Harmon Brown nominated Abigail for the position of treasurer. Someone seconded the nomination, and they voted. Abigail received a huge majority, which was a credit to Mrs. Brown's sterling reputation.

Abigail took her assignment very seriously, even though it was much more complicated than the bookkeeping she had done for Abbott's Confectionary. There were hundreds of women—clerks, consignors, waitresses, and cooks—who worked at the Exchange, and the payroll alone took her six hours to complete. To secure their privacy and to spare them the shame of poverty, they did not list names. Instead, they gave each woman a number, and those numbers organized her books and payroll records. The mission of the Woman's Exchange was to create an environment that protected the dignity of all the hard-working women there. They were employed by the Woman's Exchange due to a reversal of fortunes, which caused them to fall victim to the vicissitudes of life.

Hour after hour after hour, for a year, Abigail worked on the books, making sure her handwriting was even and legible and her numbers accurate. She worked hard at the Woman's Exchange, and the time went by quickly. She wanted to prove to Mrs. Brown that, when she nominated her for treasurer, she made the right choice.

Finally, the dreaded day came. She was expected to stand in front of the board of directors at the annual meeting and give the treasurer's report. She dressed in her very best black dress and added a white lace collar with a brooch, since she had just begun her "second-mourning" period. During this time, jewelry, white lace, and even lavender dresses with brooches were considered appropriate. It was hard to believe that two years of full mourning were already behind her.

The large meeting hall at 333 N. Charles Street filled with people. The board consisted of ten members, all of whom were women. This was innovative for the times and made way for feminine leadership. The three well-heeled men served, but without voting privileges, since they were *only* in an advisory capacity. This was a dramatic departure from tradition. The majority of the women on the board were wealthy women from Baltimore who had a penchant for charity. Abigail was the exception, since she was under their employ. Life's misfortunes ensnared her, and she had to struggle up from the bottom.

At seven o'clock, the meeting commenced. Ten proper, well-dressed ladies sat in a row near the front of the hall.

Having dined and imbibed at The Horse restaurant, the three good-humored men entered the room loudly, and found their seats to the right of the row of women. Abigail conveniently found a spot in the front row facing them. Patiently, she waited for her turn to give the treasurer's report.

She glanced at the men, and to her surprise, she spotted a familiar face. *Would he recognize me? Do I look okay?* She began trembling, and her papers rustled as her hands shook. *I must get myself under control. I'll take some deep breaths, and I'll imagine I'm in a calm place … like a meadow.*

"Abigail, please read the treasurer's report," Mrs. Harmon Brown said.

Wrestling herself out of her deep reflection, she stood up and read the summary of the numbers she had worked on all year. She practiced her presentation so much it was almost memorized. So, in spite of her nervousness, it went smoothly. When she told them there was a surplus of funds, they interrupted their usual decorum with applause.

"Respectfully submitted," Abigail said to punctuate the end of her report. The women on the board responded to her conscientious presentation with titters of appreciation. Abigail sat down, relieved that the report had gone well.

She carefully raised her head to sneak a look at Bill Garrett, whose eyes were fixed on her. He smiled. She demurely smiled back and quickly glanced away. She had not seen him for over two years and the memories of him brought back thoughts of those difficult times. The destruction of Medford Quarry, restitution for the mine workers, and Avery's drinking and ultimate death came rushing through her mind.

She waited patiently for the meeting to adjourn and then accepted the handshakes and compliments of the women on the governing board. As she turned around to leave, she saw Bill Garrett standing just behind her.

"Good to see you, again, Abigail," he said. "How have you been?"

"I'm doing well, now that the treasurer's report is finished."

"How long have you been with the Woman's Exchange?" he asked.

"It's hard to believe, but it has been almost two years."

"I've been advising the board for about two years now. I haven't seen you."

"I've been doing other jobs like waitressing, cooking, and lace work," Abigail shared.

"They have you doing a lot of different things. You *are* in demand."

"Are you still working for the railroad," Abigail asked.

"Yes, I enjoy my work, so I'll be there for a long time. Do you see yourself at the Exchange for a long time?" he queried.

"I like my work, but some days are better than others. Today was a good day."

Bill, emboldened by their easy conversation, decided to pose a question.

"Abigail, I would like to see you sometime."

"I don't think it's possible now," Abigail said, clearly uncomfortable with his statement. "I'm pretty busy being the Treasurer for the Exchange," she said as she hurriedly said good night while slipping out the front door. *Why does he want to see me? I'm still in mourning.* Abigail hopped in her buggy and headed home, trying hard to slough off the unwelcomed complication. She forced herself to focus on going to work the next day.

৯৯৯

"Good morning!" Mrs. Brown said. It was hard to believe, but the next day had already arrived. "There's a surprise for you on the counter."

Abigail noticed red roses carefully arranged in a crystal vase gracing the counter. Beside the vase was a white card trimmed in gold that read,

Dear Abigail,

I would be pleased if you would accompany me to the Annual Railroad Baron's Ball the evening of Saturday, March 7, 1891.

Cordially,

Bill Garrett

R.S.V.P. by March 2, 1891

"Oh, Mrs. Brown, what should I do?" Abigail exclaimed, her hands covering her mouth. "I'm still in mourning, and I shouldn't be doing anything social like that."

"Your feelings do matter as well," Mrs. Brown said. "Are you done grieving?"

"I don't feel deeply sad any more, but what will people think?"

"Do you feel that you've grieved enough?" Mrs. Brown said in a gentle voice. "What you think about yourself is just as important. What I have seen with women at the Exchange is that they work through their grief sooner."

"So, what you're saying about mourning is that it depends on the individual?" Abigail asked.

"Yes, when women have to work hard for a living, they don't have a lot of time to feel sorry for themselves. Life becomes a very practical matter."

"Do you think it would be proper for me to go?"

"It's up to you, whether *you* feel ready or not," Mrs. Brown replied.

"I'm curious about Bill Garrett," Abigail said "All I know about him is from his involvement with the destruction of the railroad supplies at Medford Quarry. He did a good job representing the railroad company, and was able to quiet the crowd. He was an effective leader. What do you know about him?"

"Well, he comes from the well-known Garrett family of Baltimore," Mrs. Brown said. "Elizabeth Garrett, who is a very generous philanthropist, is a distant cousin. She is credited with starting the Bryn Mawr School for Women, and John Hopkins University Medical School is indebted to her because she was largely responsible for the initial funding. We were recipients of her help, too. She was a board member about five years ago. Her father, John Garrett, owned the Baltimore & Ohio Railroad, so they are wealthy, and fortunately for us, generous with their money. She was the only daughter of John Garrett and the "apple of his eye." Philanthropies and railroading seem to be in their blood."

"So, *that's* how he got involved in the railroad industry!" Abigail said. "Has he been married before?"

"No, he was engaged a few years ago. The women on the board were so excited for him. She was a lovely lady from England, but she fell ill and died after a trip to Africa. They assume it must have been Sleeping Sickness."

"Oh, that's terrible," Abigail said sadly.

"It seems like he's finally coming out of his grief, kind of like you," Mrs. Brown said. "Perhaps the two of you are coming out of your grieving periods at about the same time."

"Well, that's too much to think about right now," Abigail said. "I've got to get to the books. The month of February has to be organized."

❧ ❧ ❧

Abigail put off the decision as long as she could, because it was such a difficult one. Wisely, Mrs. Brown left the decision up to her, but it was hard to reflect on it, because so much pain surfaced. *Am I done grieving? Does a person ever get over something traumatic like a loss of a husband, especially under those horrible circumstances?*

Abigail recalled a letter from a reader published in the *Ladies Home Journal.* It made so much sense to her. The writer said you could tell when you are coming out of grieving, because your thoughts shift from the gloom of the loss to thinking about future dreams. The Woman's Exchange had been a perfect place to keep her financially viable, to use her skills, and to meet new people. The Exchange also helped her formulate new goals and dreams. Maybe it *was* time to make even more changes to live life to the fullest.

In all honesty, she hoped that she would be given a second chance at love, and maybe even have a family. When she locked up those dreams, she lost her zest for living. Giving her dreams permission to surface energized her and gave her a freedom that she hadn't felt for a long time. Yes, this was the time to start living again. Yes and yes, she was ready to mobilize those dreams

She would R.S.V.P. in the affirmative by March 2, 1891.

⋩⋩⋩

It was time to visit Florence, her "other mother," and Rosemary, her best friend. Their friendship was a stabilizing influence whenever there was a big change in her life, and maybe they could help her sew a lavender-colored dress. She would start wearing something other than dull black.

Abigail carefully bundled up to survive the bitter cold weather and caught the streetcar to St. Ann's Parrish. Climbing up the steps to their house, she had a premonition that something was wrong. She knocked, but no answer. *I don't even see their buggy here. Something must be wrong.*

Determined to see them and wanting to know what happened, Abigail decided to wait an hour in one of the chairs on the front porch before she would head back home. The damp cold went right through her, so she was happy to see her friend Rosemary coming up the road in a buggy just five minutes later.

"It's so good to see you," Abigail said. "I'm pretty cold."

I had to bring Mom to the hospital," Rosemary said. "She had severe pains in her abdomen. I came back home because a customer is dropping off a dress for alterations."

"Oh, I'm sorry to hear that! Is she going to be okay?" Abigail asked. "Do they know what the problem is?"

"They think it might be her appendix, because the pain is on her right side," Rosemary said, shaking her head. "She's probably going to have to have surgery."

"Oh, that's too bad. It sounds like she'll be laid up for a while."

"I don't know how I can manage without Mom," Rosemary said, tearing up. "But our customers demand perfection, and the work must be in on time."

"Maybe I can help you," Abigail offered. "I have time in the evening, and I can do some handwork for you."

"That would be wonderful!" Rosemary exclaimed. "A friend in need is a friend indeed. Are you sure you have time?"

"Yes, I can make it work with my schedule. I have time now, so is there something I could take home to work on?"

"There is a gown that has to be hemmed, and they need it by Monday," Rosemary said.

Abigail left with the gown inside a garment bag, caught the streetcar back to her home, and began working on the hem. With the unexpected turn of events, she knew that she couldn't burden her friend with sewing a dress for her, so she never even mentioned it. By helping out, she would be returning the favor of all their kindnesses over the years. They had always remained generous and thoughtful. It felt good to be the giver rather than the receiver for a change.

She would have to purchase her dress for the ball,

and she recalled a beautiful lavender dress in the store window at Hecht Brothers. She decided she would check it out the next day.

అప అప అప

Her eyes were glued to the statuesque mannequin in the Hecht Brother's window. It was an elegant dress made of satin and lace. The bodice was gathered at the waist with a large bow in the back. The neck was a high-collared lace design with covered buttons decorating the lace inset. It was a modest dress, which is what she wanted. There was no cleavage or off-the-shoulder skin showing, but it was still lovely. *Could I see myself in that dress? I'm so used to black now that a lavender dress would be a big change for me.* Abigail thought about relinquishing her black mourning attire and changing to lavender trimmed with off-white. It felt right. Opening the door to the clothing store and trying on the dress would be taking the first step toward her new life.

Abigail met the sales clerk, pointed to the dress in the window, and divulged her size. She stepped into the dressing room to slip on the dress. The attendant fastened the many buttons in the back and tied the bow. Abigail cocked her head in the mirror and, in her mind, acknowledged that lavender was not her best color. Her skin and hair color did better with browns, yellows, and certain shades of blue, but, she had to admit that lavender was better than black and the off-white lace around the neck and hair made her look okay. The bodice fit well, and she admired her small waist and good-sized bust. She concluded that she was attractive enough to go to the Baron's Ball with Bill Garrett. The hem had to be shortened, so the clerk called the tailor over to take the measurements.

"I'll have the dress shortened and pressed in two days, and it will be ready to be picked up," the tailor said.

"Thank you," Abigail replied. "That will be fine."

Finding the dress was the first big step, but now she had to let Bill Garrett know that she would accompany him. She wrote a note of acceptance on lavender parchment paper and sent it to him.

☙☙☙

The night of the event came, and she put on her new dress and added a cameo at the center of the lace around her neck. She pulled her hair into a gentle upsweep with a loose bun in the back. Looking in the mirror, she smiled at her newfound elegance and approved of her "post-mourning" self. The doorbell rang, and her older sister Mary answered the door.

"Good evening, Mr. Garrett," she heard Mary say warmly. "I'm Abigail's sister, Mary. Please do come in."

Looking down from upstairs, she noticed Bill Garrett enter. He looked all spiffed up, with his tall, silk hat, stiff, white-collared shirt, a cravat, and impressive black frock coat … what a sight to behold! He carried himself with authority, and he had done a masterful job with his facial hair. He had a neatly trimmed, full beard, and a drooping mustache.

"Good evening, madam," she heard Garrett say. "Is Mrs. Avery Johnson here?"

"Yes, she'll be down shortly," Mary said formally, reacting to his formal manner.

Abigail slowly walked down the stairs. The lavender satin dress was modest but moved gently as she carefully found each step to the bottom of the stairs. She felt lovely in her new dress and appreciated by Bill ... emotions that she hadn't felt for a very long time.

"Good evening, Abigail," he said, bending to kiss the top of her gloved hand. "You look beautiful."

Mary handed Abigail's hooded, woolen cape to Bill, and he placed it around her shoulders. This special moment didn't need words. Abigail offered only a warm smile as she slipped her arm through his. They walked to the carriage silently, he took her hand, helped her up, and off they went to the Railroad Baron's Ball.

When they arrived, Abigail could see carriage after carriage bringing noblemen and wealthy heiresses from far and wide. The air was electric with anticipation as they made their way to The Tremont Grand Ballroom. Elegant chandeliers welcomed them as they walked through the halls bedecked with elaborate frescoes and embossed ceiling tiles. Round tables, seating eight, had been carefully set with flowers displayed in porcelain vases.

Amid the diamonds, emeralds, and rubies, Abigail felt so very plain. Her tastefully tailored lavender dress paled in comparison to the brilliant reds, emerald greens, and sunbursts of yellow. Nevertheless, she sensed Bill Garrett was proud to be with her and treated her like a queen. He introduced her to dignitaries in the transportation industry and other influential members of the railroad community. Following the sumptuous meal, dancing began.

"May I have this dance?" Bill Garrett asked confidently.

"Yes," she said, matching his confidence. She stood, touched his hand, and they moved gracefully toward the dance floor.

He wrapped her up in his arms and twirled her around the floor. She just knew he would take care of her always and forever. Light as a fresh breeze, Abigail felt free from the constraints of mourning and her past life.

In so many ways, he was stronger than she was, socially confident, well respected and financially secure. Most of all, she liked the way he treated her. Even at the beginning with Avery, she had never experienced that level of respect and care.

Maybe he will be the next chapter of my life.

࿇ ࿇ ࿇

Life took a welcome turn. Bill Garrett's courting started as a quiet, dignified affair. Mary and Louise invited him for a humble Sunday meal at the Abbott household, a pot roast dinner with potatoes, carrots, and onions complemented by a Jell-O salad. His social versatility was always apparent. He could dine with the three Abbott women as easily as he could with the Baltimore elite.

"Do you know how I met your sister?" he asked Mary and Louise.

"We just know that it was a couple of years ago," Mary responded.

"She found herself right in the middle of a quarry and a railroad mess," Bill continued. "Workers were fuming with anger, so Abigail sized up the situation and developed a plan that calmed the protestors. She helped the workers and saved the quarry. Your sister is quite a remarkable young lady."

"Her husband didn't make it," Mary said.

"Yes, that was a very sad outcome," he responded with concern. "I'm sorry that happened."

"Sad events happen in life, but we move on, always trying to make life better for tomorrow," Abigail said with conviction.

"Let me tell you what happened to me a couple of years ago. I asked Mary Thorpe to marry me. I love that name Mary," Bill said as he smiled at Mary. "She went to visit her aunt in Sierra Leone before we married, and she came back very ill with a fever. The doctor said it was either Yellow Fever or Sleeping Sickness. She struggled to stay alive for two weeks, but she was overcome. Everyone who knew her, especially me, deeply mourned her. My Mary was an independent and spirited young lady, very much like Abigail in that regard."

"Mrs. Harmon Brown told me you lost Mary at about the same time I lost Avery," Abigail interjected. "I wasn't sure I wanted to go to the ball with you, but she advised me to decide for myself and determine if I was ready. Mrs. Brown thought we were at the same place in our grieving."

"So, *she's* the one who encouraged you to accompany me. I'll have to make sure I thank her. The way you turned around and walked away from me when I talked to you after the annual meeting, I was sure the answer was going to be 'no,' but that wasn't going to stop me," Bill said with a chuckle. "I like strong-willed women."

After dinner, Mary and Louise cleaned the dishes and then offered to give Bill a tour of their home and garden in back. They had filled the upstairs with mementos from their parents, Martha and Pinky, and their former family business, Abbott's Confectionary. The bedrooms were adorned with splendid handmade quilts and graced with crocheted doilies on each nightstand. To visit the garden, they had to follow a brick path to a fenced-in area. Mary and Martha spent hours plowing, planting, fertilizing, and weeding their vegetable and flower gardens. Because of their hard work, the rows were perfectly plumb, and the plants were strong and healthy.

"This is one of the nicest gardens I've seen," Bill uttered. "Thank you for the tour." With that unexpected compliment, Mary and Louise smiled from ear to ear.

"When is Abigail going to visit *your* family?" Louise asked impulsively. When Bill fixed her with an appraising look, she blushed. "I know you like strong, outspoken women, so I took the cue."

"You're beginning to understand me," Bill said, smiling. "I'm hoping your sister will be able to meet my family next Sunday. Would that work for you, Abigail?"

"I was planning on visiting my friend Florence after church. She just got home from the hospital."

"Oh, in that case I would be honored to take you to church, and I can wait in the carriage while you visit."

Abigail smiled at his courtesy. "You are such a gentleman. How could I refuse you?"

❧❧❧

That Sunday morning, Abigail woke with some trepidation. What would Bill Garrett's family be like? The consolation for her was that he chose her for the right reasons and not for her money or status. He saw her at the worst time in her life, but he respected her nevertheless. Her strengths intrigued him, and that was his most endearing quality.

At this juncture, there was a *comme ci comme ca* feeling about their relationship. If it would work out, that would be great, but if it didn't, that would be okay, too. She knew that whatever happened, she could stand on her own two feet. Taking that perspective alleviated the fear she might have about the family visit.

His carriage arrived promptly at nine o'clock. He met Abigail at the door and helped her with her coat. She smiled as she tucked her hand through his arm. They were all smiles as they rode to church. Once inside, heads turned as they walked down the aisle to sit in an empty pew. Church attendance seemed to be familiar to Bill, since he seemed comfortable with the order of worship. After the church service, it was time to pay Florence a visit. Abigail was anxious to see how she was doing. Like a true gentleman, he helped Abigail out of the carriage and, as promised, he waited for her in the carriage.

"Hello, Abigail," Rosemary said. "Are you here to see Mama?"

"Yes, how's she doing?"

"Not so well," she whispered. "Her appendix ruptured, and she was very sick. The doctor said she is getting better, but it'll be a long recovery."

"How are *you* doing?" Abigail asked.

"This has been a trying time for both of us."

"Let me know if I can help you with the sewing," Abigail said.

266

"Thank you. It would help so much if you could hem another dress. Do you want to see Mom?"

"Yes, but only if she's up to it."

"The medication gives her headaches, so please talk quietly," Rosemary said as she opened the bedroom door.

"Abigail, my dear. It's so good to see you," Florence said with a thin voice.

Abigail smiled at her dear friend and nodded to Don, who was standing guard beside the love of his life. Abigail cared deeply for both of them, and it was hard to see them stressed by the post-surgery complication.

"Has it been a difficult recovery for you?" Abigail asked.

"Yes, it has," Don chimed in. "She's been battling an infection that just doesn't want to go away."

"Is she out of danger?"

"I hope she is," Don said emphatically. "Her fever is going down a little bit every day, so I believe my favorite gal is getting better."

Florence looked at her husband and gave him a wink.

"Thank you for helping Rosemary with some of the sewing," Florence said. "She's been overwhelmed with all the work."

"You're welcome. You both have helped *me* so much, I just want to return the favor. You better get some rest now. I'll see you at another time. I'll come back soon." Abigail squeezed Florence's hand and gave Don a hug.

"Thank you for taking such good care of my 'other mother.'" Abigail said.

On her way out, Rosemary handed her another garment to hem. "I'll need it after next weekend. Thank you, Abigail."

Bill saw her leave the house, readied the carriage door,

and lifted her inside. They headed north to Roland Park, where Bill's family had just recently built one of the first homes in a newly planned development. A circular driveway curved gracefully in front of a two-story Georgian-styled home. The balanced lines framed with pilasters outlined the brick and wood structure, and the chimney at each corner of the house added to the symmetry. There was noticeable warmth about the place. Margaret Garrett, Bill's mother, greeted them.

"Abigail, welcome! I have heard so much about you," she said, opening her arms for an embrace. "Come in."

In the back part of the house, there was a playful sound of children dashing about. The noise stopped, and then laughter, followed by shouts of, "You're it!"

"Camille! Andrew! Susie!" Margaret called out. "Come here. I want you to meet our guest."

"Is it Abigail?" they asked with child-like enthusiasm.

"Yes," Margaret said. The children scampered to meet her.

"Uncle Bill said he met a lovely lady, and that she would be coming to Sunday dinner," Camille said, curtsying. "It's nice to meet you."

Andrew followed suit, "It's nice to meet you," he said, bowing like a gentleman.

Little Susie gave her a big hug. "Uncle Bill said you're a very nice lady."

"Oh, what a wonderful welcome! Thank you, children," Abigail said as she smiled at Bill.

"Bill's sister, Virginia, is traveling with her husband, so the three children are spending time with grandma *and* grandpa," Margaret said. "Well, my husband, Paul should be down soon, he's in his study. We usually have dinner promptly at one o'clock in the afternoon. I'll finish up in the kitchen."

"May I be of help?" Abigail asked.

"Let me show you around, first," Bill said.

The tour was perfunctory, but what surprised Abigail was how bright the colors in the house were. Some walls were a wine red, the kitchen a pale yellow, and the living room a French blue and white. It was a happy, welcoming place, so different from the dark-green walls and mahogany furniture in her family house.

"Dinner is ready," Margaret announced. "Abigail, you can sit between Bill and Paul, and the three children each have their own spot on the other side of the table. Where are the children?"

Abigail heard the study door open, and the children ushered their grandpa to the dinner table, giggling all the way.

"Children, you can sit with me on the other side of the table across from Abigail and Bill," she said.

"Dad, I'd like you to meet Abigail Johnson," Bill said.

"Welcome to our home," his father said. "Bill has told us a lot about you. It's good to meet you. He even told me how you met. Now, *that's* quite a story."

Dinner conversation was a fun, chatty affair with adult laughter and children's giggles. Paul and Bill shared stories that verged on the preposterous. Abigail enjoyed the family banter so much that she felt like part of the family. She didn't want the visit to end.

"Well, it's time I take you home," Bill said.

"I had a wonderful time. Thank you," Abigail said to Paul and Margaret. She looked at each of the children and gave them a hug. "I liked getting to know you as well."

Arm in arm, Bill brought her to his carriage. During the ride home, they replayed the time spent with his family. The antics of the children made them laugh all over again.

"Abigail, have you ever been to New York City?" Bill asked.

"No, I haven't."

"I'd like to take you there next month. There are two places I'd like to show you."

"Will you tell me, or are you going to keep it a secret?" Abigail asked.

"I'll give you a clue. One is the tallest and the other is the tastiest place in New York City. How does that sound?"

"It sounds like fun. You *do* bring out the child in me."

CHAPTER 12

Harvest Moon

ശ്രശ്രശ്ര

The days slipped by so quickly when Abigail was with Bill. The relationship was such an easy one, and she laughed most of the time when he was around. Laughter was something she thought would surface only on rare moments. Her last memories of truly joyful laughter were in the candy store with her friends after school.

What she liked most about Bill was how the children gravitated to him. Sunday dinners became a weekly routine, and they frequently played tag with Camille, Andrew, and Susie. The play was rowdy and replete with giggles and laughter.

Even when Bill was with his friends and other adults, he embodied respect and fair play. His colleagues in the railroad industry introduced him as a key person, someone who was able to make good decisions. They described him as "unflappable." Historically, his family had substantial philanthropic interests and had particular interests in medicine and institutions of higher learning. Margaret, his mother, was an impressive, intelligent, and well-read woman. Most importantly, she was kind and a trusted advisor and a confidant to her husband, who was also a very important person in the railroad industry. Their view of the world was an expansive one, which was very different from Abigail, who had always lived in Maryland. What Abigail found most appealing was their mission to serve others and to make the world a better place for all.

"We'll be going to New York City the beginning of next week if that works for you," Bill announced on the carriage ride home from dinner one Sunday. "Are you ready for an adventure?"

"I'm always up for an adventure with you, but please give me some details," Abigail insisted. "How long will we be gone?"

"We'll be there about four days, so bring some comfortable walking shoes."

"You mentioned the two 'ts'. What were they, again? Oh, I remember. The tallest and the…"

"Tastiest," Bill interjected, "and it's the tastiest that I like best! We'll be taking the Baltimore & Ohio Royal Blue Line to New York City. That line has been on the tracks for only about a year."

"So, I need to bring comfortable shoes. Should I be prepared for rain, too?"

"Probably that would be a good idea. Bring your water-proof parasol, and a warm cape," Bill instructed. "I'll bring the carriage to your house around nine o'clock, so we can catch the ten o'clock morning train to New York City."

As usual, Bill came around and opened Abigail's door and helped her down, but this time, she gazed at him just long enough to prompt him to kiss her. Her heartbeat quickened, overpowering her attempts to keep her emotions tucked away. They both sensed a change, and he wrapped his arms around her in a big bear hug; his embrace was warm and strong, convincing her that he had what it took to keep her out of harm's way. Kissing him made her heart feel huge inside. They separated with a smile, and arm in arm, they walked up the stairs.

"I'll see you Monday morning at nine," Abigail said as she waved goodbye.

ȣȣȣ

Monday morning couldn't come soon enough for Abigail. She scurried around packing this and then unpacking that—she wanted everything to be just right. After all the frenzy, she sat down and her commonsense took over. She decided that being practical was the best way to go. Her nightgown, her toiletries, her comfortable shoes and her warm cape, and her jewelry were carefully placed in her carpet bag. With some hesitation, she found her favorite evening gown tucked way back in her closet, and with some hesitation, she packed that, too. It was a bit provocative with some shoulder and cleavage showing. Her thoughts would turn to Bill and her anticipation of spending almost a week with him in New York City.

A Hansom cab, with its driver on top, pranced up to her front door. Bill jumped out, grabbed her carpet bags, placed them in the back hatch, and hurried around to join her in the cab. His enthusiasm matched hers as they embarked on their New York adventure. Arriving at the depot, Abigail immediately noticed the Royal Blue Line on the tracks outside the cab window. With its deep royal-blue color and gold-leaf filigree trim, it looked massive and elegant. Clearly, it was designed for wealthy dignitaries, maybe even royalty. The interior was just as majestic, with its mahogany paneled walls and royal-blue carpets with ceilings to match. Ornate gold filigree highlighted the curves and lines of the Pullman car. Such grandeur was more than she expected.

Abigail and Bill settled into two plush seats and viewed the rolling landscapes as they passed through the countryside. The train movement and the scenery mesmerized them. They sat as close as they could without being improper, and both felt they had known each other their whole lives.

"Which New York hotel did you choose?" Abigail asked.

"Do you really want to know, or do you want it to be a surprise?" Bill teased.

"If I didn't want to know, I wouldn't have asked you."

"We'll be staying at the Fifth Avenue Hotel. In my estimation, it doesn't get any better than that," Bill replied.

"I've read about that hotel in *The Baltimore Sun*. It seems to be the gathering place for many famous people."

Bill looked at the scenery passing by them. "We've already gone through Philadelphia, so it won't be long before we see the skyline of New York City."

"Do you spend a lot of time in the city?" Abigail asked.

"Yes, I come here about once a month for meetings," he said. "It's a wonderful city. There's always something new. I'm never bored. The planners of the city set aside some land, and Frederick Olmsted designed a large park called Central Park. I want to show it to you. They had foresight, because, now, there's so much building going on that park land is disappearing. Oh, I forgot to tell you. There will be a ball at the hotel later in the week. Hopefully, you brought a ball gown. If you didn't bring one, we'll have to go shopping."

Abigail smiled. "My practical mind was working, so I did bring a ball gown, but does that mean we won't go shopping? I would enjoy going shopping too," she said.

"If you want to go shopping, we will. There it is!" Bill pointed out. "The New York skyline. It *always* inspires me."

Abigail peered at the uneven rectangular buildings. At first, they looked small, but they grew into huge skyscrapers as the distance decreased between them and the city. The smell changed too. It reminded her of the smell of coal dust near a smelter, or rail yard. The bustling sounds of the city intensified with each mile, as they approached New York City.

The train chugged to a halt, and Abigail and Bill disembarked. The porter from the Fifth Avenue Hotel noticed them and placed their luggage into the carriage and transported them to the hotel.

"I chose this hotel because it's known for the best service in town," Bill said. "Each room has a private bathroom and its own fireplace. I've always been pleased with the place."

The driver drove beneath the outside portico of the main entrance of the impressive Italianate building trimmed with extravagant amounts of white marble. It was the quintessence of elegance. The porter gathered their luggage, and Bill opened the carriage door for Abigail. Arm-in-arm, they walked through the front portico into this grand hotel.

The lobby offered a visual smorgasbord: rich crimson and green velvet curtains draped large windows outlined by lavishly gilded wood. Warm rosewood panels highlighted the richly brocaded wallpaper. On the wall by the reception area, a well-appointed portrait of the Prince of Wales greeted them. The statement underneath the portrait read: "The Fifth Avenue Hotel is a larger and a more handsome building than Buckingham Palace."

The porter escorted them to their rooms on the fifth floor. They rode the elevator powered by a steam engine and a revolving screw they could see on the ceiling of the passenger cab. Only a locked door separated their adjoining rooms. The rosewood theme continued throughout the high ceilings in the bedrooms. Abigail's room had gold brocaded drapes and navy wallpaper with gold flocking. For Abigail, it was the most opulent place she had ever seen. Soon after she had taken off her shoes and stretched out on her luxurious bed, she heard a knock on the door.

"Who is it?" Abigail asked.

"It's Bill. Can I come in?"

Abigail was silent, because she knew this was a pivotal moment. From this point on, the terms would change. "Let me get my shoes on first," she said as she fussed and dawdled over getting them on her feet. Slowly, she walked toward the door and opened it. "Come in."

"I'd like you to be my guest at a little deli on the Lower East Side of Manhattan. I have looked forward to their pastrami on rye sandwiches for a month. They are *so good*—probably the tastiest sandwich I've ever had!"

"What *are* pastrami sandwiches?" Abigail asked, laughing at his gusto.

"Pastrami is highly seasoned smoked beef that is cured up to thirty days. The Iceland Brothers started this little deli on Ludlow Street in 1888, and they've perfected pastrami on rye."

"I'm not sure I'd like spiced meat. Do they have anything else?" Abigail queried.

"Yes, they have lots of different meat sandwiches, *and* they have egg creams as well."

"I know I'd like *that*. Let me get my purse—and my comfortable shoes."

They enjoyed a fun evening walking to the Iceland Brothers' Deli and trying out the sandwiches. Bill seemed to travel with ease from the lap of luxury to the grind of immigrant neighborhoods. He made Abigail laugh as they walked down the streets together, hand in hand. Their respect for each other was always there, but now their shared affection added a wonderful dimension.

After the "tastiest" day, the next day would be the day of the "tallest," and Bill wanted to surprise her with that secret. They dressed warmer to brace themselves for the chill that was in the air.

"Where are you taking me today?" Abigail asked in the cab.

"You'll find out in just a few minutes. We are almost there."

Bill helped her out of the carriage, and she noticed the impressive building that was in front of her. Fortunately, her bonnet was tied on, because she tossed her head back to find the top of the building. There it was, in the clouds some twenty stories up!

"What building is this?" she asked.

"This is the New York World Building, also known

as The Pulitzer Building," Bill said. "This is the head-quarters for the *New York World* newspaper, owned by Joseph Pulitzer. The newspaper empires had a competition about who could build the tallest building. The New York World Building beat out the Tribune, the old Times Building, and it's even taller than the spire of Trinity Church next door. Let's go to the top."

"I'm game," Abigail said enthusiastically.

The elevator ride to the top was smoother than the one in the hotel. The twentieth floor had a dome with a three-hundred-and-sixty-degree panoramic view of the city. They could see the Trinity Church spire, the East and Hudson Rivers, the other two newspaper buildings, and the Brooklyn Bridge. They could also see Central Park and the rest of the city's skyline. It was a breathtaking sight!

"Well, we've done the tastiest and the tallest and, tomorrow, we can go shopping if you want," Bill offered.

"I would very much like to go shopping," Abigail said, "but *only* if you're interested."

"It would be my pleasure," Bill said, bowing slightly and smiling.

Back at the hotel, they had a nightcap after supper and talked at length about what they saw twenty stories up. They discussed the different architectural styles that caught their eye and marveled at the variety. The two of them agreed that it was a wonderful day, and they walked back to their rooms holding hands.

"I had a fantastic time. Thank you," Abigail said.

"I really enjoy being with you," he said as he kissed her on the cheek. That wasn't enough for Abigail, so she turned her head and they kissed again on the lips, not wanting the night, or that kiss, to end.

ॐॐॐ

The next day was "shopping day," and Bill and Abigail caught a cab to the Ladies' Mile. This mile was created mostly for women's shopping needs. Exquisite department stores side-by-side occupied the entire street, each containing a myriad of beautiful dresses and breathtaking jewelry. Abigail had to pinch herself to make sure she wasn't dreaming through this part of her life.

The businesses there had built an elevated train that transported people from store to store. This area was considered safe for women to shop by themselves. On the train, they passed the Ehrich Brothers' store, B. Altman & Company and Tiffany & Company, to name just a few.

They made their first stop at Ehrich Brothers. The inside of the store was five floors packed with freshly designed dresses and jewelry. Abigail's eyes were transfixed on displays at the jewelry counter.

"I'll take you to Tiffany's for jewelry," Bill said. "They have better quality and more of a selection."

"I'll go check out the ball gowns, then," she said.

The sales lady ushered her to a private dressing room and asked her what kind of dress she wanted and had her describe the occasion. The service was excellent. Bill sat in an overstuffed pink boudoir chair, waiting patiently for "The Abigail Fashion Show." Because it was early autumn, the sales lady suggested that velvet would be a good fabric choice. She went into another room and came back with three elegant dresses on padded hangers, one red, the other bronze, and yet another in emerald green. Each one had a distinctly different style. Abigail tried on the red one first. Her shoulders and cleavage showed, and what she liked most about the gown was the sleek skirt made with less fabric. She went out to show Bill and to get his opinion.

"Wow, that's very becoming on you!" Bill exclaimed. "You look like a princess."

Abigail blushed demurely. "I'm not sure I'm ready for this," she said.

She tried on the bronze-colored one next. The collar covered the whole neck, with billowy sleeves and a full bustle in the back. She didn't like the gown, because it looked too old-fashioned. Without modeling it for Bill, she took it off and just shook her head at the sales lady.

The emerald dress looked more promising. It had a square neck and an empire waist with long sleeves. She tried it on and showed Bill, but he shook his head. They both agreed that it was time to move on to another store.

B. Altman's was another store on the train route. A six-story building with high, arched windows on the first floor that had all the amenities Abigail could ever want. The sales lady gave a personal greeting to Bill, which indicated that she had seen him many times before. He introduced Abigail to her, which prompted even better service.

During their walk to the dressing rooms, Abigail described the kind of dress she wanted, and the sales lady found just the perfect gown in royal-blue velvet. It was simple but elegant. The blue velvet was so soft, and the color reminded her of the royal blue on the train. The bodice cinched tight around the waist with a design that was slightly off the shoulder and trimmed with white lace. Abigail loved it. The gown was sexy and pretty at the same time. She modeled it for Bill, and he wholeheartedly approved. The sales lady carried it to the counter, and Bill paid for it, something Abigail guessed he would do.

"We have one more stop, and then we'll come back to pick up the gown," Bill said to the sales lady.

"Certainly, sir," she said, nodding her head in deference.

Tiffany and Company was a store that contained perfectly crafted jewels. It often was referred to as "the Palace of Jewels." Abigail couldn't take her eyes off the diamonds and the sapphires.

"Why don't you look for a necklace that will complement your gown?" Bill advised. His suggestion helped her focus, and she found three beautiful necklaces that were more than suitable.

"Bill, I can't decide between these three. Would you please make the final decision?" Abigail asked.

One was a single pearl on a silver chain, and another was a faceted sapphire on a silver chain. The third one, which for Abigail was really too expensive, was a string of pearls with a star sapphire in the center. Bill admired each one, then, carefully put each necklace up to her neck. He cocked his head to determine which one he liked best, making Abigail giggle.

"I like the pearl and sapphire necklace best," he announced.

His choice surprised her, but she was ecstatic. It was the most beautiful, but also the most expensive. "I don't know what to say," she said. "Your generosity is overwhelming."

Bill smiled. "It's the least I can do … considering the one who will be wearing it."

Abigail blushed, and her lip quivered. She was too overwhelmed to speak at that moment. *It's hard to believe, but Bill respects me even though my life was so messy when I first met him. He must be able to see my love for him inside my heart.*

The two of them headed back to the hotel for dinner with shopping bags in tow. It was a pleasantly exhausting day. After a brief time together, Abigail retired for the night. She dropped into bed and slept soundly.

જાજાજા

Deciding to sleep in on her last day in New York City, she immersed herself in all the luxuries that were around her. She knew that the following day she would be back in Baltimore, going to work, and living in her humble abode with her sisters. Bill had a few people he had to call on, so he didn't knock on her door until two o'clock.

"Would you like to go for tea?" he asked through the door.

"That would be nice, since I haven't had breakfast," she said.

Arm-in-arm, they glided downstairs to the small dining room prepared for tea and crumpets.

"Are you often a two o'clock 'lazy daisy'?" Bill asked in jest.

"No, only when I have a lot to think about," she said

"And, fair lady, what do you have to think about?"

"I'm trying to figure out why Bill Garrett is treating me like a queen," Abigail said coyly. "I don't deserve it."

"Clearly, you don't see what I see."

"What *do* you see, kind sir?" she asked.

"I see a beautiful, intelligent young lady who rose

above difficult circumstances. I see a diligent treasurer who has garnered the respect of the women at the Woman's Exchange. I see someone who, when confronted with the misery of the quarry workers, had compassion. I see someone who is generous and warm-hearted. Most of all, I see someone with whom I want to spend more time."

Abigail blushed and looked at him, teary eyed. "Thank you," she said quietly.

Bill smiled contentedly, realizing that what he said made an impact on her. He had those feelings bottled up inside for a long time, just waiting for the right time to say them.

಄ ಄ ಄

Getting ready for the ballroom event could not be rushed, and bathing in her private bathroom felt so luxurious. The hotel offered luscious perfumes, so she infused them into her bath water. She savored the full sweetness of the rose scent as she soaked in the warm water.

Time flew by. She closed her eyes and considered the events of the past few days, until she heard a knock on her door. Her eyes opened wide, and she wondered who it might be.

"Who is it?" Abigail said firmly.

"Madam, I'm from the hotel staff. Mr. Garrett asked us to check to see if you needed help with your gown."

"What time is it?"

"It is five o'clock, Madam. Dinner is at six o'clock."

"Please come back in thirty minutes," Abigail instructed. She dried off and put on a small bit of dusting powder, and put cream on her hands. She quickly flipped the petticoats over her head and tied them. Her corset was the next piece of apparel, which she fastened tightly in the front. Combing her long auburn hair was the first step in securing a fashionable upsweep. Taking hairpins off the vanity, she placed them where her fingers felt loose hairs. As she laid her long white gloves over the chair, she heard a knock on the door.

"Come in," she said.

A young lady in a long, black dress covered by a white, starched apron walked in. "Madam, may I be of service?" she asked.

"Please help me with my dress," Abigail said.

The lady, careful not to mess up Abigail's hair, lifted the gown over her head and fastened the many buttons in the back.

"You look beautiful, madam," she said.

"Thank you," Abigail said politely. She reached inside her jewelry box and gingerly lifted her new necklace out of its cushioned box. Marveling at it one more time, she gave it to the attendant to place around her neck and fasten the catch.

"Oh, madam, this is a *perfect* match for your dress!" the woman gushed.

Abigail did have to admit that everything came together well. This was so much better than her widow's weeds. She put on her white gloves, collected her purse, and sat on a chair waiting for Bill's knock.

"You may leave now. Thank you for your help," Abigail said to the attendant. As she opened the door, Bill entered and offered her a tip for her work. Abigail was so pleased to see him.

"Here's the 'dinner bill,'" Abigail quipped.

"You're in good humor tonight," he said.

"Yes, and it's so good to see you!" she said. "Hungry?"

"Always," he replied.

The dinner buffet was a lavish affair with a warm ambience generated by candlelight. Overhead chandeliers were turned off, and the dim lighting enhanced the food. The appetizers and entrees were delectable and arranged artistically. First, the appetizers replete with colorful salad greens, other fresh vegetables, and a variety of cheeses. Maine lobster, prime rib, and Chicken Marsala comprised the main courses. Au gratin potatoes, stuffed peppers, and green beans followed. The steam transported the rich savory smells of the meat, cooked to perfection. The dessert table was magnificent with five different kinds of trifles. The triple berry trifle, Abigail's favorite, caught her eye.

The staff switched on the electrified chandelier above the center of the dance floor as the dance music began to play. An outstanding string quartet provided the music for the evening. Abigail's flamboyant blue dress was striking, but she felt nervous and self-conscious. *Would anyone here know that I am a widow? Am I being impertinent or improper?*

The smooth, lovely sound of the music beckoned her to dance. They played waltzes, slow dances, and a new dance called the "sliding two-step." Bill and Abigail watched the accomplished dancers twirl around the floor, while Abigail summoned her courage.

"My dear Abigail, may I have this dance?" Bill asked with a slight bow.

"Yes, my dear Bill," Abigail replied. "It would be a pleasure."

The first piece they danced to was a beautiful waltz with a myriad of dips and swells. The quartet stressed the three-four rhythms, and Bill confidently moved Abigail around the floor. Like so much in their budding relationship, he handled himself with poise and grace. His aplomb and optimism drew her to him. His formal embrace signaled to her that he was in charge and yet attentive to her. When another waltz began, they stayed on the dance floor. Just as the music swelled, to her surprise, Sam Abrams, tapped Bill on the shoulder to take his place with Abigail.

"Hello, Abigail. How's everything going?" Sam asked.

"Very well," she said. "What brings my Esquire to New York?"

"I did some business in the city today, so I'm staying the night," he said. "I knew the two of you were going to be here, so I wanted to say hello." The music subsided. "My dear, thank you for the dance. I'm sitting at the table by the quartet. Why don't you and Bill stop by, and we'll have a toast."

"I'll mention that to Bill," Abigail said and walked back to their table a little bit wary. *Would he be possessive like Avery?*

"Wonderful! You danced with my good friend, Sam," Bill said.

"Yes, I did, and Sam wants to do a toast at his table," she said. Arm in arm, they headed to his table. Bill and Sam shook hands and, as they sat down, Sam asked the waiter to bring a bottle of champagne to his table. There was no indication of jealousy.

"I'd like to toast my good friends, Abigail and Bill," Sam said gallantly when the champagne arrived. The waiter filled their flutes. "May Abigail and Bill always bring out the best in each other."

"I don't know about bringing out the *best,* but Bill *does* bring out my fun side," Abigail said, laughing.

Later that evening, they said goodbye to Sam, and as a tribute to their relationship, they danced one last dance before heading back to their rooms. They floated around the dance floor enthralled with each other. It was heavenly. This dance signaled the end of the night of wining and dining. Holding hands, they walked to the elevator to take the ride up to their rooms. In the elevator, Abigail recognized someone from the Woman's Exchange in Baltimore. This woman looked at her from her feet to her head, giving her a silent condemnation. Abigail wanted to disappear through a hole in the floor. *Maybe this woman saw me in full mourning dress and doesn't think I'm ready to wear jewels, a gown, and go out to dances. She just doesn't understand.*

Bill sensed Abigail's distress and held her hand close to him. The elevator ride to the top of the hotel seemed to take forever. Bill held her close as he escorted her to the room.

"I don't feel well," Abigail said.

"I'm sorry that happened," he said. "What can I do for you?"

"Please, just stay close to me tonight."

"I will, my love," he said as he kissed her.

After all the excitement of seeing New York City on the top of the Pulitzer Building, the good food at Iceland Brothers' Deli, and the fabulous shopping spree on the Ladies' Mile, that kiss proved the most loving memory of their time together. Bill's strength and understanding melted her heart as they lay together on her bed wrapped in each other's arms until morning.

❧ ❧ ❧

The usual Baltimore routines resumed when they returned. Abigail went back to her work at the Woman's Exchange, and Bill continued his job running the railroad. Except for the ache in their hearts from being apart, life went on as usual. Sunday afternoons at the Garrett house were a highlight of their week, and Bill became a familiar face at the Abbott household as well. He liked Mary's cooking, especially the pot roast and pies.

They strolled in the parks, took afternoon excursions on the waterways of Baltimore, and, occasionally, took the train into Washington, D.C. They enjoyed picnics, musical performances, and, whenever they could, they played games with Camille, Andrew, and Susie.

On one unusually warm autumn evening, they took a stroll in Roland Park. They always admired how well-groomed the flowerbeds and trees were. They sat on a bench and saw a harvest moon rising in the east. It was huge, orange, and brilliant. They folded into each other's embrace and were mesmerized by its glow.

"I think this is the right time," Bill said.

"The right time for what?" Abigail asked.

"Will you be my wife?" he asked, presenting an exquisite engagement ring.

She admired it and smiled. "Bill, you know you make my heart melt, and I love you so much, but I have a question that I need to ask before I give you my answer."

"Fair enough, what is it?"

"My first husband, Avery, was upset that I didn't want to have all my assets under his control. I explained to him that I needed to help my sisters and that I wanted some of the money to reinvest in the store. He did agree, but he was not happy about it. Where do you stand on such matters?"

"Abigail, as far as I'm concerned, what you make is your money, and I admire you for wanting to take care of your sisters." Bill said. "I have enough assets for the both of us, and I'll take care of you forever and always."

Deep in her heart, Abigail knew she could trust Bill. His business dealings were always honest, he didn't try to control her, and she felt cherished by him.

"I know I can trust you, and *yes,* I want to be your wife."

Bill's face creased into a broad smile. They embraced and sealed their love with a passionate kiss.

"You've just made me the happiest of men," he said as they walked arm-in-arm back to his house in Roland Park to share the joyful news.

After their announcement, word of their engagement spread like wildfire. Bill's mother and father, Abigail's sisters, Camille, Andrew, and Susie, and the ladies she knew at the Woman's Exchange celebrated with unrestrained happiness.

"When's the wedding?" they all asked.

"Christmastime," they answered.

જાજાજા

Rosemary, Florence, and Don were the last ones to hear about Abigail's engagement. They mixed with a different group of people, and it was up to her to visit them and keep them informed. She boarded the streetcar and headed to St. Ann's Parrish to visit her lifelong friends. She danced up the stairs and knocked on the door.

"The door is open. Come in," Florence shouted.

Abigail pushed the door open, and it seemed that everything was back to normal. Florence was sewing, Rosemary was hemming a dress on the dining room table, and Don was in the backyard, raking leaves. It pleased her that all of them were doing so well.

"Hello friends," she said. "Florence, the glow is back in your cheeks. My, it's good to see you all working together."

They greeted her with open arms. "Don, Abigail's here!" Florence yelled to him in the backyard,

"I'll be right there," he shouted back. Don trudged up the back stairs and gave Abigail a big bear hug. "How's my girl?"

"I'm just fine. I have a big favor to ask of you," she said to Don.

"What's that? You know I would do anything for you."

"Would you walk me down the aisle when I get married?"

"When did this happen?" he responded, smiling.

"I met Bill Garrett when he was trying to reason with the mob after the destruction of the quarry, and I met him again when I presented the treasurer's report at the last annual meeting of the Woman's Exchange. We've been courting since then."

"Oh, Abigail, we are so happy for you!" Florence and Rosemary said in unison, practically jumping up and down.

"My, my! You *are* full of surprises," Don said. "Of course, I'll give you away. It would be an honor. Are you sure you want me there? My face and body are so … well, *ugly*."

"But not your heart, and that's what is important," Abigail said as she hugged him.

"What are you going to do about a wedding gown?" Florence asked.

"I don't know. Do you have any ideas?"

"You *know* I do," Florence responded. "Let me show you something."

She took Abigail into her sewing room and showed her a shiny satin, somewhere between ivory and light gold.

"It's beautiful!" Abigail exclaimed. "I do have some ideas about the veil, though. I saw a mantilla in the *Ladies Home Journal* that I liked. My thought was to create roses from spun gold to trim the veil. I don't want to cover my face this time, so the mantilla would flow down my back. What do you think?"

"It sounds like it would be a one-of-a-kind veil for a one-of-a-kind person," she said. "Where's the wedding going to be?"

"At the Presbyterian Church on First and Franklin."

"That sanctuary is grand," Florence said. "I'll make sure Don looks spiffy. Do you want *me* to make your dress?"

"Yes, of course," Abigail said. "I'll pay your going rate."

"We'll see about that," Florence said with a twinkle in her eye. "I'll show you some patterns that I think would work."

Abigail found three that she favored and asked Florence for her opinion. The one both of them liked was a simple dress, with a snug bodice, long sleeves, and a slight bustle in the back, which created a gentle draping effect on the front.

❧ ❧ ❧

Abigail's life bustled. The festivities of the holidays, the fitting of her dress, and helping Mary and Louise plan the reception following the wedding service filled her days to the brim. The three of them decided that the luncheon reception would be at the family home. Fortunately, the church would be festooned for Christmas, so more decorations were not needed. Invitations were sent in the mail in a timely manner. They invited only close family and friends, but because Bill's family and circle of friends was large, the end result was a lot of guests.

When the day finally arrived, Abigail felt so sure of Bill, she could hardly wait to become his wife. He passed all her tests and questions with flying colors. Both of them had successfully moved through their dark grieving periods and stood ready to create new dreams.

Mary and Louise had cooked and baked up a storm the week prior, and the merriment was contagious. Camille, Andrew, and Susie were giddy with anticipation. The same was true for other family members and friends.

The church looked exceptionally beautiful, and the organ opened with *Handel's Water Music*. Bill stood by the altar with the minister and, when all the guests were seated, Abigail peered out from the bride's room and saw Don patiently waiting for her by the door. He welcomed her with his usual bear hug and teary eyes.

"You look like an angel," he said. They stood by the door waiting for the music to change, announcing their time to enter. The organist loudly trumpeted the *Wedding March* (from *A Midsummer Night's Dream*) by Mendelssohn. The audience stood and, despite the limp, Don carried himself with dignity, his face beaming as he walked Abigail down the aisle. She looked at Bill and saw him smiling from ear to ear as well. Abigail's eyes became watery, knowing her dear father, Pinky, would be proud of her. She loved Bill so much and was deeply grateful for another chance at love.

Don's disfigured face reminded her of the horrors of being a railroad worker in the 1800s, but on the other hand, Bill's face represented all that was *good* in the railroad industry. Those two images represented in Abigail's mind a tale of two lives joined together by the love of family and friends.

It was a tale Abigail looked forward to living.

AFTERWORD

This is not a true story, but part of this tale is true. The Woman's Exchange movement is very real. It has been a vital philanthropic enterprise from 1832 to the present, which makes it one of the longest-running charitable organizations in our country. During its heyday in 1892 it had seventy-five active Exchanges with a presence in every major city. Currently, the number has dwindled to twenty Exchanges, but it still continues to help women become financially independent. In 1934, the Federation of Woman's Exchanges became the overarching organization for the Exchanges. Today, all twenty have a Facebook page, a physical location, and most have gift shops that sell unique items and high-quality handwork.

If you are interested in finding out more about this worthwhile enterprise, contact Judy Riggle, president of the Federation of Woman's Exchanges, at fwe1934@gmail.com.

While shopping along Saint George Street in Saint Augustine, Florida, I spent an entire afternoon chatting with the lovely shopkeepers at the Woman's Exchange of St. Augustine. Their wonderful handmade items and the charitable mission inspired me. In Abigail's Exchange, I endeavored to highlight the ingenuity and groundbreaking courage of women helping women through the Woman's Exchange. It has truly been one of the most impressive philanthropic operations in our nation.

ABOUT THE AUTHOR

KATHRYN DEN HOUTER was a teacher and a psychologist for forty-five years. Currently, she is enjoying retirement and reading all the books on her wish list. Thirty years of her professional life were spent in Grand Rapids, Michigan. Here she parented four beautiful children with her late husband Len. They raised them on a hobby farm near Lowell, Michigan, a small town east of Grand Rapids. Her children: Jon, Jenna, Jessica, and Ben are embarking on their own careers. She has remarried and lives with her husband Jim. Their summer home is in Leelanau County, Michigan and their winter home is in Indian River County, Florida. She delights in hearing from her readers. You can contact her through her email: kathryndenhouter@gmail.com.